Be My Forever

Josie N. Winters

Legal deposit: February 2025

D/2025/Josie N. Winters, editor

Copyright © 2025 by Josie N Winters

All rights reserved.

No parts of this book may be reproduced in any form or by any electronic or mechanical means, including information storage and retrieval systems, without written permission from the author, except for the use of brief quotation in a book review.

Cover by Fleurie
Dalgona coffee illustrations by Freepik
Cup by Dooder

ISBN-13: 978-9-0834-8861-5 (Paperback edition)
ISBN-13: 978-9-0834-8860-8 (Ebook edition)

*To all the girlies with an ever-growing TBR,
hi, let's be friends!*

PLAYLIST

State of Grace – Taylor Swift (Taylor's Version)
Dance the night – Dua Lipa
Call Me Maybe – Carly Rae Jepsen
Gloves Up – Little Mix
Enchanted – Taylor Swift (Taylor's Version)
Love Story – Taylor Swift (Taylor's Version)
I Can Do It With A Broken Heart – Taylor Swift
Bitch – Meredith Brooks
Treacherous – Taylor Swift (Taylor's Version)
Cupid – Twin vers. – FIFTY FIFTY
Message In A Bottle (Taylor's version) (From The Vault) – Taylor Swift
Say Yes To Heaven – Lana Del Rey
Fearless – Taylor Swift (Taylor's Version)
Perfect – Ed Sheeran
Celebration – Kool and the Gang
All About Us – Owl City
New Romantics – Taylor Swift (Taylor's Version)
Bloody Mary – Lady Gaga
Cinnamon Girl – Lana Del Rey
White Horse (Taylor's Version) – Taylor Swift

Airhead – Honey Revenge
Love Me Like You – Little Mix
Die Young – Kesha
Karma – Taylor Swift
Into You – Ariana Grande
ARTIFICIAL SUICIDE – Bad Omens
EVEN – Bad Omens
You're On Your Own, Kid – Taylor Swift
Uh Oh – Junior Doctor
Dangerous Woman – Ariana Grande
THE DEATH OF PEACE OF MIND – Bad Omens
Sober – P!nk
ME! – Taylor Swift
Black Magic – Little Mix
Antihero – Taylor Swift
Just A Dream – Nelly
Babe – Sugarland (ft. Taylor Swift)
Red (Taylor's Version) – Taylor Swift
4 In the morning – Gwen Stefani
Mess It Up – Gracie Abrams
Fortnight – Taylor Swift
Take Me Home, Country Roads – Lana Del Rey
Euclid – Sleep Token
The Heart Wants What It Wants – Selena Gomez
Missing Limbs – Sleep Token
ceilings – Lizzy McAlpine
About you now – Sugababes
FIX IT ALL – Comastatic
Back To December – Riot House, Jack The Underdog, ENZI
You Belong With Me – Taylor Swift (Taylor's Version)
No Worries – Simon Webbe
Still Falling For You – Ellie Goulding

Find the full playlist on Spotify:
https://shorturl.at/SkZJM

PROLOGUE

Two years ago

"I still don't understand how someone can have so many pairs of shoes," Theo muttered as he dragged a huge box filled with boots inside the already cluttered living room.

Jasmine sighed dramatically, looking at her boyfriend. "Of course you wouldn't. You only buy new sneakers once your toes bore holes through the old ones."

"I'd rather spend my money on other things than hundreds of pairs of shoes."

"Which is why your feet smell so bad," I shot back.

Theo turned his head to the side in fake shock, meanwhile Jasmine showed me a thumbs-up.

"Damn, Evy, that's mean."

When he turned back to his girlfriend, Jasmine just smiled sweetly. She patted his arm before getting back to organizing the boxes. We still had a month before the school year would start, but it was nicer to move in and have enough time to settle without the added stress of starting another new chapter of our lives. I wiped sweat from my brow as I dragged a few bags full of clothes into what would be my room for the next three or more years. It had been a challenge to build the IKEA furniture with just the three of us, especially with Jasmine and her tendency to be bossy. But let's be real, if it had just been me and my talent for building, things wouldn't have been done either.

As I strutted back to the living area, a loud knock made us all jump. Jasmine glanced at me, and I glanced at Theo. He showed me his palms.

"Don't look at me like that. I didn't invite anyone."

"Me neither," Jasmine added.

"Don't look at me. You know I don't talk to anyone except for you guys." I sighed.

We opened the door as one. In front of us stood a very tall young man who was smiling brightly. His bright blue eyes sparkled with curiosity.

"Hi, I'm Danté. I live across the hall."

Jasmine pushed us aside to let him in.

"I'm Jasmine, and these are Evy and Theo. But Theo won't be bothering you too much."

"Rude, babe."

Danté shook their hands before taking mine. His grip was firm and confident. And man, was he cute. I had always liked tall guys who had more of a slim build. They marked bonus points if they were blond, and this guy had checked all the boxes.

Sensing his attention linger a bit too long, I took my hand

back and squared my shoulders. I wasn't shy per se, but I didn't like more attention than what was necessary. Jasmine jumped back in; she knew socializing with strangers wasn't my strong suit.

"How long have you been living here?"

"Three years. I'll be starting my master's year of physiotherapy."

Theo whistled in amazement. He and Jasmine told Danté what they would be doing: Jasmine had always wanted to be an elementary school teacher, and Theo wanted to study communication. Danté turned to me, silently asking me to say more.

"I want to be a dietician. I know. It sounds rather boring but…"

Most people had made a face when I told them I wanted to go down that road. "Why would you want to spend your life telling fat people to go on a diet?" was a question many had asked, if not with those exact same words. And every time, I had told them to fuck off, if not with those exact same words. Food was more than just a diet or an obligation, and everyone deserved to have a healthy relationship with food. I was readying myself to bite back, but the questions or annoying comments never came.

Our new neighbour shook his head, still the epitome of golden retriever energy inside a human body. "Oh, not at all. It sounds rather complicated. Good luck."

Said the guy who was about to start his master's degree. He had one dimple in his right cheek, and two in his left. I found myself smiling back.

"Anyways. I just wanted to welcome you. And if you need

any help, don't hesitate."

Jasmine thanked him. Danté waved one last time before crossing the hallway. Once both our doors were shut, Jasmine and Theo turned to me.

I rolled my eyes, already aware of what was coming. "Please don't."

"He's cute."

"And he seems nice," Theo added.

"He's totally your type! We all know you can't resist blond guys."

She had a point, of course. I shook my head. There was no need to get ahead of myself.

"Chill. We barely met the guy."

Theo and Jasmine exchanged a look. They had been together for about a year and a half, and were friends before that. They could basically use telepathy. She put a gentle hand on my shoulder.

"Just don't let this chance ruin itself. I don't want you to be lonely."

"I am eighteen! There is plenty of time for me to find someone."

Because I knew myself. I would fall head over heels, and there would be no turning back. Jasmine gave me an unconvinced glance.

"If you say so."

Theo didn't stay the night, which I was grateful for. Even though we had been friends for most of our teenage years, it was nice to know that this apartment was for Jasmine and me. And occasionally Theo. I wasn't bitter about the fact that my best friends were dating. If anything, I had pushed Theo into Jasmine's arms so they would finally acknowledge their feelings. *Literally* pushed him. That didn't change the fact that I didn't want him around every second of every day. Jasmine wanted us to settle on our own. We would be together for as long as we would be at college. And I was fine with that.

When "Sweet Melody" from Little Mix came on, Jasmine turned up the music, making it blast through our little kitchen. She danced to the song, spilling some of her third Passoa on the counter. She quickly wiped it clean before getting back to dancing. Even the alcohol in her blood couldn't keep her from being a maniac.

"You know what we need? Some snacks."

I looked in our fridge. The only thing that could be a snack except for raw courgette or bell pepper was a block of cheese.

"Want some Gouda cheese cubes?"

"Sure."

After going through our three kitchen drawers, I finally found a sharp knife. *I'm definitely going to move the knives when she's not looking.*

Jasmine bumped into me. Before I could let go of the tool, it went straight into my finger. I hissed from the sharp pang as I let the knife fall back on the counter.

"Oh my goodness. Evy, are you alright?"

"I think it touched my bone."

Jasmine grabbed my hand, and blood started gushing out of the wound. Her face became pale at the sight of it.

"I am fine."

But to be fair, it really hurt. And there was a lot of blood leaking from my hand. Probably too much. There were already white spots dancing before my eyes.

"I am taking you to the ER."

She grabbed her car keys, and I stopped in front of our door.

"Absolutely not!" I snapped. "You are swaying as much on your feet as I am, and I am the one bleeding out."

Jasmine bit her lip, fighting against the alcohol in her blood. She looked at her phone, then sighed. "There are no more trams nor busses at this hour."

Great. I opened my mouth to ask her for a cab, but Jasmine stopped me.

"Evy, grab your wallet and something to stop the bleeding."

I did as I was told and followed her outside of the apartment. Jasmine pounded on Danté's door, and I could feel panic rise in my stomach. *Oh shit.* A few seconds later, his door opened ever so slightly. He wore nothing but a pair of grey jogger pants and a frown. Which was normal. It was past 1 AM now.

"Is everything alright?" he asked.

My eyes landed on his lean stomach, and I quickly looked away. If he noticed my flushing cheeks, he didn't say anything.

"You told us we could come to you if we needed help. Right?"

"Yeah, sure. But now is maybe not the best time."

A feminine voice could be heard from the other side of the door. Then a gorgeous blonde woman appeared next to our neighbour. She wrapped her arms around his waist.

"Babe, what's taking you so long?"

She was wearing the exact same shirt he had been wearing a few hours ago, and lacy black underwear. Her eyes stopped on my Chiantos t-shirt. She raised a mocking brow.

"Cute shirt."

I coughed from embarrassment. So this was my first night of independence: standing in front of my very handsome neighbour, tipsy and bleeding out, while his girlfriend's fingers were dragging lower and lower *and lower*. We hadn't woken him up – we had interrupted something else entirely. Something that had been going on for a while if I counted the red marks on his neck. I could see the muscles of his stomach move.

I panicked as I almost yelled "I need you to take us to the hospital."

That seemed to get them both out of their trance. Danté's eyes shot wide open.

"Why?"

"Because Jasmine's drunk."

"And why do you ask us if she's drunk and you're not?" Blondie asked.

For a second I debated whether or not I wanted to strangle her with the bloody kitchen towel I had wrapped around my hand. I hadn't asked *them*; I had asked him. Big difference. Instead of committing a murder on the very first day, I showed them the wound. Some more blood leaked out, and the girlfriend made a disgusted face. Danté's brows knitted together.

"I'm the one bleeding. But Jasmine's in no state to drive me there."

As for me, I didn't have a license, so I was plain useless here.

"Fuck. Let me grab a shirt and I'll bring you."

The pretty girl started to sputter complaints, but Danté just asked her to get dressed and leave. When she wanted to kiss him goodbye, he just dodged her altogether. Jasmine winked at me as we followed him. I lost my balance several times before we made it to the car, Danté and Jasmine always staying within reach.

Jasmine climbed in the back. Some part of me wanted to hide in the back with her, though that would've been ridiculous. I breathed in and hopped in the car on the seat next to Danté.

Brussels by day was a city buzzing with energy, so much that the peace and quiet and the free-flowing traffic at night were impressive. He drove quietly for a few minutes, but maybe he wasn't one to like silence.

"So, how did that happen?"

I shrugged. This couldn't get worse anyway. "I was cutting cheese, and Jasmine was dancing. Then she bumped into me while I was holding the knife."

I took the towel off to inspect the cut under the night lights. Too much blood was still gushing out of my flesh, and yep, I could definitely see the bone. This was oddly fascinating.

"Keep pressure on that wound," Danté ordered me, his voice tight.

"Relax. I won't die because of a cut. I only need stitches."

"I'm pretty sure you're not helping yourself by fiddling with that wound."

"Fine."

Jasmine was singing along with the radio, still as drunk as a skunk. Everyone knew she couldn't take alcohol very well. I let my head rest against the window, only to regret it immediately as we drove over a bump in the road. As we arrived at the ER, a nurse urged me to follow her after she saw the bloodied towel.

"You can wait here," I offered. "It won't be long."

Jasmine thanked me and fell down on one of the benches. Needles had always been something that made her uncomfortable. Danté, however, shook his head and followed me.

"I'm pretty sure that if I let you out of my sight, you'll injure yourself even more."

The nurse came back with the equipment for the stitches, followed by a young doctor. The doctor made a face as he looked at my hand.

"How did you manage a cut that deep?"

"I tried to cut cheese."

My cheeks reddened at the look he gave me, which was fair, I guess. This whole night was just getting ridiculous. Danté laughed quietly, and I hit him with my foot.

"Stop laughing. This is embarrassing enough."

"Sorry. Want me to hold your hand? You're not going to puke once you see the needle, right?"

I rolled my eyes, but couldn't help but smile back.

"Are *you*?"

"I might."

"You can still wait outside," I told him.

But he stayed right where he stood. He was even looking over the shoulder of the doctor to watch everything. The doctor numbed my hand before stitching it. Two stitches. Two stitches for a midnight snack. If I'd had any chance at looking good in front of Danté, it had been shattered in less than a few hours.

When we walked out of the ER, Jasmine gave us both a coffee. In other circumstances, I would have refused; coffee tends to keep me awake if I drink it too late. Now I accepted the hot drink without any complaint. Once the adrenaline subsided, I'd be too tired to even care about the caffeine anyway. Dua Lipa danced the night away on the radio, and I bopped my head to the beat.

"Didn't think I would end up in the hospital on the very first night just because Jasmine got wasted. But thank you for helping me out."

"I am not wasted!" Jasmine sputtered. "Just too dizzy to drive."

A small smile played on his lips, but he made no comment. Jasmine was right. He was completely my type. I cleared my throat.

"Anyway. I'll try not to annoy you during your sexy time anymore. Your girlfriend is very pretty."

A surprised laugh bubbled out of him. Oh yeah. I was an introvert, so that was probably what misled most people. In fact, I had no real filter once I started talking. Luckily for me, Danté didn't take it seriously.

"Not my girlfriend."

Whoops. Not only had I interrupted an intimate moment, but one he had with a one-night stand. What a wild night. I opened my mouth to apologize when he pointed a finger at me. Part of me wanted to bite it, but that would've been weird, even for me.

"Admit it, you did it on purpose," he said in a fake offended voice.

"Oh yes, I wanted that bitch out of my way. And what better way to do that than guilt-tripping you with my blood?"

Danté shook his head, making his hair messier than it already was. It wasn't fair how he looked so fine with sweatpants and an old hoodie, while I looked like a goblin coming back from battle. Especially with the shirt I was wearing, now splattered with blood. Not that it mattered anymore. I would forever be the girl who cut her hand instead of the block of cheese.

"Here I thought your intentions were pure. But you were trying to get in my pants the whole time."

I gulped but played it cool. I pretended to look if my glasses were dirty before putting them back on. I only wore them when I had to look at a distance.

"A girl can dream," I told him in what I hoped was a sultry voice.

Jasmine let out a strange laugh from the backseat, and my cheeks burned even harder than they already did. It seemed to also sober Danté up. His expression got serious.

"Promise me you won't do that again any time soon."

I put a hand on my heart, ready to take the pledge. "I'll try not to chase your sex friends away next time, I promise."

"I meant you hurting yourself."

"He is absolutely right," Jasmine chimed in, and I shot her a dirty look.

"You hurt me like this again and I'll stab you."

She flashed me her toothy smile. "Noted."

"Just so you know," Danté added, "I might have told you I would help if you needed anything, but I won't help you hide bodies."

I put on my most charming smile, not sure if it would work. "And if I ask very nicely?"

For a second, it looked as if he didn't know how to respond. Danté let out a breath, drumming his fingers on the wheel. "It's still a no."

Jasmine coughed. A second later, the screen of my phone lit up.

Jasminnie: *Since when r u such a shameless flirt?!*
Me: *I'm not flirting!*
Me: *Wait, I am?*
Jasminnie: *U SO ARE! Go get him, tigerrrr :D He likes it*

I glanced at my best friend, and she nodded her approval. Before I could come up with something new, Danté parked his car in front of our building. So that was it. Once we stood in front of our doors, Jasmine slipped inside, pretending that she needed to throw up because of the alcohol. Then it was only us. Now that we were both standing under a bright light,

I didn't know what to do. The booze that had given me courage until now had fled my system.

"Uhm, thanks for the ride. It means a lot."

"Anytime." As soon as he realized what he said, his eyes widened. Danté showed me the palms of his hands. "I mean, please let's not do this again. But you're welcome."

"Then I'll see you another time?"

"Yep."

Why was this suddenly so awkward?

As I opened my door, he shot back, "Nice shirt, by the way."

It was hard to believe that he wasn't mocking me. Yet there was no judgement on his face.

"Thanks. Good night."

"Good night."

He gave me a little smile before heading inside his apartment. I closed my door as quietly as possible and let myself slide to the floor, grinning like an idiot. This night might have started as a disaster, but maybe things would go just fine.

CHAPTER 1

Now

It was 9:30 PM. Most students and young adults were still wide awake at this time, probably getting ready for a night out. This was why Jasmine and I had insisted on having an apartment a bit farther away from school and the noise. So when the music on the other side of the hall got too loud, and the laughter too, my best friend and I looked at each other. Jasmine sighed. Then her sigh turned into a yawn.

"I hope they'll calm down sooner than they did last time."

"They probably won't." I shrugged.

We weren't against parties and noise. I loved a good party and nice cocktails, just like I loved a good night of sleep. Especially if I had a shift that started at seven in the morning afterwards. Jasmine let her head fall back against the couch, and we waited, hoping that the noise would die down eventually. It didn't. After a while, the floor even started to tremble. I could see Jasmine wanted to go to bed. She had morning classes to attend but was too kind to complain.

"Alright, that's it."

I jumped from the couch and put on my dino slippers my older sister Eleanor had given me for my birthday. Jasmine followed as I knocked on the door in front of us. We waited, but no one answered. Maybe they hadn't even heard us. I knocked louder and longer until the door finally swung open. Danté leaned against his doorframe, a smirk on his lips.

"Yes, Squirrel?"

I fought back a scowl. He had been calling me Squirrel since the day he had spotted me taking out the trash in a squirrel onesie a few months after we moved in here. It was the same onesie I was wearing today.

"Alighieri."

Now it was his turn to bite down a retort. His parents loved philosophy and literature, hence the name. So if he could call me Squirrel, I could call him Alighieri. You know, just to keep some balance. We looked at each other, seeing if the other would continue the banter. Then his gaze stopped on my slippers, and his smirk turned into a catlike smile. I instinctively crossed my arms, ready for the blow that might come.

"Interesting combo."

"Yes, yes," I said ironically. "I am sure you prefer me and my outfit to a girl wearing nothing but your shirt and see-through underwear, but that's not why we're here."

"Oh Squirrel, if you are jealous, I can lend you a shirt too."

I could feel my cheeks heat. Jasmine bit her lip to keep

from laughing. This was not what I had planned. I cleared my throat and smiled back.

"Am I jealous, or is this just an excuse for you to see me with a thong?"

A little laugh escaped him. It didn't matter how much time had passed since we got here, he was still as charming to me as when we arrived here two years ago. If not more. Danté still had his cheery, playful smile, but the boyish immaturity had vanished when he graduated and started working in a medical practice. Now he was a man, and that had only made my crush on him grow bigger. Sad, I know. You'd think that after all this time, I would've been able to stop pining after him.

"Alright Evy, what can I do for you?"

"You're too loud."

"It's not even 10 PM yet."

Which would mean I could not yet complain. Officially. I looked at my watch as the clock ticked ten.

"It is now."

He rolled his eyes. His door opened wider, and one of his friends, Alex, popped his head out.

"Brother, what's taking you so long?"

As soon as he saw us, he smiled. Jasmine's eyes scrunched shut as she smiled back. Yes, she had a boyfriend, and yes, she wanted to live with him as soon as they graduated. That didn't change the fact that she always had had a thing for Alex. Not something where feelings were involved, but something like a celebrity crush. Innocent, unlike mine.

"Hi, Alex!"

"Oh, hey Jasmine! 'Sup, Evy?"

I just waved back, not making the effort to talk back. He closed the door behind him, leaving the other friends still inside. I never had that thing for Alex that most girls seemed to have. He was handsome, in a rather generic kind of way. Like, really handsome. The man could probably feature on one of those romance book covers where the guy wears no shirt, has a very sharp jawline, and mysterious eyes. And I'd probably buy those books. The thing was, I just didn't like him personality-wise. There was something about him that made me uncomfortable. Alex was too cheerful and observant. I never knew if he was making fun of me or not. But apparently, I was the only one thinking so, so instead of fawning over him like the others, I used my social awkwardness as an excuse not to talk to him.

"What's the matter?"

"Oh, actually…" Jasmine started but didn't continue.

I let my head fall back, sighing. Had it been just Danté, she wouldn't have hesitated. Danté watched me closely, waiting to see if I would stand my ground. I crossed my arms.

"We want you to turn down the sound. Jasmine has morning classes, and my shift starts at seven."

"No please?" Alex asked.

"Thanks," I said instead, plastering a fake smile on my face.

People sometimes called me a grump, or even rude. The thing was, I just didn't like people to walk over me. Especially when all that mattered to me was graduating and starting the job of my dreams. While Alex raised an amused eyebrow, Danté shook his head. There was no use in trying to impress him. It had been clear from all the girls that had walked in and out of his place that I never stood a chance. I didn't see myself as unattractive, more like average: average height, average body that wasn't slim nor large. The only feature I thought made me unique was my strawberry blonde curls that loved to defy the laws of gravity. And never had I seen Danté with a girl who looked like me.

Alex waved before getting back inside. Jasmine left my side and went back to our own apartment too, leaving just the two of us in the hallway.

"You truly are something," Danté said, leaning against the wall.

My heart skipped a beat before beating painfully. Knowing that that was how he saw me was rather disappointing. Not that there was anything left to do about it. I gave him a curtsy.

"I am sorry to ruin your night with your friends. I just really need to go to bed."

And I meant it. I didn't like to be a bother for others. I just stood my ground, because no one else would do it for me.

"Don't worry, Squirrel. I remember what it's like. We'll turn down the music."

"Thank you."

Danté nodded before going back inside. Once I was completely alone, I let out a breath. What a great way to start a new week.

CHAPTER 2

"You should stop making all those lists," Jasmine shot me from the stove.

The air in our kitchen smelled like eggs and burnt toast. I had offered to make breakfast, but Jasmine wanted to do it herself. *Just great.* Hence the original arrangement: I cook, and Jasmine does the dishes. It has always been a win-win situation, as I have a real hatred for washing the dishes, and my best friend has always been a terrible cook.

"I might forget something," I answered without looking up.

There were so many things to do this week, and I had to make a new batch of kimchi, which would take me quite some time.

"You never forget anything. Plus, no one is going to die if you don't do groceries at 3 PM on a Tuesday. Live a bit on the wild side."

Yeah, how about no? The store would mostly be empty at

that time of day. Going later would mean more people. More people in the store would mean having more annoying parents holding up the queue with their kid while they are still roaming around the place. And I had better things to do with my time than to spend thirty minutes in an endless queue. Like, I don't know, studying. I'll have some leftover time when I die.

"You know I just want to graduate and get a job. Then I can stop worrying."

"We both know you'll never stop controlling everything."

I also hated the word "controlling". It sounded so harsh, and so *wrong*, like it's bad to have some control over your life. I wouldn't have survived college if I didn't know how to manage my study sessions, cooking time, and gym workouts. I finally looked up, seeing the very sad breakfast that she was putting on a plate for me. I accepted the soggy eggs and burnt toast with a polite smile. People might call me a cold-hearted bitch – which I was not, just to be clear – but I actually didn't like giving critique to people who tried their best.

"You're wrong."

Jasmine sighed loudly, and I knew she wasn't ready to give up yet. I shoved some egg in my mouth. *Oh my gosh, that's way too salty. Smile, Evy.*

"And then what, Evy? You find a nice job, a boring but nice guy, and get married? You guys will buy a little house in a little suburban area and only go on holiday to Gran Canaria? Is that the life you really want?"

I closed my agenda with a loud thud, getting irritated myself. If I had to choose a destination, I'd rather go to Japan or South Korea and learn how to cook their cuisine. Those people eat a lot, but what they eat is all so tasty, yet so healthy. I had no doubt I would learn a lot of interesting things that I could implement in my career. That detail was beside the point here.

"Where is this coming from?"

Jasmine sat in front of me, also chewing on her breakfast. She made a face but kept eating. So did I.

"You are listing what you need to do for the whole week, per day."

"And that is bad because?"

Seriously. I'd been making lists since I was thirteen. Why was it an issue now?

"You only do those intricate plannings when something happens."

"Nothing happened though?"

She just gave up on her breakfast and pushed the plate aside. Her big, worried eyes were roaming over my face. I tried to stay as still as possible.

"Is this because of Danté?"

My stupid, traitorous heart did a flip at the mere mention of him. I did my best to keep a straight face. Jasmine knew I liked him. At one point, I had just stopped talking about him. It had just become too pathetic. And if I stopped talking about him, maybe people would think I had finally moved on. Then it was just a matter of time before my stupid heart understood too that it was time to get over it.

"Why would that be?"

"We all know you are crazy about him. Instead of compartmentalizing your life whenever you feel like you aren't in control, just ask the damn guy out. I am sure he wouldn't object to it."

I snorted. As if. And what was that phrase? "He wouldn't object." That wasn't good enough. I wanted Love with a capital L. The sweet kisses and holding hands while walking home from a date, and the wild sex that left you breathless. I wanted it all. I'd always been in love with the idea of being in love. What some considered unrealistic, others found romantic. I, however, saw it as my most fatal flaw. But why, you may ask. The answer was quite simple. While I loved thinking about loving someone, or even better, being loved by the person I love, real life was a tad bit different. Because being lost in my own head wasn't really doing anything for me. My name was Evelyn Somers, and I had had a crush on my neighbour for the last two years. Just that. Ridiculous, I know. The fact that I kept hoping, kept imagining how things could be, well, let's say it was getting sad. Even for me. But here was the thing: I had wanted to ask the guy out. I almost had, until a ginger girl had sat on his lap at a club. When he had taken her home that night, things had become rather clear. Yes, I liked Danté more than it was sane to admit. And no, I would not be just a one-night stand for him. Even if I had no doubt that the night would get, well, loud and *very* enjoyable.

I took another bite and washed it down with a big gulp of water. Then I pushed my plate away. This conversation had taken my appetite away, even more than the salty eggs and blackened bread. I grabbed my agenda, and Jasmine shot up from her chair, her palms flat on the table.

"Evy, please consider asking him out."

"I don't have the time to talk about this."

Nor did I want to. It had been hard enough to swallow back my pride when the ginger girl had kissed Danté in front of me. She had represented just one night. Many nights had passed, and so had many girls. All beautiful, none looking like me. And Danté had never shown me any interest, so I had accepted the reality. But accepting and moving on are two different concepts. Especially when you see each other all the time.

The time on my phone indicated I had to hurry up if I didn't want to be late for classes. I looked at Jasmine over my shoulder. She was pouting, so I stuck out my tongue.

"I am still not doing the dishes."

Theo and Jasmine were bickering over which one was the best at painting. They had been making some board games for the children Jasmine was student teaching, and it was a messy evening, to say the least. As the best friend stuck in the middle, I tried to stay out of it.

Jasmine groaned in annoyance. "Babe, there are too many streaks on the board."

"It adds a nice texture."

"It looks sloppy!"

Let them be. I did my best to focus on reading the notes from the classes I had earlier. The problem was that they were so loud it was getting harder and harder to block out the noise. The time on my watch told me Grandma would call me any second now. We called every Monday evening at 7 PM. A rule neither of us had broken since I went to college.

"Evelyn," Jasmine cried out, "please look at this board and tell me what you think."

Fuck me. I got up from the couch and glanced at Theo, who was almost ready to surrender. When we were younger, he generally had to be the mediator between Jasmine and me, since we've always had explosive personalities. Since they were dating, it seemed like Theo and I had switched roles in the group dynamic. The painted board had streaks here and there, and sure, it looked homemade. Though I wasn't so sure if five-year-old kids would notice such details while playing. Not that that was enough to keep Jasmine and her perfectionism satisfied. When I opened my mouth to answer gods know what, my phone chimed. *Saved by the bell.*

"Sorry, Grandma's calling."

"Traitor," Jasmine muttered.

Theo gave me a thumbs-up before I picked up.

"Hey, Grandma."

I was greeted with Grandma's snoot pressed against her camera. Just the silly sight made me smile.

"Hey darling, how are you?"

It took her a few seconds to hold the phone at a good distance from her face. Now I could also see her permed short hair and the strings of her pink apron.

"Good, and you?"

"Oh, same old. I thought about you today."

"How so?"

"I went to the local market this morning. They had – what was it called again? – brown sugar pumpkin blondies."

Just the idea of it made my mouth water. I hadn't tried those yet, but they sounded heavenly. Grandma had thought that adding pumpkin to pastries and coffee was weird at first, but I had been able to convince her how nice and versatile it could be.

"And I bought you a handmade scented candle," she continued.

"Really? That's so cool!"

Phone calls between us were never really long, but I cherished them. She was the person who would always fight my corner and who would always care.

"How is school?"

"Good. I can't wait for this semester to be over though so I can finally start my internship."

"Where will that be?"

"At the medical centre near my apartment. There are several dieticians there."

Several people of my class, me included, had applied there. I remembered a girl saying during the first year of college that I was too serious. An overachiever and a buttoned-up girl was what she called me. Yet only one person had been accepted at the medical centre, and it wasn't her. It was probably petty, but it felt satisfying to know that I had been the one to get the spot, and not her. Especially because there was a chance that they would hire me if the internship was a success.

"Darling, that's wonderful."

"Yes, I'm very excited."

"You'll nail it, I'm sure."

"I'll do my best."

"You always do. I am very proud."

Once the call was over, I felt recharged and ready to keep studying. She was right, I would nail it. Because I hadn't invested all my time for nothing. And nothing would keep me from reaching my goals.

I took a quick look in the mirror of the school bathroom, making sure my winged eyeliner was still looking sharp and that my septum was hidden. Then put on my thick-rimmed glasses. Call me shallow, but liking what I saw in the mirror impacted my motivation and productivity. Once I was satisfied, I hurried to the classroom of food technology.

Suzy, a lovely girl with a heart-shaped face, shiny brown curls, and a world-winning smile waved me over, and I let myself fall down on the chair next to hers. Chad, who sat in the row in front of us, greeted me. His face lit up like a Christmas tree, and I forced myself to smile back. As soon as he turned back, I let my head fall back as Suzy snickered.

"I wonder when he'll get it," she whispered in my ear.

I shot her an exasperated look, but couldn't help but agree.

"Soon, I hope."

Suzy was one of the only other students in my class I actually liked. Most of the people we had started with in our first year had dropped out. Suzy and I had gotten along pretty much immediately. The others I had never cared about. It had been a surprise to me how quickly I had been able to bond with someone who wasn't Jasmine or Theo, but here we were.

Chad was also a super sweet guy. There were not many guys who went for dietician. Apparently, it was too "girly" for most of them. It hadn't been too girly for Chad, and just like with Suzy, we had gotten along fast. There was just one tiny problem: he had ended up developing a crush on me. I had hoped that he would get over it when I dated Robert, but instead, his hopes had gotten up after we had broken up. And no amount of subtle, and less subtle, ways of letting him know that I wasn't interested had been able to make him move on. Just like I had with Danté. Which was why I had never been able to tell him to his face that he should stop pining after me. It would've been rather hypocritical of me to ask him that when I was unable to do it myself.

"I heard that Miss Leloux is in a bad mood today," Suzy said, leafing through her notes from the previous lesson.

So basically, the next hour would be hell.

"Well, fuck."

Miss Leloux was known to be a sweetheart when she was in a good mood. Gods protect us all when she wasn't. That was the very reason why students started calling her Two-Faced. Said teacher stormed inside the classroom and dropped her bag and her papers on her desk. A few students who hadn't been aware of the dark cloud looming over our teacher jumped in surprise at the sudden sound.

"Alright class, who can remind me where we stopped last time?"

Suzy and I looked at each other, silently assessing who

would answer. Leloux was the type of person to despise you if you weren't completely up to date with her classes. Suzy nodded, so we both raised our hands. Leloux looked around the class to see if someone else would answer; no one else gave a sign. She sighed, already done with this class before the lesson had even started.

"Alright girls, I'm listening."

CHAPTER 3

Two years ago

The navy shirt fitted just right. Kristen nodded, satisfied. My nerves were already overstimulated, and I felt like jumping around, or fainting. I wasn't sure what would happen first. Kristen's dark eyes softened as she put a hand on my forearm.

"The uniform suits you."

"At least I know that if I fuck things up, I still look cute in it."

Chloe, another college student who had been working here a year already, snorted, then choked on her coffee. Kristen shook her head before handing her some napkins.

"Don't worry, Evy. Chloe and I are here to help you."

"We are," Chloe agreed.

It still felt like a small miracle that Kristen, the owner of the Hot Stuff café, had accepted me as her newest crew member. I had worked in a restaurant as a student before. It had never been more than cleaning tables or doing the dishes. So when I had applied to be a barista at Hot Stuff, I hadn't expected the owner of the café to let me bake a cake to prove I could work there. Literally. It had taken an okay latte macchiato and an excellent lemon cake with icing to get me in. And the cherry on top, I got to work shifts with Chloe, a law student with a big mouth, a passion for bright make-up, and a passive-aggressive personality. Things had immediately clicked between us when she fawned over my red lipstick, and when I had fallen in love with the gorgeous colour of her eyeshadow and the glass beads in her African braids.

Kristen went back to the kitchen to continue baking some of the cakes and cookies that she sold. I followed Chloe to the counter, where she showed me how to make a chai latte, my favourite. And the perk of the demonstration was that I got the drink afterwards.

A familiar blond head sat in a booth near the window. There were many books and papers on his table, and he was leafing through a magazine.

"He comes here every few days to grab a drink and study," Chloe told me. "A very nice fella."

"I know."

Chloe arched an eyebrow.

I shrugged. "He's my neighbour."

"What a lucky girl you are."

Danté and I hadn't really spoken since the whole hospital and cut flesh episode. I had wanted to talk to him again, had stood in front of his door to ask him if he wanted to go out with me for a drink, but had walked back to my own apartment as I heard the voice of a girl on the other side of a door. Some liked to call me a bit naïve, as I hadn't dated anyone, ever, even though I was eighteen, but I could take a hint. And I had already bothered him once when he had a girl over. There was only so much a girl could do before it became a problem, right?

Chloe gave me a notepad and gently pushed me towards him. The beads in her hair clinked together in a melodious way.

"Go ahead and help him instead of staring."

My cheeks grew red. Just great. If I had wanted to be subtle, that had been a total failure. I breathed in, pushed up my glasses, and went over. Danté was so lost in his magazine that he didn't hear me come. It was a travel guide about South America.

"Going anywhere?"

The magazine went flying, and I had to jump back to avoid being hit in the face by Machu Picchu. I cackled while my very lovely neighbour pressed a hand down on his heart.

"Oh jeez! Evelyn?"

I made a curtsy. It hadn't been the plan to startle him, though it certainly was funny. I picked the booklet from the floor and gave it back to him.

"Sorry I scared you. Those are some nice pictures."

He nodded, smiling at the scenery.

"Yeah, they make me want to travel."

"Where would you like to go?"

Danté rubbed the back of his head, smiling sheepishly.

"Is it cliché to say I want to travel the world?"

Was it though? To me, it felt way more cliché to want to visit New York or Paris than to visit everything. I lifted my palms.

"Maybe, but I'd admire you if you did it for real."

I had never really travelled outside of Belgium or Morocco; the only reason I had ended up in Morocco in the first place was because Jasmine had family there. Her parents had been kind enough to take me with them during the summer. Seeing other countries was something that was on my bucket list, but that would have to wait until after I graduated. The whole point of working here was so that I could give Uncle Nadim and Auntie Aswaa my part of the rent. Her parents hadn't wanted Jasmine and me to be in the centre of the student part of the city, where there was a lot of noise and a lot of alcohol flowing in the streets. So they had chosen a fancy little apartment with two bedrooms for us, and a higher rent. But because I paid everything myself, they had only accepted for me to contribute to thirty-five per cent of the rent. So money for travelling would have to wait just a tad bit longer. It would at least give me the time to think about where I'd like to go first, and what I'd like to do.

"Anywhere *you* would like to go?" Danté asked.

He seemed really interested in what my answer would be. Well, since he had already pulled the card of seeing the whole world, I couldn't say the same. It would only make me look like a girl without opinions. And quite frankly, I wasn't sure if I wanted to see *everything*.

"Japan."

"Anime fan?"

I shook my head. My sister was the bigger fan of anime in the family. She had forced me to watch the whole first season of *Dragon Ball* with her. When she finally accepted the fact that I could not be bothered by it, she finally gave up. And *Naruto* was better anyway.

"More like a matcha and udon fan."

Danté hummed. "That makes more sense."

"Though I like some shōjos here and there." But I was getting side-tracked. I clicked my pen a few times. "Anyway, can I get you anything?"

"The sound of matcha is rather nice."

A boy who loves matcha can only be a good match-a, right? I felt myself smiling.

"We don't have that here, but I can make you some at home."

Evy, you smooth girl. Smooth like a smoothie. From the corner of my vision, I could see Chloe, who was pretending not to listen to us while she definitely was. Danté flashed me his golden retriever smile where his eyes turned into crescent moons. It was unfair to be that charming.

"I'd love that."

"Then it's a date."

In the way his eyes went wide and he was unable to say anything coherent back, I knew I'd fucked up. I shook my hands in front of me. No wonder I had been single my whole life. Smoothie who?

"It was a joke. Please don't look at me as if I asked you to marry me."

His face relaxed, and I let out a long breath. Catastrophe averted. For now.

"You are one peculiar girl."

I pouted. I was well aware of it, but if it was that clear from the start, I was pretty much doomed. Especially if someone like him saw it.

"Is that a good or a bad thing?"

"Until now, good."

Maybe I could make peculiar look cool. I squared my shoulders and flipped my notebook open.

"Perfect. If I were you, I'd get the lemon cake. Something tells me it's delicious."

Danté bowed his head. Apparently, I wasn't the only peculiar one. There was a playful twinkle in his blue eyes.

"Then I trust Your Highness's opinion."

"Dork," I muttered. "I'll bring the cake right away."

"Thanks."

When I went back to the counter and took a slice of the lemon cake, Chloe came back.

"Is there something I need to know about you two?"

I bit back a grin. "No."

At least not yet, I hoped.

The back courtyard of our building was already flooded with people when Jasmine, Theo and I got there. From what Jasmine had said, they would do a test of the fire alarms and an evacuating simulation at the beginning of every academic year. A familiar blond head appeared, followed by a few other guys. When Danté spotted us, he walked up to us.

"Hey guys, did you settle in alright?"

Jasmine shot me a quick look. As I stayed silent, she flashed him her world-winning smile.

"Yes, we did!"

They both chatted a bit. From what I heard, Danté was telling her about a nice bar he recommended, but I zoned out. I recognized one of the guys next to Danté as Jared, his roommate. Only because I had seen him open their front door with a key. And Jasmine in her full curious, social butterfly glory, had asked him who he was. The poor guy had looked a second away from combusting at the sudden attention. He had shot me a grateful look when I yanked my best friend inside our own place under the excuse that I needed her help in the kitchen. Other than that, we never really saw him. The other guy was Alex. The first time I had seen him, I thought he was another roommate. He was just a close friend, from what Jasmine had told me. For a reason I couldn't pinpoint, he made me uncomfortable. Yes, Alex was very nice to look at: perfect jawline, tall, dark-haired, and mysterious. It was his aloofness that made me pause. The guy seemed so cold and cocky. It was a bit weird that he would be such a good friend with someone who had such a sunny vibe. But maybe I was judging Alex too harshly. After all, first impressions weren't always the right ones.

I tuned back in to my friends and Danté at the worst moment.

"Thank you once again for bringing Evy to the ER. We were lucky you were there."

A strangled noise came out of my throat, my cheeks growing red. Danté turned his attention to me, his eyebrows going slightly up, probably realizing that I was still there.

"How is the wound?"

That made Alex tune in as well. Why did he suddenly look so interested when he had been so bored just seconds before? I showed him the small scar on my finger. You didn't even see the pink line if you didn't know it was there.

"It healed well. Makes me look pretty badass, doesn't it?"

The skin around his eyes crinkled when he smiled. "A badass scar for a badass girl."

I rolled my eyes but couldn't help but smile as well. People streamed out of the courtyard and back to their apartments now that the evacuation was over. I opened my mouth to say something else, but before I could, Danté gave us a sign before heading back to his place, followed by Jared. Alex lingered a second longer, his attention solely fixed on me. A cold shiver ran down my spine. The way the corner of his mouth lifted, it looked like he had me figured out. Then he disappeared as well. I just hoped I wouldn't see that one too often.

CHAPTER 4

Now

I watched Chloe fill the coffee machine, nibbling on a piece of apple. Wednesdays were always calmer than Tuesdays. The little bell at the door chimed as Danté walked inside the café. His eyes were unfocused and his hair completely tousled, as if he had jumped out of his bed straight into his jeans before getting here. A small smile tugged at my lips, but I forced it away when Chloe shot me a knowing look. Danté let himself fall on one of the tall stools with a loud sigh. It was unusual for him to be so dishevelled, or to come here on a Wednesday.

"Give me something sweet," he said by way of greeting us.

"Well, well, someone's got their panties in a twist today," I teased.

"My panties aren't in a twist," Danté shot back.

"So you admit that you are wearing panties. Is that a kink of yours?"

A spark lit up inside his eyes. "Would you like to see?"

"I got to admit, I am curious." Without thinking, I put my hand against his forehead. There was no fever, just exhaustion. The most surprising was that Danté slightly leaned into the touch. And maybe my fingers lingered a moment longer than they should've. I cleared my throat. "You don't look so fresh."

"Don't ask…"

"I wasn't going to."

He let his head drop in his hand, almost falling back asleep. I shook his shoulder from over the counter. This man truly was something. Would he even be able to get back home in his current state? I shook my head. *He's a grown man, Evy. He doesn't need you.*

"I was with a person last night. She was insatiable."

My stomach churned as an image of him and a blonde going at it all night flashed before my eyes. Chloe disappeared inside the kitchen. *Coward.* I cleared my throat, making sure my face was neutral.

"And that's why I didn't ask."

Danté's eyebrows shot up as he realized what he had just shared. Or was it my reaction that made him straighten on his chair? It didn't matter.

"Right."

I waited for him to say something. Anything to get that filthy image out of my head. He stayed silent.

"So, can I get you anything or do you want me to coddle you?"

My sharp tone surprised me as much as it surprised a customer who was sitting a few stools further from my neighbour. Danté huffed out a laugh, not even impressed.

"Your customer service is atrocious in the morning. I'll take a double espresso. With extra sugar. And a croissant."

I clicked my tongue before I could stop myself. "You know, that's a terrible order. It's not good for you."

Danté clasped his hands together, and I felt my gaze stopping on them. Unlike some guys, he had long and slender fingers. His hands were *pretty*. Shame that I now knew what those pretty hands had been up to these last few hours.

"If you're going to tell me coffee dehydrates, I am aware."

My head shot back up. *Stop staring at his hands, you weirdo!*

"Oh no. Coffee does dehydrate you, that is true. But if you drink enough water and just one or two cups a day, it won't affect you that much. It's bad for your cortisol levels."

"Jesus, Evy!" Chloe shot, tossing a wet kitchen towel at my face. "Don't say that to our customers! Plus, I'm sure he doesn't need all that information this early on."

She had been eavesdropping, huh? I scowled at my colleague, who scowled right back at me. I sighed and showed my palms as a sign of surrender. A petty part of me wanted to tell her that Danté wasn't a regular customer, and that if he shared what happened in his bedroom, I could share facts about food. Except that he was, in fact, our customer, and most people didn't care about the facts that I shared. I stared at my baby blue sneakers. Chloe patted my shoulder before helping out another customer who had just walked in.

"Sorry, she's right. I shouldn't be bothering you with all

this food stuff," I said, cleaning the wet streaks from Chloe's towel on my glasses.

"So, what were you saying about my cortisol levels?"

I looked back at him, expecting to see a bored face, but found attentive eyes instead. I rubbed my neck. Jasmine would smack me for being so bad at socializing. I waved my hands in front of me.

"It's okay if you don't care. I just get too excited sometimes."

"No, I'd like to know."

He was never playing fair. Danté knew how to make people feel special; he had the ability to give someone all his attention, as if what one had to say actually mattered. When I met him two years ago, I thought he was faking interest. But Danté wasn't fake; he was curious, and a social butterfly.

"Oh. Well, coffee increases our cortisol levels, but when we wake up, our body produces those hormones on its own. Drinking coffee during the first hours after you wake up imbalances that. So you should wait two hours to let your body do its thing. When you drink your coffee later – which you usually do – there's no issue."

Danté nodded as if he was really listening to what I had just said. And it didn't feel like he would forget the interaction once he moved on to another person.

"Alright. I'll keep that in mind next time."

"Enjoy your breakfast," I said while I gave him his order.

Instead of taking his food and sitting at his usual table, he stayed and chitchatted with Chloe and me. Probably because he would fall asleep on his own. After a while, Danté fell quiet, and Chloe went back to the kitchen. I took out my notebook and looked at everything I had to get done. In all fairness, I had been a bit lazy these last few days. It didn't happen often, but I had spent many hours on TikTok, looking at way too many Taylor Swift videos. It was time to stop fooling around and to get things done. From where he sat, I could feel Danté's focus weighing on me.

"What is it?"

"I always wondered why you have such intricate to-do lists." Danté rested his elbows on the counter, reading my list upside-down. I didn't understand how he was able to do so, especially since my handwriting tended to be rather messy, but he was. He let out a whistle. "Surely, you don't do all that?"

"No, I do."

"Doesn't it get boring to know every single detail of every day?"

The question was genuine; there was no judgement to his words. I hummed. "Not really. It keeps me prepared for when something unexpected happens."

Danté locked his gaze to mine. I could almost hear the cogwheels turn inside his head. There was an intensity burning in his eyes. That could only mean one thing: he had an opinion. He let out a long breath, but made no further comment. It was nice that he didn't feel the need to impose his thoughts. I huffed. "Go ahead, say what you have to say."

A smile tugged at the corners of his mouth. "I just think you miss out on a lot of things by knowing everything in advance."

I didn't expect him to understand. We were opposites here. I liked stability. *Control*, as Jasmine would call it. Danté, on the other hand, saw life as an adventure, and secretly, I admired him for his openness to change. It just wasn't me. "I don't like surprises. Life is easier when it is predictable."

Life had been everything but predictable the day the doctor said that my sister had to go to the hospital because she had become so unhealthy. Difficult times with a lot of emotional rollercoasters were bad surprises, and there had been nothing I could do. And I hated every second of it.

"But it is the imperfections that make it worth living," he said quietly.

There was no use in telling him that having a sister who almost died because of an eating disorder, and parents who had gotten PTSD from it and were now overbearing, was what made it worth living. Knowing Danté, he would probably say something along the lines: "Sure, life is hard, but it makes you appreciate the time you have together now even more." Which was also fair, I suppose.

For a few long, awkward and silent seconds, Danté's attention was on my face. Almost like he was searching for something. I just didn't know what he wanted to find.

"Do you think you could ever stray from the life you've planned?"

"What do you mean?"

He took his time to answer. This whole conversation was becoming too serious. Too heavy.

"How would you feel if you didn't go through with all those steps? Could you still be happy?"

His question made a pinch of anxiety bubble in my chest. Straying from my plan had never been an option. Not because I couldn't, but because I didn't want to. I loved the path that I was walking. This was what I wanted.

"I think I would feel lost. This is my calling, so I don't know what I would do if I couldn't go through with it."

Danté's expression turned blank, like he wasn't with me here anymore, but lost somewhere in his own head. I bit at the skin of my thumb, unsure of what to do. Then in the blink of an eye, he was his old self again. It was as if Danté sensed where my thoughts were at because he gave me a sweet smile.

"Don't worry, Squirrel. I'm not here to convert you."

I almost sighed in relief. Seriousness wasn't part of how we communicated.

"Good, because you wouldn't be able to," I laughed, crossing my arms.

"I'm pretty sure I could."

Now that was a bold statement. He most definitely could. If there was one person who was able to get me out of my comfort zone, it was him. I leaned towards him, the counter still between us.

"Give me an adventure, and we'll see."

His face lit up like a Christmas tree, and gosh, did that smile do something to me. Dimples appeared, ones I knew by heart, but still loved to see as much. His expression turned playful.

"Honey, I am the adventure. Didn't you know?"

I coughed from embarrassment. Well, he sure was. I was pretty certain that my face had become the twin of a tomato. Danté winked at me, and I let my head fall in the crook of my elbow.

"I didn't know you could be so corny," I muttered.

Danté patted my head. When I looked back up, I knew he

wasn't done. Danté gave me a terrible wink.

"See, now that was a surprise."

A laugh bubbled out of my throat, and he just ended up laughing with me. It wasn't the adventure I had hoped for, but Danté making fun of himself for me had certainly made my day, just like it had erased the panic his earlier questions had given me.

"Alright, you won this one."

For a brief moment, Danté's lips parted, as if he wanted to add something. Whatever it was mustn't have been that important. He merely shook his head.

"See you later, Evy."

"Bye."

In the blink of an eye, Danté had grabbed his jacket, and then he was gone. From behind me, Chloe was cackling. I held up my hand.

"Don't say anything."

She gave me a pat on my shoulder. "Oh, I don't need to."

CHAPTER 5

Two years ago

Jasmine watched my every move with too much curiosity as we walked back to our apartment. Though she never asked why I skipped more than I walked, she knew I was up to something. It had taken us a few tries before finding a store that had vanilla bean paste. Now that I had the last ingredient to make a fancy matcha latte, I could finally invite Danté over for one. It had been a few days since we talked about it, so I hoped that he would remember. The last thing I wanted was to look like a total psycho who had planned everything, when, in fact, I had simply been the only one to care. I shook my head and continued skipping when we walked inside our building. Jasmine sighed as we took the stairs, complaining all the way up until we reached our floor.

"This is really pushing it too far, Eves. You force me to eat all your creations and to take the stairs. What's next?"

Unlike me, Jasmine didn't have the time to hit the gym almost every day. I rolled my eyes as I looked at her while she climbed the last of the stairs.

"I could stay with you while you shower to tell you if there's still shampoo left in your hair."

"I hate you," she muttered.

"Sure you do."

The moment Jasmine searched for our key in the trash bag that was her handbag, another door opened. Before I could open my mouth to say anything, a girl perched on her toes and kissed the very person I was about to invite in. They hadn't noticed that someone else stood in the hallway, too focused on mixing their saliva. The yellow light made her straight ginger hair shine like in a shampoo commercial. With my heart beating in my throat, I elbowed Jasmine.

"Come on, Jazz! Search faster."

At the way her eyebrows furrowed, I could see she was about to hit me. Before she could, I pointed to the door behind us. Jasmine quickly glanced over her shoulder, and her cheeks dusted red. But instead of opening the door, she cleared her throat.

"Hi, Danté!"

The girl jumped back, and Danté's eyes went wide now that he was called back to reality. His attention was first on my friend, then it landed on me for a brief second.

"Oh, hey."

His voice was too cheerful. Had we once again interrupted a sexy time? Please, let that not become the theme of my life. I pinched the bridge of my nose while Jasmine started small talk with our neighbour and his... well, what was she? At this point, I was more confused about his girls than I was about the Belgian weather. It was then that I realized I had never greeted him back. Jasmine smoothly kept talking to them like she did with her friends. The girl was smaller than I was by a few inches. No wonder she had needed to stand on her tippy toes. She looked nothing like the blonde girl we had seen here on our first-night catastrophe. And she looked nothing like me. When Danté's gaze fell back on me once again, I felt like a deer caught in the headlights. What was I supposed to do? What should I say? The bag I was still holding seemed to become heavier by the second. At least now I knew I could stop hoping. It would never be a date. I lifted the bag.

"I can make you a matcha latte, as promised."

The girl's head whipped in my direction. I let my arm fall back, unable to respond to the hostility that she was sending my way. Danté didn't notice, or didn't care. A smile lit up his face. A genuine one this time. Even though I felt like I was about to barf up the inside of my stomach on his black Vans, I smiled back.

"I thought you'd forgotten."

So he had remembered? Jasmine and the mean ginger lady looked between the both of us. I bit my lip. All this attention was overwhelming.

"I couldn't find vanilla."

"Don't worry."

A part of me, a very petty part, if I do say so myself, wanted to invite him over, just because I could. It just didn't feel right. I shrugged.

"Anyway, you can come whenever you want."

Jasmine understood the finality of the statement and gave me the key. Another part of me wanted to strangle her for keeping that key from me even though she had found it minutes ago.

When I waved, Danté said, "I'll come in a few minutes, if that's okay with you."

So he wanted to spend his time with us? The girl on the other side of the hall understood it too. I found myself unable to answer something smart, so I just nodded like a dumb bobblehead. Jasmine opened the door and discreetly pushed me inside. When we were out of their hearing reach, Jasmine shot me a wry smile.

"I know."

This was getting too complicated. Because I wasn't the type of girl who was confident or hot. If anything, I was the cute kid no one took seriously. I blamed it on my very round cheeks. And it seemed like I wasn't the type Danté went for. But for some reason, we always ended up in each other's orbit. My best friend patted me on the arm.

"You, my dear, are in for a wild ride."

And an emotional one too, it seemed.

Chloe had been talking for a while, not that I could recall what it was about. At some point, she waved a hand in front of my face.

"Why are you moping?"

"I'm not moping."

"You definitely are."

"No, I'm not!"

Chloe raised her palms to show me she would drop it, but at the way her eyebrow raised, I could see she didn't believe me. She was right, of course. I was moping. I had been for the last few days. Danté had come over to our place for the matcha latte. Jasmine had been the real hero, trying to figure out if the girl we had seen was his girlfriend. She wasn't, which would have been a reassurance if Danté hadn't also said that he wasn't ready for commitment because he had gone through a tough breakup a few months earlier. All he wanted right now was just to have some fun. I couldn't blame him. I also couldn't help the disappointment that pinched inside my chest. It wasn't love, sure, but there was something about him. Danté was a light, and I was a moth.

The bell chimed, and a group of students walked in. Chloe silently assessed me, probably trying to feel if I was able to muster enough sweetness to deal with customers.

"Why don't you go and help that one out?"

A rather handsome fella stood at the counter, with blond dishevelled hair. The guy was having a staring contest with the drink list on the wall. I plastered a smile on my face. He didn't even hear me approach.

I cleared my throat. "Hello, can I help you?"

The guy turned to me, his gaze bewildered. He laughed nervously and rubbed the back of his head. "I'm a bit overwhelmed at the amount of drink choices you have."

I found myself smiling. I was the kind of person who had to see the menu days in advance so I could make a choice without the pressure of choosing on the spot. So I knew how he felt.

"Can I help you or do you want me to come back in a few minutes?"

He ended up sliding on one of the bar stools. "What would you recommend?"

"I personally love chai lattes the most."

"Alright, I'll take one on the go."

Though he was a bit smaller, understandably, he looked a bit like my annoyingly good-looking neighbour. Jasmine and Theo had a point: I had a type. But where Danté was a flirt and as confident as one could get, this one seemed to get easily lost in his own head.

"Can I have your name please?"

"Oh, it's Robert."

I put his name on the paper cup. A few other customers arrived, so I started preparing the orders.

"Robert?" I called.

"You can just call me Rob."

"Alright then. There you go, Rob."

Instead of taking his cup and leaving, he stayed.

"And you are?"

"Evelyn, but you can call me Evy."

He laughed quietly. His eyes roamed over my face, and I started to feel self-conscious under the scrutiny.

"That piercing really suits you."

My hand went to my septum, and I winced at the contact with the fresh piercing. It had been on my bucket list for quite a while. So when my mother had said that septum piercings made girls look like ugly cows, I had dragged Chloe to the nearest piercing shop after our shift yesterday, just because I could. My mom was so going to have a shock, and I was all here for it. The fact that someone actually said that I looked good with it was nice.

"Thank you. Anyway, enjoy your drink."

"Thanks, I'll see you around."

He gave me a small smile and waved before turning back. "I'm sure you will."

CHAPTER 6

Now

My phone rang, distracting me from my paper. *Eleanor*. Why was she calling me now? We called every Thursday.

"Hello?"

"Evelyn! I've been knocking on your door for the past minute. Why aren't you opening it?"

"Hold on. I'm coming."

I hadn't heard anything. Had I been so focused on my paper I hadn't realized there had been knocks? As I opened the front door, I saw my sister glaring at Danté's door. I let out a snort.

"That's the wrong door, El."

Eleanor winced. Though we sometimes met for lunch or a coffee, my sister and parents never came here. It probably had something to do with me never inviting them over.

"No wonder you didn't answer."

My sister jumped in my arms and we both squealed.

"Oh my God, I missed you," she said, hugging me tighter with her small arms.

I smelled her familiar Marc Jacobs perfume. When we were younger, when I was still a kid and she was a teenager, I loved to slip into her room and use her perfumes. They always smelled so nice to me, especially since I was forbidden to enter her room. I smiled at the memory and hugged her back just as hard. Danté's door flew open. His eyebrows were knitted together and his hair was dripping wet.

"What is going on…"

He stopped mid-sentence as his eyes landed on us. Eleanor shot me a side glance, and I cleared my throat.

"Sorry. My sister banged on the wrong door."

"I thought there was an emergency. The knocks were loud, and there was some yelling."

I bit my lip to keep from laughing. From the corner of my eyes, I could see my sister blush from embarrassment.

"Eleanor, this is Danté, our neighbour."

"Nice to meet you," my sister said, taking his hand in hers.

All signs of embarrassment were now gone. Danté smiled warmly at her. His eyes darted between both of us, probably trying to see how much we looked alike. Spoiler alert: we didn't look alike at all. Not the hair, not the eye colour, nor the body type. I had taken after Mom, and Eleanor after Dad. The only thing we had in common was our height, if that even counted. Eleanor's hair was almost black, shiny, and oh-so straight; my lighter curls defied the laws of gravity. Not that her hair would've suited me, or my lion's mane her. Once Danté was back inside, Eleanor flashed me a cat-like smile.

"What a cute boy."

"The boy is twenty-four."

She hummed. There was a sudden interest in her behaviour. Danté was older than the both of us.

"Is he single?"

My stomach churned at the question. Eleanor was beautiful. Most guys turned to look at her when she walked past. Which made me wonder why Danté hadn't. Instead of showing how her question made me feel, I wrapped an arm around her shoulders and led her inside my own apartment.

"Don't waste your breath. He isn't the kind that does serious relationships."

Never had I seen Danté commit to a serious relationship. He had seen a girl a while back, but it hadn't lasted more than two or three months. All the others that I had seen walk over the floor were one-night stands. Eleanor sighed as if it were a real loss. It was to me.

"He's delicious to look at."

I couldn't lie about that, even if I wanted to.

"That he is."

Jasmine ran out of the kitchen and hugged my sister like she was her own. I guess she sort of was. Jasmine and I had been friends for so long that of course she and Eleanor were family. Eleanor jumped with my best friend, just like she had done with me a few minutes before. Once my sister and I were in my room, I closed the door. Even though I was happy to see her, she wasn't around often for her visit to be casual.

"So, what brings you here?"

"Do I need a reason to visit my baby sister?"

I hated it when she called me baby. It was supposed to be an endearing word, yet it never felt so to me. I had never told her that, not wanting to vex her. But I hated being referred to as the baby of the family when I always felt like I was the outsider of said family. How could I be the baby when I had grown up without them? She flashed me a sheepish smile, so I knew that there was something she wanted to ask me. I waited a few seconds, but Eleanor didn't elaborate. Did she really think I hadn't realized she wanted to ask me something? My sister plopped down on the bed, looking at my lessons.

"Mom and Dad want to know if you'll be there for Christmas," she said casually, flipping through the pages strewn over my bed.

So that was what she wanted to know. I looked at her warily. I was so going to kill her if she crinkled one of my papers. No matter how much I loved her.

"Christmas is more than two months away. Why do they ask that now? And why don't they ask me personally?"

It wasn't like I ghosted them often when they called me. They could've asked me. Not that I had anything planned for Christmas. It wasn't as if I cared about that holiday that much. Not like Eleanor did.

El shrugged. "I was at home last weekend, so they asked me." My sister finally looked up. "They also asked when you're coming home."

This apartment was my home. Jasmine was my home. I rolled my eyes.

"I went not so long ago."

She clicked her tongue. "Evy, you went home more than

two months ago."

I blinked. Had it been that long? A hint of guilt crept up in my chest. Maybe it was indeed time to visit my parents. Then I could stay home again for two months without having to worry about that.

I sighed. "When are you going?"

"Next weekend."

Eleanor went back every weekend and during all the holidays. That was proof of how different she and I were.

"Alright, I'll come with you."

"You know, Evelyn, they are the only parents we have. You should cherish them more."

"So you came here to scold me," I observed, crossing my arms.

It had been naïve to think Eleanor had come here on a whim just to see me. So why was I disappointed when I knew? Eleanor's expression shifted into something softer. She put a hand on my cheek. Once again, she looked at me as if I was the baby that needed to be protected. A shiver ran down my spine.

"I didn't come here to scold you. But I want you to remember everything they did for us."

Her words left a bitter taste in my mouth. Everything they did for us? No, everything they did for *her*.

"Don't forget they are paying your tuition. Show them you are grateful."

Which was literally your duty as a parent. I kept from saying that. Otherwise, she would smack me. It wasn't that I didn't love my parents. I knew they had gone through hell with Eleanor, so I never held them accountable for their absence. I knew that if I had been the one who had almost died, the situation would have been reversed. But I was the healthy one, who stayed at home while my parents had spent many nights at the hospital. They had given up everything to help my sister get over her eating disorder and the many downfalls she faced while getting better. It had taken a few years, but Eleanor had gotten better. When things had started going better, my parents suddenly remembered they had a second child, a *younger* child. And by the time they tried to bond again with her, she had moved on. She didn't need them anymore to help with homework or to cook a meal or get to school. The girl had grown up at a too young age without them seeing it. Others had taken her in when her own parents hadn't come home. Mom and Dad hadn't been there when I had dance recitals or baking contests. Grandma and Jasmine's mom were though. Now I just didn't feel the need anymore to have them around as regularly as my sister did. And that was fine. My parents had saved her life. That was wonderful. But I had survived on my own, and I hadn't faked the fact that we had become strangers in those years we barely saw each other.

I could still remember my mom coming home from visiting Eleanor in the clinic, asking me if she needed to show me how the washing machine worked. Except that I had learned to do so on my own three years prior. Had she even realized that I had been doing my own laundry at sixteen for more than three years? It didn't matter anymore. I hadn't felt lonely in those years, because other people had filled my parents' shoes. That was the tricky part: they now wanted to fill that space again, and I couldn't pretend like I wanted to give them that space back as if nothing happened.

"Whatever." I shrugged. "I have a paper due tomorrow. I'll see you this weekend. Do I need to bring anything?"

My sister wanted to protest at the not-so-subtle dismissal. Except that this was a fight she would not win. We had both inherited our mom's stubborn nature. She smiled ruefully.

"Try to bring some manners."

"Keep on dreaming."

My alarm beeped at 9 PM, like it did every Monday. *Take out the trash*. I got up from my desk, sighing and stretching. My neck cracked in a satisfying way. Jasmine laughed quietly when she saw me walking to the door with the trash bag.

"You look smashing."

"Thank you, my lady."

I went outside to the back of our building. Steps were echoing on the ground behind me, and just by the rhythm of those steps, I already knew who it was, and bit down the smile that my face tried to make.

"'Sup, Squirrel."

"Hello, Alighieri."

Danté grabbed my bag and threw it in the huge bin, so I gave him a little curtsy. We often met here on Mondays. It had sort of become our own private joke to meet here so that he could rate my funny pyjamas. The first time it had happened, a bit more than two years ago, I had felt mortified.

Can you imagine walking around in Lion King pyjamas and glittery pink fairy slippers in front of the guy you wanted to ask out? Yeah, well, it had happened to me. But unlike what I had feared, that Danté would mock me or judge me, he had laughed and said that my outfit had brightened his then not-so-nicely going day. So instead of playing it cool, I continued to show off my collection of terrible outfits, if it could bring a smile to his face. Today I wore a new one: fluffy green pyjamas with Homer Simpson disappearing inside a hedge. Danté observed me, and I did a little whirl to show every part of it.

"This one is new. You like it?"

He let out a long blow, pouting. "To be fair, I'm jealous to not possess the same outfit."

"Can you imagine if we had the same? It could be our costume for when we take over the world."

Danté pretended to think. He was always quick to follow with my quirky jokes. "I don't know about taking over the world, but I'd gladly take over Hot Stuff and have all the free cakes in the world."

"You need to think bigger, Alighieri. Why stop at more cakes if you could also have more alcohol and money?"

He crossed his arms, and although Danté had a rather slim build compared to other men, the gesture made his biceps bulge. Or was it his triceps? I wasn't good with human anatomy, unlike him. The only thing I cared about was being allowed to touch said body parts.

"It seems like you thought it through."

I had to force myself to stop gawking at him and looked back up. There was a knowing smirk on his lips, but he didn't make any comment. Good. It would've been too awkward if I had to admit that his anatomy made me want to tear his clothes off. And lick every part of it.

"Oh, you know, never let them know your next move. Or something like that."

"And yet you shared your evil plan with me."

"Well, I'd hope you couldn't resist me, or my cute smile, and would participate."

"Alright. Let's say that I help you in overthrowing the world to make the Evelynian Empire. You'd at least give me half of the power and the goods, right?"

The Evelynian Empire? Now that sounded like an apocalypse. My mind visualized the world after Doris had taken over in *Meet the Robinsons*, everyone being controlled by bowlers. Except with me, it would be rabid squirrels instead of hats. Danté leaned against the metal fence, laughing quietly.

"Of course, but I'd throw you under the bus if our plan failed, just to save myself."

My beautiful neighbour gasped, and I found myself giggling. This was why I came here every week. Because when it was just the two of us, I could be myself, quirks and all, and it felt right to be like that with him.

"How dare you!" he shot back, falsely outraged.

"Sorry babe, but a sweet girl like me wouldn't survive in prison."

"So I really am your scapegoat, huh?"

"Only in worst-case scenario." I winked at him.

He flicked me on the forehead. "I see how it is, and here I thought you'd at least try to break me out of jail so that we could be runaway criminals."

"Watch us become the new Bonnie and Clyde."

"Squirrel and Alighieri. It has a nice ring to it."

"No one will take us seriously with those nicknames."

"That can work to our advantage."

I snorted as another image popped up in my brain: me with a squirrel mask, and Danté with a Venetian carnival one. We're driving in an old-school convertible filled with stolen money and jewellery, disappearing into the sunset, never to be found again. How romantic and thrilling that could be.

"I like the way you're thinking."

A cold wind blew, making the skin on Danté's arms pimple with goosebumps. Even though I enjoyed being here with him, where it was just the two of us, I didn't like seeing him cold. I wasn't his girlfriend; I couldn't be the one to warm him up. As if he could sense that the time for jokes was over, he motioned to the door of our building. We both took the stairs to our level. Back in front of our doors, Danté turned back to me.

"Have a good night."

"You too. Try not to think about me, or how I get you out of jail in a skin-tight leather outfit, too much."

I didn't know if I dreamed it or not, but I could've sworn that his pupils dilated. Danté shook his head, his blonde locks flying around his head, creating a halo.

"I wasn't, but now I might."

A soft warmth crept up my cheeks as I kept my gaze low.

"Good night then."

"Good night, Evy."

CHAPTER 7

My parents' house loomed over me like a dark cloud, and it wasn't even that high. And yet, it felt as if I were going to climb Mount Everest without the necessary equipment to do so. Oh, fuck me. I entered the house and put my backpack and small luggage near the staircase. The house still smelled like it did in my memories: wooden furniture and polished floors. I waited for the olfactory recognition to awaken some nostalgia. Nothing came. The door from the kitchen opened, and Eleanor ran towards me. My sister crashed into me, and I hugged her back.

"Evy! You're early."

My parents appeared in the hall too. I could almost touch the awkwardness that floated in the air.

"Hello," I tried, a polite smile plastered on my face.

Mom gave me a quick hug, and Dad gave me a peck on the cheek. When they were done, I took a step towards Eleanor. If she saw the awkwardness, she pretended like it wasn't there, and pulled me inside the kitchen. There were a lot of ingredients and spices strewn on the counter. I whistled at the sight.

"My my, are you cooking?" I asked, impressed.

"I am. I've been trying out a few recipes so I could impress you during your next visit. Plus, that way, we can avoid Mom's cooking," she added conspiratorially.

I let out a quiet laugh. My mom was not a bad cook. She just had the bad habit of overusing butter, heavy cream, and oil, which made the food heavy. The amount of fat always gave Eleanor the jeebbies. My sister had come a long way, but my mom's cooking was still a step too far, so Eleanor had learned how to cook a few things herself. I felt pride bloom in my chest as I looked at her preparing a white chili.

"This has been my favourite dish for the last few months," she told me as she cut some bell peppers into tiny cubes. "Beans are so versatile."

"They are," I agreed. "And they are packed with fibres and protein."

"Beans are life."

My sister and I kept chatting and laughing as I helped her cook. Even though I had to admit that she had the same tendency as I had: being bossy and not enjoying having someone else roaming in our kitchen while we were cooking.

The most awkward part was once we were all seated at the kitchen table for supper. There was silence save for the sound of cutlery scraping against the plates.

"How is school?" asked my father.

It was his way of doing small talk, so I had to give him some points for trying. The problem was this: I had been at the top of my class since I entered secondary school, so there weren't many options I could choose from.

"Good. I'm still nailing it."

Eleanor wiggled her brows, then cocked her head towards Dad as if to say "Come on, say something more". I sighed internally, sipped my water, and took a deep breath.

"I am excited to finish the semester. We have to do an internship in a dietician's practice after our exams."

"Oh, that is wonderful!" my mother said.

I nodded before shoving some food in my mouth. This time, when my sister looked at me, I shook my head ever so slightly. I sucked at small talk. Eleanor had always been the chattier one of us. Though I didn't like pity on a regular day, I enjoyed the fact that she took pity on me now and talked with our parents in my stead.

When supper was over, Eleanor and I cleaned the table.

"Let's see a movie tonight?" she suggested.

"Sure."

Even though I had told her I would be just fine, Eleanor grabbed my backpack and we went upstairs. We passed the wall full of pictures, and I halted. Many of those pictures had been there for as long as I could remember. A house where the last picture of me dated from when I was twelve. There were newer ones of Eleanor, who still lived here. I, on the other hand, had changed my address as fast as I could to have a clean start. It felt weird to look at those memories now. They felt so distant, as if they weren't really my own anymore.

"Evy, are you okay?"

Eleanor's voice got me out of my head.

"Yes. I'm fine."

We both nestled on my sister's bed. Her room was still so very her. The walls were still lilac, and her room smelled like monoi. As a kid, I was always so happy when Eleanor let me inside her room to watch a movie with her or even be allowed to sit in her room. When I was younger, I thought my sister was so cool, and the fact that I could spend the evening with her made me feel rather awesome as well. I slipped under her soft comforter, and Eleanor gave me a hug.

"I'm so glad you're home."

I couldn't trample her happy bubble; I couldn't tell her this wasn't my home anymore. So instead, I hugged her back and enjoyed the evening we had together.

Eleanor dropped two fake sugars in her coffee before taking a huge bite of her breakfast: a toast loaded with avocado, cottage cheese, herbs, and a royal amount of sriracha sauce. I watched her take it all in. She let her cat-like eyes fall on me. I grinned at her.

"You're cringing."

My sister could read me like an open book. My smile became genuine.

"I guess I am."

She let out a sigh. Her nails clicked against the white mug. "Fine, what am I doing wrong this time?"

Unlike with Jasmine, I had spared El most of my

knowledge about food. But if she was asking, how could I refuse?

"You're putting fake sugars in your coffee."

"So? It's fewer calories than real sugar. And this way, I can drink my coffee without feeling guilty."

She took another bite of her toast and hummed from contentment.

"I love that you enjoy eating again, but you should not count calories. Your two avocado toasts are almost as much as a cheeseburger from McDonalds. They are nutritious, yes, but they also contain lots of calories."

Her face blanched, but before I could continue explaining anything, my mom intervened.

"Evelyn!" She tutted. "Don't try to scare your sister. She's eating well, and she's healthy."

I didn't even try to hide the scowl on my face. Mom's eyebrows shot up at my displeased face. Here she was again, trying too hard to now be the mother she should've been years ago. Next time I'd have to time how long it would take her before getting her feathers all ruffled up because I spoke to my sister.

"I never said that she was doing something unhealthy. What I am trying to explain here is that she shouldn't look at the calories because they don't tell the whole truth about what you eat."

As if she could sense my mood shifting, Eleanor put a hand on my arm. "Alright, I'll keep that in mind."

I stared at my bowl of cereal; I had barely touched half of it. Now just the idea of eating the rest made my stomach feel leaden. I pushed it away.

"Lost your appetite?" Mom asked in a teasing tone.

It was meant as a joke, yet I nodded. Like I would be able to joke with her after her useless remark.

"Indeed. Now if you'll excuse me, I need to study. I wouldn't want to scare my patients away by being unprofessional."

"Why is she always so defensive?" Mom asked as I left the kitchen.

If that was how family breakfasts were going to be, perhaps I shouldn't do those anymore. This was such a waste of time and energy. It often went like this: Mom would build an invisible wall around Eleanor, wrap her in an emotional blanket, and if anyone dared say anything she didn't like, she thought Eleanor would break. It made most people feel like assholes, and sometimes I wondered if my sister felt like Mom was keeping her from toughening up. Eleanor was twenty-three. She was a strong woman. Still, Mom saw her as if she were made of glass.

Back in my room, I let myself fall on the bed. How much longer before I could go back home? I glanced at my phone. It was barely 10 AM, and yet it felt like I had been here for ages. This weekend felt like forever. My phone buzzed.

Jasminnie: *So, how's it going?*

Oh, how I missed her. Was she at home with Theo? Or was she with her parents? If only I could teleport and get back to Jasmine and her bubbly personality.

Evy: *Regretting all my life choices...*
Jasminnie: *Want me to send you some memes?*

Evy: *Please do. I don't know how else I'll survive*

A second later, a picture of a sad cat munching on salad popped on my screen. I giggled as Jasmine kept sending memes to get me through the day. A knock on the door made me jolt, and Eleanor entered. She assessed me for a second before plopping down on the bed.

"You're in a better mood than I feared," she said slowly.

I was used to people seeing me as a grump. It was a reputation I had made for myself, unwillingly of course, but still. The fact that my own mother saw me as nothing more than a grump, or that she couldn't understand the reason I had become grumpy in the first place, was proof enough that there was nothing for me here.

"I want to go home," I answered quietly.

"Evy, this is your home."

I shook my head. I couldn't lie to Eleanor.

"No, my apartment is my home. This feels like a charade."

"Doesn't it feel like a charade because you make it so? Mom and Dad are trying, so stop being so stubborn."

Mom yapping at me every time I talked to my sister was not what I would call "trying". Eleanor picked a long hair from her otherwise perfect bangs and put it back into place.

"You know she can't help it. She worries about me."

Yes, she always worried about fragile little El. Evy, on the other hand, could take it all. She was strong enough to take it all. My nails dug into my palms, and Eleanor grabbed my hand.

"Tell me what's wrong."

My breath got stuck in my throat, and my eyes blurred. "I want to go home," I pleaded. "I just want to go home."

The only thing this place reminded me of was what had happened to my sister and how it had affected my family. How they had kept me away from Eleanor because I was too young. How it had forced me to grow up without my parents. They had walked away, not because they had wanted to; it was their duty as parents to be there for Eleanor. Now they wanted to waltz back into my life, and I found myself unable to let them back in. I rubbed my cheeks angrily, wiping off the wet streaks. Eleanor eyed me warily.

"Why do you hate it here so much?"

For a brief second, I hesitated. Would it be worth it to tell her? Would she understand? She probably wouldn't. But I was so tired of this situation, of having to keep up the façade and come back every time pretending I wanted to be here.

"Because being here makes me feel worthless, like I can't control my life. And I don't want to pretend like I am still that thirteen-year-old girl you left behind when I've moved on with my life. I have my own life with the people that were there for me. Where people don't see me as a threat to you."

I pressed my lips together, waiting to see how she would react now that the words were finally in the open. Eleanor smiled, albeit a bit forced.

"Evy, no one left you behind."

"Eleanor, you weren't here," I bit back. "I stayed with Grandma or at Jasmine's house for years."

That made her pause. I snorted. Like she knew how things had been over here. I didn't pretend like I knew how life had been for her. She drew back her hand, almost as if she was afraid to touch me now. Was it because I had crossed a line in her head, or because she suddenly realized how much I hated it here and didn't know what to do, I couldn't tell. I grabbed my pillow and held it against my chest. Eleanor sighed.

"I'll tell them you need to go back home to work on a school project. If it comes from me, they won't complain too much."

More tears escaped my eyes, so I just nodded. My sister gave me a hug. I clung to her, too thankful to be able to say it aloud.

"You better work on a school project once you're home again so that it isn't a lie, okay?"

"I will."

Just like Eleanor had predicted, my parents didn't really react when she told them I had to go back to the apartment. I kissed them goodbye, trying to hide how relieved I was to leave. Once it was just my sister and me, I let out a loud breath.

"Thank you."

"Let's go grab lunch together next week, to make up for the lost night."

I could tell that she was disappointed in my behaviour. The least I could do was accept. I nodded, and my sister gave me a smile.

"I'd love to."

"I'll choose the spot," she said.

"That's fine. I'll see you next week, then."

Eleanor waved before heading back inside. I couldn't help the smile that spread on my lips as I walked to the bus stop. It was time to go home.

CHAPTER 8

The light flickered once, twice before it gave up and half of my room became dark.

"Oh, fuck me," I muttered.

But I was prepared. I grabbed a spot out of our stash of lamps and a chair from the kitchen. Changing a spot couldn't be that hard. I saw Theo do it once. This would be fine. Until I stood on the chair and couldn't reach the ceiling.

"Oh, fuck me!"

My options were rather limited. Should I wait for Theo to come and help me? He wasn't coming today, and making him come all this way for a lamp seemed a bit excessive. My dad? He'd come from even farther. For a second, I pondered over if I should study in Jasmine's room. That would barely be a temporary solution. I sighed. *Fine.* I knocked on the door. It didn't matter which one would open. There was some shuffling, then Danté appeared. His brows shot up.

"Oh, 'sup Squirrel."

I kept from calling him Alighieri. After all, I needed him.

"Hi, do you have a ladder?"

"A ladder?"

"You know, a device that makes you able to reach higher."

Danté hooked his thumbs in the loops of his faded jeans, his tongue pressing against his cheek. He always looked so much softer in light-coloured clothes. Unlike the cheeky devil that he was on the inside. It was that devilishness that I liked.

"I am aware of what it is. I was more intrigued by *why* you would need one."

"One of the lamps in my bedroom stopped working."

"To answer your question, we don't have a ladder here. But maybe I can help."

He was a full head taller than I was, so it could work. I nodded.

"I'd appreciate that."

He followed me inside my bedroom. It wasn't that I was a messy person or anything, but having him inside my own bubble felt rather weird. Danté looked at the spot and got on the chair. Yep. He could reach it without any problem. There went my dream of being an independent woman. His shirt moved up enough for me to get a glimpse of the smooth skin and the muscles moving underneath. And boy, did I want to find out if his skin was as soft as it looked. *Focus, Evy!* I shined some light with my phone. He motioned me to give him the new light bulb. While he was changing it, he stood awfully close to the edge of the chair.

"Make sure not to fall off the chair. I don't have the strength nor the driver's license to get you to the ER if you break your ankle."

He tsked. "Glad to hear you care so much about my well-being," he shot back without looking at me.

When he was done, Danté got down from the chair. Or he almost fell down off it, was more like it. My heart plummeted to the floor just like he did. I caught him by the middle and almost ended up on the ground too.

"What did I tell you?"

Was he always so clumsy? I had never noticed it before, but I had never seen Danté doing much more than standing or sitting. He patted my head like one would pat a child.

"We're still standing."

Realizing I was practically hugging him, I let go, clearing my throat. A mocking smile tilted the right corner of his mouth.

"You can breathe, Squirrel. You don't have to bring me to the ER today."

Why did that sound like it was something that would happen eventually? *Please, let the ER not be our thing.* He pushed on the switch, and the light was back. I let out a happy squeal. Who needed to be an independent woman when the light was back thanks to the cute neighbour? That was a joke. It sucked balls to have to ask such basic tasks to someone who had a penis. Not that I could complain with Danté here.

"Thank you."

"You're welcome."

Instead of leaving, he leaned over the desk. He skimmed through the pages of my lessons and papers.

"Impressive," he finally said.

"Not as much as you knowing the whole body."

He looked up, and I found myself blushing.

"I meant bones and muscles."

An evil grin spread across his face. *Shit.*

"I didn't ask for a clarification, but thank you for insinuating I know my way with a woman."

I flapped some wind at my face. This was ridiculous, so why was that exactly how I saw him? Many of those girls came back for more, so obviously he had to be good. I'd come back just for the soft, low voice and the eyes that promised nothing but trouble. Oh yeah, and a cute round butt was definitely a nice bonus.

"Oh, you know, I love to inflate one's ego. A deflated ego means a deflated dick."

It seemed like a valid nindō to have, though I wasn't sure Naruto would be proud of it. Poetry had never been my forte.

"How considerate."

I flashed him a grin. "Yes, I wouldn't want you to have that misery."

Danté let out a breathy laugh. His eyes turned into crescent moons, and that adorable dimple made its appearance. How could one be hot and adorable at the same time? It seemed like an interesting formula, but as I had always sucked at mathematic formulas, I just loved the result without losing too much thought about it. Danté put his hands together and made a mock bow.

"I am forever grateful."

"You are so very welcome."

We went back to the living room. Before he could leave, I ran to the kitchen to grab the cookie jar and offered him a chocolate chip cookie.

"As a thank you for your precious help."

He let out an appreciative hum. Danté and sweets had always been a love story.

"Self-made?"

"Always."

His brows slightly scrunched. Danté hesitated before taking one that had the least amount of chocolate in it. So he wasn't a fan of chocolate but was too polite to tell me no.

"I'll see you around."

I waved and waited until he was back in his apartment before closing the door. How was it that he made perfect scores when he wasn't even in the competition?

A spoonful of lemon zest and a drizzle of honey made most things in life better. Though every test cake I had made had been fine the last few days, there was always something off. So instead of doing a lemon frosting, I put a honey glaze over the baked goods. And it smelled heavenly. Jasmine's hand ventured too close to the cake, and I had to pat it away. She still managed to get a little chunk of it, humming.

"This one is perfect, Eves. The cardamom gives it a nice dimension."

Theo also tried to take a piece of cake, but this time, I was prepared. I hit his hand with my spatula. He yelped; no piece of cake was lost. Theo shot his girlfriend a desperate look and got a cackle as response.

"You ought to have better timing when stealing from Evy."

I took a bite from the cake, analysing the taste. The proportions were just right. The cardamom gave it a nice little twist. Had I added more, it would've tasted like perfume.

"Alright, I'll quickly change and we can go to the market," Jasmine said before vanishing.

Theo shot me a glance. I got more of those the last few weeks, so I ignored him until he glanced at me again.

"What?" I asked, his behaviour unsettling me.

Suddenly he couldn't look in my direction anymore. It had been a while since he and I had spent time together, just the two of us. Jasmine and Theo were a duo, just like Jasmine and I were. The Theo-Evy duo had ceased to exist, so when it was just the two of us, I didn't know what to say. It seemed like I wasn't the only one to feel that way.

"Stop being so mysterious and just tell me what's on your mind."

"I hoped to go to the market with Jasmine, just the two of us."

For a few seconds, I didn't know what to say. It wasn't like I had asked to go with them in the first place. Theo saw something shift on my face and immediately shook his hands in front of him before I even opened my mouth.

"I know she asked you to come. She always does."

And he never did. I couldn't remember the last time he actually asked me to come. Theo's expression turned sad; he knew his words hurt me.

"Evy, you know that I love you. I just want to go outside

with my girlfriend every now and then, and not with my two best friends."

"Well, maybe you should tell her if it bothers you," I snapped.

My eyes went wide as my tone became harsh, and so did his. Unlike with Jasmine, Theo and I never fought. Jasmine and I were both fire, he was soothing water. Me snapping at him was something that hadn't happened in years.

"I know. I'm not implying that you did anything wrong. Jasmine can't plan something without having you in it. You guys are like twins. But I'm not dating you…"

My shoulders sagged. That was probably something that was bound to happen while growing up, I guess. I had never wanted to interfere or be their eternal third wheel. Especially since it bothered Theo to have me around twenty-four seven.

"Fine, I'll stay."

"You don't mind?"

I didn't mind not going. I understood where he was coming from. What I did mind was that he had waited so long before telling me this was how he felt. Not that I could blame him. Theo had never been one to hurt others. He was too kind for that. So I just shrugged.

"Enjoy your date."

I took another bite of my cake. His eyes lingered on it, and I couldn't resist giving him a petty smile.

"But no, you still can't have my cake."

Theo engulfed me in a bear hug. It had been so long since it had been just him and me.

"You're a bitch," he muttered in my hair. "But know that I still love you as much."

"So are you."

My eyes prickled, but I wouldn't cry. None of us needed that right now. Jasmine cleared her throat, and in the blink of an eye, the moment was gone. She observed us with a frown.

"Did I miss something?"

My friend's mouth opened, probably to tell her what we just talked about, but I quickly intervened. There was no need to go that way and ruin their afternoon.

"No, nothing. I just told Theo to enjoy the market."

"You're not coming with us?"

I shook my head, smiling. "I need to write my recipe down. You can go."

Jasmine looked at Theo and me, unsure of what just happened. When she wasn't focused on us anymore, Theo mouthed a quiet thank you. Once they were both gone, I looked at my dessert.

"At least I have you, buddy." Then I plopped down on the couch, ready to eat away the afternoon.

CHAPTER 9

I reached for my pocket, but my key wasn't there. Uh oh. I took off my jacket and searched all the pockets. This couldn't be. *No no no no no.* I knocked on our door several times, but my call for help stayed unanswered. Jasmine also didn't pick up the phone. In a desperate last attempt, I tried to open the door, even if you couldn't unlock the door from the outside without a key. Why oh why did I have to forget my keys the night Jasmine had to go to bed earlier? I let myself glide to the floor. This was going to be such a long night. The cold of the floor seeped through my leggings, and I curled into a ball. I still knocked every now and then, hoping she would take out her earplugs and hear me. She never did. At one point, I must have fallen asleep. Something warm brushed my cheek, and a shiver ran down my spine. It was soft and felt nice. The feeling continued, stirring me from my sleep. I opened my eyes to find Danté looming over me.

"What are you doing?"

I looked up at him, not getting why he was there when I woke up. The light around him gave him a halo, and I beamed at the view. Then as I looked past him, it felt like the hallway looked back at me. Danté was frowning, his warm hand touching my cold forehead.

"Were you so drunk you couldn't even get inside?"

"Of course not," I mumbled, rubbing the sleep off my face.

"Then did something happen?"

A yawn escaped me, and as I stood, my whole body was aching. And cold. Danté's brows knitted together in concern.

"No, I just forgot my keys inside. And my roommate always sleeps with earplugs."

"Have you been there the whole night?"

Was it morning already? I glanced at my phone. *Fuck*. I *had* been here the whole night.

"Yep."

Danté sighed loudly. It kind of felt like he wanted to scold me, but he didn't.

"Why didn't you come to me? I could at least let you crash on the couch rather than the floor."

Well, that was a thought that hadn't even crossed my mind. I avoided knocking on his door after 10 PM.

"I didn't want to disturb you and your lady."

I could still see the blonde, model-like girl tracing her fingers over his bare torso until the fingers were low enough to play with the waistband of his pants. And even though looking at Danté without a shirt on was a gorgeous sight, I preferred it much better if no one was touching him in front of me. He leaned back against the wall on his side of the building. He raised an amused eyebrow.

"There was no lady last night."

"Look, I've already bothered you once when there was someone. I don't want to do that again."

Otherwise, I might need bleach for my eyes and my memories. It was one thing to know what was going on behind that door and another to see glimpses of it. Danté locked his gaze on mine. He couldn't read my mind, right?

"It wouldn't have bothered me," he simply said.

That couldn't be true. How many times would I have to give him blue balls before he actually admitted that I bothered him?

"You sure? Because last time, she stormed off because of me."

"I didn't mind. Now please come inside."

He opened his door, and the warmth of his home seemed so inviting. And yet, I couldn't bring myself to accept.

"Why? My roommate will wake up soon enough. I don't need your couch anymore."

"No, but you need a hot drink. Tea or coffee?"

How could I say no when he truly looked concerned about my well-being? I ended up nodding.

"A hot chocolate would be nice."

"Perfect. Now get inside."

His apartment was the mirror image of ours. The only difference was the layout. Where our home had lots of warm colours and mismatched pillows on the couch, everything here was toned down. With two guys living here, I guess that's as good as it could get. Many papers on the salon table caught my attention. Some looked like travel brochures, so he hadn't given up on his dream to travel. Was he going on holiday?

Before I could ask anything, Danté shot from the kitchen, "Are you team regular milk or oat milk?"

"I am a sucker for dairy," I admitted while plopping down on one of his bar stools.

I couldn't complain. Danté went all out. He took a saucepan out of his cabinet and put it on the stove, about to make hot chocolate milk from scratch. With dark chocolate. He ended up sprinkling some cinnamon on the hot beverage before handing it to me. He looked at me expectantly as I took a sip. It was *so* good. I wrapped my hands around the mug, enjoying the heat that crept back into my body.

"It's perfect. Thank you."

While I sipped my hot cocoa, he put together a protein shake and grabbed a banana from the fruit basket. I stayed silent as I watched him. He was wearing his gym attire. Then I glanced back at the disgusting-looking shake.

"Please tell me you've already eaten something else this morning."

"No, why?"

"You mean to tell me that this sorry excuse of a meal is supposed to be your breakfast?"

Danté sat in front of me, still not touching his shake. As if he was scared of what I would do. I knew it wasn't my place to make comments on what he did with his life, and what he did to his body. And yet my instincts were screaming.

"Bitch, are you dumb?" I cried out, getting up from my chair. "What the fuck?"

"Did you just call me a dumb bitch?"

"Yes! And I'll do worse! If you don't start eating healthy stuff, I'll throw a butternut at your head!"

"That sounds oddly specific, and premeditated. Was that something you already had in mind?"

"Not really. I thought about throwing melons at people once, but never butternuts. Until now, it seems."

Danté looked at his "breakfast".

"I can't believe she called me a dumb bitch…"

"Well, you're blond, tall and skinny. So the profile kind of fits anyway, unfortunately."

"And she keeps insulting me. Dude, I let you in and gave you a hot drink. Can't you be a bit more thankful?"

There was no bite in his words. If anything, Danté seemed to find the whole situation rather amusing. My lips twitched towards a smile.

"I don't do uselessly polite, and you know that. Do you have to be somewhere in the next hour?"

"No," he dragged with a sceptical voice. "Do you?"

"I had planned to go to the gym, but it can wait."

"Will you survive if you stray from your plan?"

I glared at him from over my hot chocolate. He had a point. I didn't like to stray from my plan, not that I would give him the satisfaction of admitting that. I quickly glanced at my phone. Jasmine was last seen a few minutes ago. Perfect.

"I'll live. Now throw that shake away and follow me."

I grabbed his mug and went to the door of my apartment. Danté followed silently.

"Jasmine, open the door!" I yelled, fist pounding on our front door.

There was some shuffling inside, then the door was thrown open. Jasmine glared at me, her toothbrush still in her mouth.

"What are you doing outside?"

Her eyes landed on our neighbour.

"I forgot my keys inside," I explained.

She shrugged before going back to the bathroom. Danté sat down at our kitchen table as I got everything out of the fridge.

"Do you need help with something?" he tried.

"I am good. Don't worry."

It was easier for me to do everything in the order I had in mind, rather than having to wait for someone to do things in their own way. And he was my guest. Sort of.

"Just for your information, carbohydrates are actually a primordial part of our diet. Why would you cut them off?"

"I dated a nutritionist a while back. She told me it was better to cut those off and pack up the protein."

That explained a lot. Wait, when did he date someone?

"Let me guess. She also told you it was healthy to drink water with lemon juice?"

"How'd you know?"

My eyes rolled so far up it almost gave me a headache. I bit back a salty comeback and went for the educational explanation instead.

"Lemon water doesn't do anything for you except destroy your tooth enamel."

Danté leaned back in the chair, arms crossed. There was a small, knowing smirk on his face.

"Alright Squirrel, tell me what I need to know. I know

you're dying to tell me."

I let out a breathy laugh, shaking my head. And here I was trying to not be a know-it-all, as Chloe often called me. I quickly blanched the bean sprouts and spinach before turning back to him.

"Our bodies need carbohydrates to function properly. If you stop eating them, your body will find its needed energy in the lipids it has stocked, which isn't bad, as long as you have some extra weight. If you don't, your body will suck the energy out of its own proteins, which are your muscles. Do you see where I am going?"

"Which is the reason why I don't bulk up, I imagine?"

"Exactly. Tell me you haven't been doing this for a long time."

"Not religiously, no."

"You know, if you really want to do it the right way, you should eat things such as wholegrain bread or pasta. They have lots of fibres, which help to evacuate the lipids you take in more easily. Just make sure to drink enough water if you eat wholegrain foods because otherwise, you'll end up being constipated."

A loud laugh escaped him as Jasmine walked inside the kitchen, a towel wrapped around her hair. Her olive skin glowed from the moisturizer.

"Why are you talking about him being constipated?"

I'll admit that was probably not the sexiest conversation topic to have if you're trying to impress someone. On the other hand, there was nothing I could do to impress this man. All my chances had flown out of the window when we met. And if there was still one teeny tiny chance left, I had thrown it out of the window myself by calling him a dumb bitch. Which made me question who the real dumb bitch was in this room,

"This genius thought it was wise to stop eating carbohydrates."

"Bitch, are you stupid?" she yelled.

Danté shot me a questioning look as if to ask "Not her too?" I shrugged. Of course I had drilled my best friend. Jasmine had quickly followed my instructions without complaining and was now an advocate of my cause. Especially since she lost quite some fat tissues and gained some muscle instead. I finished the three bowls of bibimbap and put them on the table. Jasmine added a whole lot of gochujang to her food. Thanks to her Moroccan roots, she could handle way more spice than I could. Danté dug in his bowl and made an appreciative hum.

"Well, thanks for the life lesson, and the nice food."

I nodded. We ate in a comfortable silence until we were all done. It was nice to have Danté over at our place. Then I remembered something.

"Are you going somewhere?" I asked.

Danté looked back up. He always watched people as if he was genuinely interested in what they had to say. Right now, his attention was solely fixed on me.

"What do you mean?"

"There were brochures on your salon table."

"Oh right. I forgot to tell you. I'll be going overseas to volunteer as a physical therapist. It's something I've been wanting to do for years, and now seems like the perfect time to go."

As if I couldn't like him more than I already did. Of course that was something he'd be into. Jasmine hummed.

"That's so cool! How long will you be gone?" I asked.

"I don't know yet. Most volunteering programs are six months or a year. But since I want to travel a lot, I might go from one program to another. We'll see where I end up, I guess."

A year? The joy I felt was short-lived. It was selfish to even think such a thing, I know. But Danté being gone for a whole year was a long time. Jasmine must have sensed the shift in my behaviour because she asked the question for me.

"Oh, it will be weird without you here. Will someone be staying in your room while you're overseas?"

Danté shook his head. The light-hearted openness in his eyes had subdued. "No, I'll move out before going. I'm not from Brussels, so there's no reason for me to come back after my trip."

My heart rate spiked up painfully to the point it felt like I would faint. *Danté is leaving. Danté is leaving. Danté is leaving.* The words were spinning in my head, making me dizzy. As if he could feel my thoughts getting out of control, Danté looked back at me. He watched me as if he was waiting for me to say something. I just didn't know what I could possibly say. This couldn't be. In a few months, he would be gone, and there was nothing I could do about it. I swallowed down the sudden panic and showed him a wavering smile.

"That's awesome."

His jaw tightened, but he nodded. Danté kept looking at me, but his gaze was too strong. I dropped mine and looked at my hands. What else was I supposed to say? It didn't matter anymore. He got up from his seat.

"Thank you for the delicious food, but I need to go to work."

And then he was gone. Jasmine hit me in the shoulder. I glared at her.

"What was that for?"

"He is leaving, you dumbass!"

She hit me again, and I couldn't muster the energy to fight back.

"Yes, I registered that."

"Now was the perfect moment to ask him out!"

Was it though? It felt like my time had run out already. I got up on unsteady legs.

"Evy, are you alright?"

No. I wasn't. How could I be? Part of me wanted to run after him and ask him out, or ask to stay in touch. Anything, as long as I could keep Danté in my life in some kind of way. I also knew that it wouldn't be fair. He was about to live his dream, and I wasn't a part of it. There was no point in pretending like I was.

"I will be."

CHAPTER 10

Danté, Alex, and a few other of his friends were sitting at one of our round tables. They had been at it for an hour already, and they didn't look like they were about to leave. At one point, they even hooted, not that I heard what it was about. Every now and then, I glanced at the table. Well, not at the table, but at the blond guy sitting there, laughing and cracking jokes. How much time did I have left? Now that I knew that this sight would end up disappearing, I found myself looking more and more. Maybe that was a tad bit creepy. I just didn't want to miss a minute of him. Especially now that he might slip away from me. My heart was still beating painfully fast in my chest, beating so fast it felt like I would pass out from fear and panic. I had to do something. Anything! Even though my head was running three hundred miles an hour, I felt absolutely, utterly stuck. Danté and I had never worked out, so what could I possibly do to make it work now? The only thing I was certain of was that I would never forgive myself if I didn't try my luck. Because I'd had two years to do something, and I'd wasted those two years pining after him, then dating a guy just to try to stop the pining.

When Alex made a sign for us to take their order, my heart squeezed from the panic. I glanced at Chloe. As always, she just shook her head.

"I'll leave them to your good care."

Since the very beginning, she never wanted to take Danté's orders if I was around. I swallowed, then grabbed my little notepad and went to their table. I plastered a polite smile on my face.

"Can I get you anything?"

"Can you bring us a few slices of chocolate and coconut cake?" Alex asked.

What can I say? My chocolate cake brings the boys to the yard. Most guys nodded in agreement. Everyone, except for one. I caught Danté's blue gaze. My smile became genuine when he made a face. Chocolate wasn't his favourite. Though he had never said so out loud, Danté had always avoided our drinks and pastries that contained chocolate. It had taken a chocolate chip cookie for me to understand it.

"Alright. Five slices of chocolate cake. Anything else?"

They looked at each other, then at me with confused faces. There were six, so of course it looked like I got the order wrong. Instead of explaining, I looked back at Danté.

"I made a lemon cake with icing. Would you prefer that?"

Danté nodded, thankful. If the others had an opinion, they at least had the decency to keep their mouths shut.

"Sounds great."

Chloe raised a questioning eyebrow when I got back to

the counter.

"Since when are you so kind to him?"

"Don't be so dramatic. I am a kind person."

"Oh, please."

I turned back to her, arms crossed. Chloe flung her arm around my shoulders. When I had started working here two years ago and said I missed having my sister around, she had taken it too seriously. Two years later, Chloe was still pestering me on every occasion, just like she had also become a dear friend.

"You know what I mean, Evy. Of course you are a kind person, but you coddling Danté is unusual."

"I am not coddling him," I tried. "The guy just doesn't like chocolate."

A knowing smile played on her plump lips. I had to admit, my excuse sounded weak, even to me.

"You would know that, wouldn't you?"

I couldn't help the heat creep up my neck and cheeks. Chloe had always known I liked him. Probably anyone could see it, anyone but one. She had even slapped me every day with a towel on the shoulder when I had started dating Robert. At least the first month. When she realized I was rather serious (well, sort of), she gave up.

The six men were in deep conversation when I put their pieces of cake and cutlery on the table.

"I was convinced that Alex would be the first one of us to get married."

Some of them laughed at that while Alex's cheeks went beet red.

"Still working on that," he muttered.

Of course, I knew Alex was seeing someone. I just had no idea that it was that serious. Sometimes I wondered what kind of creature would date Alex. Not that he was a bad guy. I simply had a hard time figuring the guy out. The man next to him, Jamie, clapped his shoulder.

"Sorry brother, I didn't want to wait any longer. Will Elena be there?"

"No, she's still in Russia. I'll come alone."

His girlfriend was in Russia? That was one hell of a long-distance relationship. I grabbed the empty cups and put them on my tray.

"And you, Danté? Who is your plus one?"

My head shot up, the empty coffee cup still clutched in my hand. My heart clenched at the question. It was none of my business. I knew that. And yet, I waited for his response, steeling my spine for the blow that would come. Another of his friends laughed loudly.

"He probably can't decide and will find a random girl a few hours before the wedding."

A muscle twitched in his jaw, but he stayed silent.

"Well, we never saw him with a girl," said yet another one, "so I am not even sure he'll have a plus one."

Both Alex and Jamie made a face. They had seen Danté with many, many girls.

"Nonsense," I shot back.

All eyes landed on me, and I wanted to hit myself in the face with my tray. If it hadn't been full of dirty mugs, I might have done it. Danté looked at me, curiosity dancing in his blue eyes. I swallowed and kept my customer-friendly smile as I placed myself next to Danté, putting a hand on his shoulder. There was tension underneath the fabric of his sweater. Alex watched me, silently assessing my next move.

"If you really want to know a bit more about him, Danté's favourite kind of girls are the ones with dorky personalities and funky pyjamas."

A silent laugh shook him, and the tension in his shoulders lessened. Danté nodded. "They are."

My eyebrows shot up. I shook my head and regained my composure. He was just playing, just like I had before. This wasn't real. I nodded once and went back behind the counter on unsteady legs. *Get yourself together, Evelyn! Don't take everything so seriously.*

A few other customers walked in, and I focused on them. It was easier to pretend that Danté's words had no effect on me as long as I could concentrate on something else. One by one, his friends paid, then left the café.

When everyone was gone except for Danté and Alex, I sipped on my water. Danté walked over, taking out his wallet.

"Was everything to your liking?" I asked.

"Your cake was great. Thank you."

I couldn't help but smile like an idiot. Danté smiled back, the skin around his eyes crinkling cutely.

"Sorry for having stepped in. I was joking."

Danté opened his mouth, then closed it. Had I overstepped a boundary by chiming in while he was with his friends? He shook his head, a small smile still on his lips. What was going on in that pretty head of his? I bit my lip, waiting. Danté rested his elbows on the counter.

"Would you like to be my plus one?"

I choked on my water. Worry crossed over his face as I

felt mortified.

"I beg your pardon?" I asked between coughs.

I had misheard that, right? Danté grabbed a paper napkin and offered it to me. I dabbed at my mouth.

"Will you go to the wedding with me?"

I cleared my throat. My mind had a hard time processing what was happening.

"Why would you want me as your plus one?"

"Because you're my dorky neighbour who has a whole collection of funky pyjamas."

I crossed my arms, doing my best to keep from laughing. Danté's lips twitched, but he waited expectantly. Under regular circumstances, I would've found an excuse to not go to something as official as a wedding. Or something that almost sounded like a date. But maybe this was my very last chance. And maybe it was time for me to stop pining and panicking, and to finally do something. No matter how things would go.

"How can I say no to that?"

"Is that a yes?"

"Yes."

Danté let out a loud breath. Like he had been expecting things to go differently. He quickly regained his composure, standing a little straighter.

"Great. Let's grab a coffee tomorrow, and I'll give you all the details."

Part of me wanted to do a happy dance. Instead, I simply answered, "Okay."

He hesitated as if he wanted to add something. Nothing else came.

"Bye, Squirrel."

He waved before heading for the door where Alex was waiting for him. Once they were all gone, Chloe came back from the kitchen. She patted my shoulder.

"That was about damn time."

CHAPTER 11

Just like Danté had promised, he came to the shop the next day right when my shift was about to end. He wore simple jeans and a black knitted sweater, and even so, he looked like he had walked out of one of my dreams. Which he probably had. I still couldn't believe that we were going to go to a wedding together. And if he looked so good in plain clothes, then my little heart wasn't ready for Danté in a tux.

"Hey, Squirrel. Are you ready?"

I glanced at the clock. Still five minutes to go. Chloe shooed me away.

"It's alright. You can go."

I quickly went to the locker room and took off my apron and blue shirt. Then put on some perfume before heading back to the front of the shop with my bag and jacket.

"So, do you want to drink a coffee here, or go somewhere else?" I asked.

"Well, the coffee here is way better. But if you're tired of always being here, I am up for anything."

"Agreed, our coffee is the best."

In the end, we settled into one of our own booths. It was weird to have Chloe bringing us our drinks. Once she was back behind the counter, Danté leaned forward, his elbows resting on the table.

"So, Squirrel, what's your story?"

I looked up from my coffee.

"My story?" I asked dumbly.

Was I supposed to tell him how I got bitten by a genetically engineered spider and was now superhuman? I had been bitten by a spider a few weeks back. Unfortunately, when I had gone to the gym to lift weights, it had been clear I still wasn't about to become a hero.

"Why do you want to be a dietitian?"

Oh right.

"Because I love food."

As far as I could remember, I had always wanted to do something with food. Although at first, I had wanted to have a cupcake and macarons shop. Which was still something I intended on doing one day, just not as a full-time job. Danté raised an eyebrow, not entirely convinced.

"That's it?"

How had he known? I took a sip from my latte.

"And because I want other people to have a fair chance at loving food the same way."

In the way his gaze became heavy, I knew he understood. His features softened as he laid his hands on the table.

"Who?"

I didn't mind talking about it; I just avoided it because

people always saw it as a sob story. The thing is, every family has a sob story, and ours has a happy ending, so why hide the truth?

"My older sister Eleanor had an eating disorder when she was a teenager. She struggled with it for years. It's under control now, so there is no need to worry. But where I've always seen food as something that makes me happy, she saw it as a struggle and something that would hurt her. And I just want to be able to help people like her enjoy eating without the guilt."

Danté hummed in understanding. There was a calmness about him that felt nice. Danté didn't comment on how sad it was, just like he didn't brush it aside as if it were nothing. He just waited for me to decide if I wanted to continue that conversation. I took another sip from my drink, and he nodded without pushing it any further. I hadn't been able to help Eleanor, because I was thirteen when she had been diagnosed. Seeing her body turn into a skeleton had been a nightmare. One that still haunted my parents and one that had given me a purpose. Hopefully, I could help other Eleanors who needed to learn how to accept themselves and the food they had to take in.

"That's valid. What's your favourite food?"

"Like most Belgians, fries," I admitted.

"Friet met mayonnaise?"

I made a gagging noise. Chloe would smack me for my lack of manners. I just couldn't help it.

"Oh yuck! I hate mayo."

Danté placed a hand on his heart, face contorted in fake shock. "Excuse you?! How could you want to help people love food and hate mayo at the same time?"

Someone turned around at his suddenly loud voice. I giggled.

"Hey listen, I never said that I had good taste."

"Unbelievable. I feel personally attacked."

I leaned over the table like I was going to tell him a secret. "Wanna know something more? I don't like beer either."

Danté threw his used napkin on his empty plate, completely done. "Are you even human?"

He poked my nose, and I made a weird cracking noise with my mouth.

"Oh no. I am an alien trying to trick you into believing that I am human."

"Ah yes, that explains the green shine of your skin. Here I thought it was because you only eat greens."

"Asshole."

"Only for you, Squirrel," he replied, wiggling his left eyebrow.

I hid my smile behind my mug.

"And what's *your* story?" I asked.

"Oh, mine is not half as interesting. One day, my grandma had to babysit me, but she had to go to the therapist, so I had to accompany her. For some reason, I was fascinated. And that's how I became one myself."

"Because you love to massage grannies?"

"I prefer massaging pretty women."

I rolled my eyes at that. *Men*. "Of course, you would."

Danté shook his head. "Don't even think that. I would never do anything with a patient."

"Never?"

"Never."

"So you really don't like to massage grannies?"

His laugh was easy, and I found myself laughing back. Oh, why hadn't I asked him out for a coffee earlier?

"No, I do like to massage grannies. They are the easiest ones to please. But I prefer cracking bodies to massaging. It's more fun."

Something told me Danté was a favourite with grannies. I could practically see them pinch his cheeks after a massage before leaving the medical practice. I wondered if they even offered him those old sticky lollipops they always have in their handbags.

"So, that means I can't ask you for a massage then?"

Danté leaned back in his chair. "How about I crack your neck instead?"

"Why would you crack my neck?" I asked, panicked.

I suddenly felt very uneasy. Never had I had to go to a physiotherapist. I didn't even have to go to the doctor once a year because I rarely got sick. And this dude wanted to crack my *freaking* spine?

"I am sure it's stuck in some areas," he continued.

"How would you know?"

Was I walking with a hunched back? Was there something bad in my posture? Danté smiled.

"Stop stressing. Most students have their neck or back that needs to be cracked at some point. May I?"

"Wait, you want to do this here?"

He nodded. I looked around. Most of the café was empty, except for an elderly couple and a student sipping coffee while working away on her laptop.

"I won't hurt you. Do you trust me?"

Did I? I found myself nodding before I even thought it through. Danté positioned himself behind me. I saw Chloe looking at me weirdly, and I just shrugged. What could I even say? He kneaded my neck and shoulders. His fingers trailed down my spine, his touch gentle. Danté wrapped his arm around my face and positioned the other hand on my shoulder. The skin of his hand felt soft against my cheek.

"I hate pumpkin spice," he said, still holding my head.

Call me basic, but I was an advocate for pumpkin spice. It didn't matter if it was in coffee, in cakes, or even scented candles.

"How could you hate pumpkin spice?" I sputtered.

Before I could say anything else, he cracked my neck. Tension I didn't even know I had left my body. That was it? When he finally sat back, there was a satisfied smirk on his face.

"You said that to distract me."

"I did," he confirmed.

"So you don't hate pumpkin spice, right?"

The little hope I had left was completely extinguished when he shook his head. "No, I really don't like it."

And the chance I had to impress him with homemade pumpkin spice cookies had been *crushed*.

"That's worse than hating mayo. Your taste is just as bad as mine."

"I disagree. My taste is great."

I squinted at him. Danté watched me, waiting for me to take the bait. So obviously I took it. It wouldn't have been fun otherwise.

"Are you talking about food or your taste in women?"

"Especially my taste in women."

And as if to emphasize his words, Danté winked. He fucking winked. At me.

"Then I hope you're referring to me: your favourite dorky neighbour with the awesome squirrel onesie."

A soft smile played on his lips. "You know I was."

And maybe it was a lie to not bruise my fragile ego, but for once, I just smiled and appreciated the warm feeling that his words gave me.

"Perfect."

"Now that we both agreed on something, let's talk about the wedding."

"Alright, I'm listening."

CHAPTER 12

"Ouch!" I yelped as Jasmine yanked at my hair.

"Sorry," she muttered.

We had been at it for hours. I enjoyed taking care of myself to a certain extent, for a student with a limited amount of time, that is. But scrubbing, shaving, and then doing hair and makeup was a lot. I also didn't enjoy being tortured by Jasmine. Except that she was way better at doing hair than I was. She had been able to mostly tame my unruly curls and create a hairdo that looked stylish. Now most of my hair was in an elaborate bun, with just a few strands hanging loose around my face. When she was finally done with my hair, Jasmine grabbed her makeup pouch. When she plucked some hairs from my eyebrows, I yelped again.

"This is getting ridiculous! I should've said no to the wedding if I knew this was the kind of torture you would put me through."

Jasmine pulled back, arms crossed. "Then why didn't

you? You knew exactly what I would do to you."

I glared at my best friend; she just glared back.

"So?" she asked again.

"You know why," I mumbled, ready to drop the subject.

"I really don't," Jasmine said, a knowing smile on her pretty face. "So please, enlighten me."

Part of me wanted to call her names. On the other hand, Jasmine had gone out of her way to go dress shopping with me. She even had given up on sleeping in today to help me get ready. The least I could do was take the jab like a grown-up. Especially since we hadn't talked about it. Jasmine had jumped with me when I told her that Danté had asked me to be his plus one, without pushing it further. I guess now would be the time to finally talk about it. I inhaled deeply, nestling back in my chair.

"I couldn't say no. You know how much I like him."

"Does that mean you'll finally get your head out of your ass and ask the guy out?"

Was I so afraid of committing that the mere idea of saying to Danté how I felt gave me nausea? Or was it the fear of being rejected? I pushed the panic aside. It would come back later anyway. For now, I just wanted to enjoy the day Danté and I would spend together. I could look back at the grey clouds in my sky later.

"If things go well today, I will."

"Promise?"

I swallowed. I wasn't one to break promises, so I hesitated. The problem was that I could still feel the clock ticking in the back of my mind. I wouldn't have much more time.

"I promise."

An hour later, I looked like I stepped straight out of a magazine for brides and bridesmaids. Jasmine had done wonders to my face. I hated having a full face of foundation and the whole rigamajig. Not because it looked bad per se, but I never found that a lot of makeup suited me. I never recognized myself. I enjoyed having a long, thick cat wing and my lips in a bold red, which were not really the best style for a wedding. So instead of layering the foundation and powder, Jasmine had just put a bit of concealer under my eyes to brighten up my complexion. The soft champagne-coloured highlighter that she had added was also gorgeous. My lips matched the cinnamon rose of my dress. Even my eyeliner was thinner than what I usually did.

Dress shopping had been rather chaotic. I had never been to a wedding, so I had no clue what I was supposed to wear. I had wanted to find a long dress, but it had to be simple enough so I wouldn't be mistaken as a bridesmaid. That would've been rather awkward, especially since I probably wouldn't know anyone at the party except for my date. All hope seemed lost until we saw *her*. A beautiful cinnamon rose, asymmetrical chiffon dress with just a tad bit of ruffle. It looked as if the dress came straight out of a vintage prom night, and both Jasmine and I had agreed that it was perfect.

"Should I take a picture? I feel like a proud mom."

I gagged at the idea.

"I'd rather die."

There was a loud knock on our front door, and Jasmine *actually* squealed from excitement. How was it that she was even more hyped than I was? She ran out of my room to open the door while I grabbed my black velvet pumps. I quickly put them on and did a few steps inside my room to adjust to the ten-centimetre high heels before walking to the door. Danté and Jasmine were talking in the living room. Both turned their heads when they heard my heels click against the floor.

"There she is!" Jasmine exclaimed. "She looks like a dream, doesn't she?"

I bit back a sigh, just ignoring her. When I looked at Danté, he was smiling softly. The way he looked at me made my heart do a few flips.

"She does," he agreed.

Heat crept up my cheeks, and if his ever-growing smile indicated anything, the red cheeks didn't go unnoticed. Danté was wearing a black tuxedo that hugged his body perfectly. There was even a black bow tie around his neck. He had always been handsome to me, but now he looked ravishing.

"You clean up rather nicely yourself."

The only thing I would change was his hair that was slicked back. It made him look like Jack Dawson in Titanic, but I preferred him when he was just Danté.

"Are you ready?"

I took my jacket and purse off the hook. *Well, there we go.*

"Yes."

He offered me his arm, which I gladly took. Jasmine raised her eyebrows in a suggestive manner, and I just waved at her before going out. She would grill me later tonight to know how things went. I just hoped I'd have juicy details to share with her.

Danté took rather big strides, and I had to almost jog to

keep up. There was a noticeable height difference between the both of us, and with high heels, it would be even harder to keep up.

"Can we slow down a bit? My shoes are rather uncomfortable."

He flashed me a sheepish smile. "Sorry."

He slowed down so much as if he were walking with a granny, but that was the pace I would have all day.

"Why did you take those if they're uncomfortable?"

Ah, men. They didn't understand how much pain we could inflict upon ourselves to look the way we sometimes do.

"I wouldn't look half as elegant if I had put on something else."

"I can't disagree with you on that one."

Ever the gentleman, Danté opened the door of the passenger seat and even helped me get in. Once seated in the car, I discarded my shoes. We drove in silence for a few minutes. Not one to like silence, I touched the screen of his dashboard to put some music on. Danté shot me a wary glance that I didn't understand. Since he didn't comment, I left it at that. Several sounds with a slow and steady beat played. They all had the same vibe, and none of those songs were metal, unlike Danté's usual music taste. Then came "The Death of Peace of Mind", and I turned up the volume. That song was so good, and *so* sexy.

"Damn, those are all very intense sounds you're listening to."

"It's my sex playlist."

I choked on my saliva. No wonder he had been so jumpy when I turned on the radio.

"You have a sex playlist?!" I yelled, unable to control my shock.

At least he had the decency to blush. I felt myself grow red as well.

"Of course, you have!" I scoffed.

"You don't?"

I shrugged. Our tastes were so different.

"Having sex to Taylor Swift isn't really something I ever considered. Plus, I don't need music to get in the mood."

The idea alone to get undressed to *Love Story* made me giggle. Danté let out an overdramatic gasp.

"Are you saying I *need* music to get in the mood?"

"I wouldn't know."

Though I wished I did. As the music got more intense, images of him in a dark room, with messy hair and no clothes on, kept flashing before my eyes. I had to do something to keep them at bay.

"Do you keep the same playlist for all the different kinds of girls?" I blurted out.

"Mostly," he answered, eyes on the road.

Jealousy roiled in my stomach. It was bad, I knew that. Yet I never stopped wondering how Danté brought home so many girls, all different looking, and still I had never caught his eye. Especially since he was always on my mind.

"So, how many girls has this song seen?"

"None. I just added it."

A weird feeling of relief cooled down the green jealousy in me. I looked out of the window as I felt a smile creep up my face.

"Perfect. Keep it that way."

"May I at least ask why?"

"I love that song. So now you'll only think of me while listening to it."

Danté laughed, and it made goosebumps erupt over my arms and legs. The sound of his laughter was low and addictive, and I wanted him to laugh more. With me.

"Possessive much?"

Touché. Maybe it was stupid to want something that was just ours. Without the idea of it being stained by someone who had been able to make him see stars, unlike me.

I shrugged. "Maybe."

"It's still a sex playlist."

One he intended on using again, was what he meant.

"Want me to remove it?"

He shook his head. "Leave it."

"You sure? I wouldn't want you to get blue balls."

It would be rather funny if I was the reason he got blue balls. At least, with someone else. Not that I was even in the picture, but that would be a huge blow to my ego. And self-esteem. And everything in between.

"I am sure you wouldn't."

The sarcasm dripped from his voice. I took the phone and opened the app. Danté's hand twitched towards me. I probably should've asked for his permission before unlocking his phone as if I had any right to do so. I waited, but he put his hand back on the steering wheel. I looked at the songs that were in that damned playlist. Who the hell calls a sex playlist "vibin'"? Most of them were very, well, hot. And I wouldn't mind doing it with that music in the background. I snickered when I put his phone back.

Danté shot me a worried glance. "What did you do?"

"Nothing."

The only reason he didn't take back his phone to check what I had done was because of the traffic. His eyes regularly drifted towards his device, his fingers tapping against the wheel. When we finally arrived at a red light, he unlocked his iPhone. I saw him search until his head fell back from laughing. The sound sent a jolt of joy through my system.

"Are you serious?" he asked, handing me back the phone instead of putting it back down.

"Very much so."

"The horizontal lambada – Squirrel's version."

"It's just what you need to put you in the mood, isn't it?" I asked, poking him in the shoulder.

"Or to get me out of it."

I grinned at him, and Danté flashed me his dimples. I took a selfie of me blowing a kiss at the camera and made it the picture of the new playlist. My antics made him snort.

"You are one peculiar girl."

"You wouldn't like me half as much if I wasn't."

After all, I was his dorky neighbour. I had to live up to the reputation.

Danté gave me a satisfied nod. "Very true."

I bit my lip to keep from squealing like a schoolgirl. When I glanced at Danté, his gaze was so filled with joy that I let go of the pretence. This was going to be a wonderful day.

The bride and groom were still at the photoshoot when we arrived at the venue. Danté helped me get out of the car. I felt like a newborn foal on wonky legs with my high heels. I wasn't sure if Danté had noticed how uncomfortable my shoes were, but even once I got my stability back, he kept holding my arm. Needless to say, I enjoyed every second of it.

I thought the wedding would be something rather small, as the couple was around the same age as Danté. Instead, the rest of the wedding took place in a large, fancy festivities room decorated with white roses and forget-me-nots, and a huge buffet that could feed an army. My eyes immediately fell on the whole dessert table. There was a towering cake covered in white and baby blue icing that they would probably have to cut together. It was the cupcakes that took the cake. Bad pun intended.

"Damn, they went all in." I whistled in amazement.

I wasn't sure I wanted to get married someday. That didn't keep me from taking mental notes of how fancy this was. If one day I ended up tying the knot with the love of my life, if such a thing even existed, this would be the dream.

Danté laughed quietly. "Jamie's family is quite rich."

"That makes sense."

The place looked more like a ballroom; it was that big. The parts that caught my attention were the huge dancefloor and the circular bar. A hostess walked to us to ask our names. We followed her and sat at a round table near the dance floor. Even our name cards were fancy, thick cards with an elegant silver font.

I was behaving, if I do say so myself, minding my own

business while waiting for the bartender to serve me my apple juice, when someone slid on the barstool next to mine.

"So, when are you going to tell him how you feel?" Alex asked in a too-laid-back tone that grated on my nerves. "Playing hard to get doesn't really seem to work."

I bit my lip to keep from lashing out. The audacity. I squinted at him. *Breathe, Evy*. I could tell him to fuck off in a polite way. I put on my customer smile.

"I don't like you, so let's not pretend like we're friends."

Alex choked on his drink, shaken by laughter. Had I looked like that when I had choked on my drink in front of Danté? Goddamn it.

"Wow," he breathed.

Okay, mayyyybe I had gone too far. But just a little.

"It's nothing personal," I tried in a kinder voice. "Something about you makes me uncomfortable. You always look at people as if they have no secrets for you, and it feels invasive."

He shook his head, still laughing. To my surprise, there was no judging edge to him. Alex accepted it like a gentleman. How curious.

"That's fair. I didn't mean to give you the impression that I want to invade your life and thoughts."

"Alright."

We both stayed silent for a bit. Silence with Danté felt comfortable at times. With Alex, I could almost taste the awkwardness. And maybe he had the answer I was looking for.

"Does he like me?"

Alex traced the rim of his glass with a slender finger, an

eyebrow raised. There it was again, the impression that he knew me too well.

"I was wondering when you'd have the guts to ask."

My foot tapped nervously against the floor. Should I wait for him to answer me, or just head back and leave it at that? Alex kept his heavy gaze on me until I felt like I would melt from embarrassment before he ended up shrugging.

"It's not my place to answer for him, so you'll have to man up and ask him for yourself. Just know that waiting for Danté to make the first move is not what will make him get the message."

I hated how much Alex was right. I had waited for him to ask me out for years. Not because I believe that guys are the ones who need to make the first move. Hell! I would've asked him out if there hadn't been a different girl in his bed every other day. But there was only so much a heart could take. So tonight had to be the night. I couldn't hold back tonight. Because I wanted him to know that I wanted more, if that was something he wanted too.

"I'll keep that in mind. Thank you."

Alex made an appreciative noise. There was an evil twinkle in his eyes. "So she has manners. I was wondering if you had any."

I made a face but didn't fight back. I deserved that. Instead, I bumped my shoulder with his. "I'll accept that one."

"And she can be humble. This must be my lucky night."

I laughed. Maybe I had judged Alex wrong. Maybe there was a chance that I could like him.

"Don't push your luck. At the next jab, I will stab you with a dessert fork."

"May I at least know why the dessert fork is your chosen weapon?"

"I'd like to get to the dessert before having to commit a crime. I won't get fancy food in prison."

Alex let his head fall back, a long, dramatic sigh leaving him. "Why am I not surprised that you thought it through?"

I shrugged. "If you can't be strong, you gotta be smart."

The bartender gave me my drink, and I clinked my glass with Alex's.

"Enjoy your evening, Evy."

"Oh, I will." I savoured every second of it, and I would hold on to the memories of tonight for a very long time. I gave Alex a smile. "Don't bother me tonight."

"Go for it, girl."

Once the plates were all cleared, the lights dimmed. Danté took that as his cue to get up. He, Alex, and a few other guys went to the little stage, and a picture of what I could only assume was baby Jamie appeared on the wall. The crowd laughed at seeing the cute, chubby baby that he was. His friends all gave a little speech, all while the pictures kept coming. I found myself melting at one where he and Danté were still kids, seven years old at best, both smiling with missing teeth, trying to crawl out of an outdoor swimming pool. Once Alex was done talking, he gave Danté the mic.

"Hello, I am Danté. Most of you know me, but for those who don't, Jamie and I have been best friends for over two decades. So it's only fair that I come here to show his most embarrassing pictures, and give you a few juicy facts about our lover boy."

The crowd laughed, and I found myself hanging on every word he said. Danté was a social person; he was also very good at capturing a crowd's attention. He smiled at his best friend, then sighed dramatically.

"Where to start? Jamie has always been popular with girls. Ever since he was able to talk, he's always been able to charm his way out of trouble, and to convince the girls in kindergarten to marry him. This charm was a skill that he honed as a teenager as well. So imagine my shock when he told me a few years ago that he met the one."

The picture changed from a toddler version of Jamie giving flowers to a teacher to one of him and Sophie, probably when they started dating. They were sharing a milkshake in the booth of a café, as happy as can be. I glanced at the bride and groom. Jamie hid his mouth behind his hand, afraid of what would come, unlike Sophie who was cackling at her husband. After all, she was now living the best day of her life, so she had won the lottery. Danté leaned against the wall, one hand in the pocket of his tux pants, looking at the picture of the young couple.

"I'll admit I was sceptical when he wanted to introduce us to Sophie. I thought it was just infatuation, until I met her. Then everything changed. It was the first time that I saw Jamie so happy and carefree, like he was finally complete."

There were ooooh's coming from the crowd, and now

Sophie was tearing up. Jamie put an arm around her shoulders and kissed her temple, ever so sweetly. Danté noticed, and his dimples appeared.

"Jamie, it's an honour to be your best friend, and I wish you and Sophie all the best. You both deserve it. I love you."

People applauded. This had been a lovely speech. Jamie wiped his eyes and gave his best friend a hug. It was also nice to see that none of them worried about hugging each other in front of so many people. Danté gave the mic to someone else before getting back to me.

"You are very good at this," I said as he let himself fall back in his chair.

"Thanks."

And when he looked at me with bubbling happiness in his eyes, a small part of me wondered if he would ever look at me the way Jamie looked at Sophie. How would it feel to know that you met the love of your life? I pushed the thought away. It was better to not think about that tonight. So I focused on the other speeches their friends and family gave. They were all just as kind and wonderful. Gosh, I loved weddings.

Sophie and Jamie opened the ball by slow dancing to "Perfect" by Ed Sheeran. Maybe it was ridiculous, but I teared up at the scene in front of me. I had always been a sucker for happy endings. Danté noticed. For a second, I thought he would laugh at how silly I was. Instead, he laid my head on his shoulder, letting his hand rest on my waist as we watched the couple dance. He hummed along to the song, and my heart squeezed.

Once the first dance was over, I almost got an emotional

whiplash when the music changed, only to be "Celebration" by Kool and the Gang. I quickly patted my eyes dry while people swarmed the dancefloor. Danté jumped up from his seat.

"Will you accept this dance?" he asked, offering me his hand.

My eyebrows shot up at the request. That was a part of him I had yet to discover. "Of course. I didn't come all this way to sit at a table all night."

I accepted his hand and followed him to the dancefloor.

"You could've sat at a table and looked at me all night."

Which was exactly what I had been intending on doing until now. I winked at him as Danté took my hands.

"Now why would I do that if I can actually dance with you?"

The corners of his mouth twitched up while he rolled his eyes. "Smooth."

I let Danté guide me, following his rhythm. It became clear quickly that the guy knew how to move, and if I hadn't been falling for him already, his moves might have made me. He made me twirl.

"Look at you," I crooned. "You're not half bad."

Danté slightly pinched my forearm, rolling his eyes. "Just be honest and say that I am a good dancer. I know you're thinking it."

Was he wrong, though? No, not at all.

"Fine. You're a good dancer. But you know what that means then, don't you?"

His face came awfully close to mine. I just hoped that the dimmed light would hide the flush on my face.

"That you'll offer me a drink?" he asked playfully.

"That you'll have to dance with me all night."

"I think I'll survive. If you offer me a drink."

"Fine. Let's go."

I followed Danté to the bar, where he asked for sparkling water with mint. Feeling a tad bit more fancy, I asked for another apple juice. If there was one night where I didn't want alcohol to dampen my senses or my memories, it was tonight. Then we went outside. The cool air felt nice against my clammy skin.

"Why did you ask me to come?" I asked. "You surely had more than enough options?"

Not that I was complaining. If anything, I was grateful. It didn't change the fact that it was weird for me to be his plus one at an event where no one knew me. Especially when Danté had plenty of girl friends. Danté cocked his head to the side, his hair finally getting messy again.

"Why would I want to do this with anyone else?" he asked, like it was obvious why I was his plus one.

"That's what I'd like to know."

His cheeks turned pink. One thing was clear: that wasn't because of the cold.

I cocked an eyebrow. "Go on, tell me."

"Fine. I had another date, but she injured her foot a while back. In the end, I'm glad that you are the one who came."

That made so much more sense. There was no way that I would've been the first choice.

I gaped at him in fake shock. "So basically, I am your stand-in."

Danté bumped his shoulder with mine in a playful

manner. "If I have to be stuck at a wedding and show off my dance moves, I'd rather do that with you than with anyone else."

That wasn't exactly what I wanted to hear, but it was better than nothing, I guess. The little voice inside my head urged me to ask who would've been his original plus one. For once, I ignored it. I may not have been the first choice, but I was here now. And all in all, we were having a marvellous time. That was good enough. It had to be. I pouted, and his eyes softened.

"You look stunning."

Even if he had already said so earlier, his words still gave me a warm, tingling feeling. I found myself smiling, though I tried not to.

"You already told me so."

"Now more than this morning."

Was he drunk? I thought he was drinking sparkling water, but maybe it had been alcohol this whole time. I was positive that what he said wasn't true. If anything, I was getting sweaty. And I hadn't even checked to see if my makeup had smudged. I crossed my arms.

"How could that even be possible?" I muttered.

The skin around his eyes crinkled as his eyes turned into crescent moons. "A bit breathless and smiling at me is how."

My skin turned hotter than a furnace. He wasn't playing fair.

"You shouldn't say that so lightly."

"I didn't mean it lightly."

"Just so you know, I am a nightmare dressed like a daydream."

We both laughed. He even got my references.

"Trust me, I was well aware."

An older woman in a skirt and jacket waved at us before almost running towards Danté. "Danté, it's lovely to see you."

Danté took the woman in his arms, his touch as gentle as if he were touching glass. Seeing the endeared face of the woman, I knew I had been right. The grannies just loved Danté and his golden retriever energy and kindness.

"Hello, Agnes."

"The wedding is wonderful, is it not?"

"It is," he agreed, his hand still on her shoulder.

Her attention focused on my presence. "Who is this charming young lady?"

"Agnes, this is Evelyn. She is my date."

Date. I forced my eyes to not widen as he knocked the air out of me. Danté had never used the word "date" to describe me. I was just his plus one. Plus two? His hand found the small of my back. Even if it felt like I had been overcharged, the physical contact grounded me. The movement didn't go unnoticed by Agnes. She took my hand in hers and shook it; she could barely hide her curiosity and excitement.

"Nice to meet you, Evelyn. I am Jamie's grandmother."

No wonder Danté knew her. I tried to show her my most charming smile. For some reason, I wanted her to approve of me.

"Likewise."

She turned back to Danté. "She is a stunner."

"I keep telling her so, but she doesn't believe me."

This time my eyes almost fell out of their sockets. Danté

noticed it and winked. The old lady chuckled.

"Good," Agnes said.

Then she pinched his cheek, and in the blink of an eye, she was gone. Danté's hand was still on my back as he led me back inside. My shoes started to really hurt. When I looked down, the back of my pumps had cut through the sensitive skin of my heel. Danté noticed it too.

"Please take them off. It's hurting you."

"But won't it be weird if I am barefoot?"

"Want me to take off my shoes so you're not alone?"

I giggled at the idea. "That won't be necessary."

As soon as I took them off, Danté took the shoes from my hands.

"I can carry them," I tried.

He just shook his head. "So can I. Do you need some Band-Aids?"

"I'll be fine as long as I don't put them back on."

"You're sure?"

His concern was absolutely adorable. I knew Danté was a gentleman; there had never been a doubt. I just never realized how considerate he was about my well-being. It felt nice.

"Yes."

And since I was his date, I slipped my arm around his, holding him closer. Danté smiled down at me, and for a second, it felt like it was just the two of us.

"Let's dance?" I asked.

"I would love to."

It was cold when we went inside the car. Little white clouds escaped our lips when we got in. Danté noticed me shivering and immediately gave me his jacket before turning on the heat. The jacket smelled like soap and just the tiniest amount of perfume. It smelled just like him.

Unlike when we were in the car earlier, Danté let the music play ever so softly. I let out a yawn as I looked at the passing lights. This whole day still felt so unreal.

"You can sleep if you want."

"Don't you need me to talk to you to keep you awake?"

He shook his head, fingers drumming on the wheel. "I'm often the driver when my friends and I go out. I'm used to driving in silence during the night."

I wanted to talk to him, but I let out another yawn, then another one. I wouldn't be able to keep up. Danté gently squeezed my knee.

"I'll wake you up when we get home."

I took out my earrings and nestled in my seat. It was to Danté's soft humming that I fell asleep.

There was a weird pressure under my calves. At first, I batted it away, but the pressure kept coming back. That wasn't just pressure; someone was touching me. My head jerked up, and my heart rate quickened. Danté loomed over me, his eyes wide, like he had been caught doing something illegal. His hand was still under my knee.

"What…" I started.

When I looked behind him, I could see where we were. My body immediately relaxed. I had been so fast asleep that I hadn't even noticed that we were back at our parking lot. I must have been the most boring person to be with on a drive. My gaze fell back to his hand.

"What are you doing?"

Danté crouched, letting his elbow rest on my thigh. The bow around his throat was long gone, and the first few buttons of his shirt were now open. It was hard not to stare.

"I tried to carry you out of the car but you kept hitting me."

My cheeks warmed up. "I'm awake. I can carry myself now." I flailed my arms in front of his face.

Danté's lips went up, but he made a sign for me to move.

I grabbed my shoes; I just never got to put them on.

"If you're going to put them on even though your feet are now open wounds, you'd better let me carry you inside," he said from where he was leaning against his car.

"Don't be ridiculous. It's not that far."

Except that when I put the pumps back on, even just a few meters and a few levels of stairs felt like a whole punishment. And I must have done a terrible job at hiding my wince, because the next thing I knew, Danté swept me in his arms.

"You can put me back down. I'll survive."

"So will I."

We both sized each other up, waiting to see who would give up first. Danté's face was too close to mine. His breath tickled my skin. Under the light of the lamp post in the middle of the night, the temptation to lean closer and kiss him was growing bigger. I gave up.

"Fine. Carry me home, peasant," I ordered him.

Before I could understand what was happening, Danté's body jerked, and his arms disappeared from under me. I let out a scream and nearly choked him before he caught me again. His chest shook from laughter, but I found myself unable to let him go.

"Don't worry, Your Majesty, I wouldn't dare let you fall for real."

My arms relaxed a bit around his neck. I smacked him on the back of his head.

"Don't ever do that again."

His evil grin turned sweet. Danté carried me to the back door of our building. Once we were inside, I let him put me down and took off my shoes. Being carried like a princess was nice. Seeing Danté puff after dragging me up several flights of stairs seemed a bit too cruel.

Once we stood back in front of our doors, the magic of the night dissipated a bit. I didn't want it to end and pretend like this night hadn't happened. I just didn't know what to say. Danté beat me to it.

"Thank you for coming. It meant a lot." He gave me back my shoes.

I stood on my toes and dropped a kiss on his cheek. "I had a wonderful night, so thank you."

Danté's eyebrows went up in surprise for half a second, but his smile returned full force. It was that dimpled smile I clung to when I closed my eyes and fell asleep.

CHAPTER 13

Jasmine and I were watching *The Princess and the Frog*, singing along to every song, just like we always did when watching Disney movies, when my phone rang. *Mom*. Jasmine looked at my screen, grimacing.

"Are you going to answer?"

I rolled my eyes. If only it were so simple to not answer and to forget about it.

"Honestly, I'd rather not, but she'll keep calling until I answer, just to tell me it is unacceptable to have a mobile phone and to not be available at all times."

I breathed in to give myself some courage and picked up. Jasmine put the movie on pause to listen.

"Hi, Mom."

"Hello darling, I feared you were not going to pick up."

Damn right, I had wondered if it would be wise not to. I plastered a fake smile on my face. I read somewhere that if you smile, even if it is a fake one, your voice sounds friendlier.

It was at least worth a shot.

"How are you?" Mom asked.

"I am fine. How are you guys?"

"Oh, you know, your father needs to go to the physiotherapist."

"Is he alright?"

"Except that he has trouble accepting he's not thirty anymore, he's fine."

The sass in my mother's voice made me laugh. Okay, this wasn't so bad. Mom continued to talk about how their life was going. Like every time she called, she also wanted to know if I finally had a boyfriend. My mind wandered to the other side of the hall. Maybe I should also go see a certain physiotherapist, in lingerie. Would that also be worth a shot? I hadn't seen him since the wedding a few days ago, so I had no clue how things were supposed to be between us now.

"No, I don't have anyone."

She would get a heart attack if she knew how many men walked in and out of my bedroom.

"You should've stayed with Robert. He was a sweet guy."

Jasmine sighed loudly, and I bit my lip to keep from laughing out loud. My mom was the only person to think it had been a mistake to let him go. Even Dad had been glad I left him. Robert had indeed been a decent person. More than decent even. I just didn't love him, and that alone was reason enough to call it quits. If there was no love after a year of dating, there never would be.

"Robert and I were not meant to be."

"What a shame. Oh Evelyn, don't forget to wish your sister a happy birthday."

The comment was not supposed to be more than a simple reminder; to me, it felt like a bucket of iced water.

Jasmine let her head fall back against the sofa, muttering, "Here we go."

"Like you forgot mine two years in a row?"

My mother clicked her tongue, not happy about that reminder. Like I cared.

"We already apologized for that."

Right. Because a quick apology was worth so much. I rolled my eyes, thankful that my mother wasn't here. Otherwise, she would've given me a bombastic side-eye. And everyone who knew my mom knew how bad those were. A nasty look from her made you feel like a cockroach, and the only thing you wanted to do then was to disappear.

"I already sent her a message. I don't forget things like this."

I had even promised to make her a birthday cake that wasn't too unhealthy, which she had accepted by sending twenty-something heart emojis.

"Evelyn, that's enough," my mother snapped.

Her light-hearted mood was gone, just like it had gone up in smoke for me. This was why I didn't like to call her. There was always a moment where she felt like she had to mother me or scold me, where she thought she had the right to even do so. Maybe she still had, but it still felt unfair and undeserved to know she would always scold me for something, even when it was unnecessary to bring it up in the first place. So I lied.

"Whatever. I need to go to class."

"Already?"

"Yes."

I could hear her breathe loudly on the other side of the call. She was probably pinching the bridge of her nose in frustration, trying her best to keep calm. People tend to say I have a bad temper. Looking at my mom was indication enough if they wanted to know where said temper came from.

"Okay, I love you," she said in a forced cheerful tone.

"Yeah," I muttered. "Bye."

I let my phone fall back on the sofa. My best friend scootched closer, her knee bumping mine.

"That went well," Jasmine tried.

"It went as well as trying to cure a headache by hitting your head against a wall."

"The good thing is, she won't call you any more this week."

At least I had that going for me. Having her call me every week was already taxing enough. Jasmine observed me with knitted brows. I sighed at that face.

"You think I overreacted."

"Not necessarily."

"Speak, woman."

She chuckled. Jasmine grabbed her long dark hair and started braiding it. She really looked like the Disney princess when her thick mane was in a plait. Whereas I always looked like the drugstore version of Merida, with the personality of Rabbit. I didn't mind. At least I could flex to others about how beautiful my best friend was.

"I think it's normal for you to feel butthurt when your mom acts with you as if you're still fourteen and in need of her education. However, I don't think that being passive-aggressive towards her is going to resolve anything."

Well, that was probably true. That didn't mean I had to like what she said. Jasmine noticed my frown.

"You can't keep doing this, Evy. Everything in your life would go better if you were honest."

If you were honest. The words made my skin pimple with goosebumps.

"Are you insinuating that I am a liar?"

Here I thought that I was rather straightforward as a person.

"Oh, hell no. You are brutally honest. Just not about what really matters."

"And what matters, oh wise one?"

"Bitch," she muttered as she hit me in the arm.

I hugged her before she could hit me again. Jasmine, like the true hero she was, wrapped her arms around my shoulders and squeezed gently.

"What matters is telling others how you feel, Evelyn. Because you are so openly honest about mostly anything, they don't know what you really want if you keep those thoughts to yourself. You are an ostrich when it comes to facing your problems."

"Are you talking about my parents or about Danté?"

Her body shook as she giggled. "Both. I'm serious, Eves. You have been abandoned before, so I get why you guard your heart and run away from people instead of facing them. The problem is, you'll only hurt yourself in the long run."

Just the idea of telling my parents how I felt, or what I wanted, felt wrong. I shook my head. This was going to be a catastrophe. Maybe it would be better to just suck it up. Because even though I didn't need my parents around like most people did, hurting them by saying so was not what I wanted either. I was a bitch, sure, but not such a mean one. Danté on the other hand... I knew we had to talk. How could we be just friends after having spent the whole night laughing and touching? It couldn't have been all in my head, right? Or was I so delusional that I saw a future where there was nothing but a dead-end street?

"I need to talk to Danté."

I had promised Jasmine that I would try to talk things out with him if things went well at the wedding. Things had gone well. Too well even. And like any drug addict, I couldn't stay away from him. I didn't want to. So if there was a chance that he liked me too, I couldn't throw that away.

"That wasn't what I hoped would be your revelation of the day, but please do! You still haven't told me the details of the wedding."

I ended up laying my head on her lap. Even from this angle, Jasmine was gorgeous. Her light brown eyes were shining with curiosity.

I found myself grinning when I said, "He almost never took his hands off me."

"Did you kiss him?"

My breath caught in my throat, and I ended up coughing while heat crept up my neck and cheeks. "Gods, no!"

"There's no need to be a prude. That would be the most innocent thing you did."

"You're right, but this is Danté. I don't want to rush and act with him as if he was any other guy."

Because he was not. He was the whole reason why I couldn't fall in love with Robert. Jasmine brushed a strand of copper blonde hair from my face.

"Then what did you do?"

I smiled as the memories of us twirling over the floor flooded my head; memories filled with people and noise, where all I could focus on was him, and his eyes filled with laughter and a softness I had never seen there before, his warm hand never leaving mine.

"We danced."

My alarm clock rang, indicating that it was once again time to take the trash out. Without wasting much time, I grabbed the bags and went to the back courtyard of our building. The sound of steps shuffling behind me made me turn back. My eyebrows shot up in surprise as Jared, Danté's roommate, walked out of the hall. Needless to say, he wasn't the one I had hoped to see. Unlike our other neighbour, Jared wasn't that tall. If I wore heels, I was probably at the same eye-level as he was. He was a bit chubby, and always had a zen and reassuring vibe around him.

He offered me a polite smile. "Oh, hi Evelyn."

He had been Danté's roommate long before Jasmine and I came to live here, and yet, I wasn't sure I had seen that guy more than six times. Was he the type of person to stay at someone else's place, or was he simply always holed up inside his bedroom hikikomori style?

"Hey, Jared. How are you?"

"Good. It's weird to have the apartment all to myself."

"Where's Danté?"

Jared threw his bags in the bin, then offered to do mine, which I silently accepted.

"He went to Greece to go rock climbing with his sisters."

So that was why I hadn't seen him at Hot Stuff the last time. Not that I kept tabs on where Danté went. Had I known that Danté would be on holiday, I might have rethought my decision to wear my infamous squirrel onesie outside of my home. Luckily, Jared was a gentleman and ignored my attire. I wasn't sure if I had to say something else; I barely knew the guy. Jared wasn't someone to care enough to do useless small talk, because he gave me one last wave before going back inside. Probably locking himself in his room, only to emerge again in a week. I shrugged before heading back inside myself. There was no reason for me to dwell outside today.

CHAPTER 14

There were voices down the hall, then Jasmine opened my door. She shot me a suggestive smile.

"There's someone for you."

Before I could ask, she went back and Danté walked in. My eyebrows went up as he got in. My room wasn't as tidy as it generally was. Since the wedding a week ago, I hadn't found the courage to do my laundry or dust anything off. Even I got lazy sometimes. We had been home so late from the wedding, and the next days, I had needed to rest, my feet hurting. After that, I had been plain lazy. It could've been worse, but compared to Danté's place, this was a mess.

"You're back!" I said as I got up from my desk.

"I came back yesterday."

I waited for him to continue. It was the first time we saw each other since the wedding, life having gone back to normal as it always would on my part, and Danté being in Greece. All that was left of that wonderful night were my memories, and a selfie of us, where we were both breathless and beet red, but all smiles. And yes, I had looked at that picture too many times for it to be sane. Whatever. Danté grabbed something from the front pocket of his jeans and gave it to me. The earrings I had worn that evening.

"You left those in my car. I hope you didn't need them because I only noticed it today."

I rubbed my neck. I could vaguely remember taking them off and throwing them somewhere in his car.

"Honestly, I hadn't even noticed I didn't have them."

After the party, I had been too tired to care. And after having been carried like a princess, those earrings hadn't been on my mind at all.

Danté was having a staring contest with the Taylor Swift poster that hung on the wall, above a little shelf where I kept all my CDs. He made a face the longer he watched the picture. If he was going to comment on my full collection of her CDs, I was going to strangle him. I didn't care how cute he was.

"The fact that she looks straight at the camera makes it very creepy."

"It's just a poster."

He moved to and fro, never looking away from it. Had this dude never seen a poster in his life? I was a hundred percent convinced that he had posters of almost naked ladies lying on cars when he was a teenager. My cousins sure had.

"A poster that looks at me all the time, no matter what I do."

"Awww. Don't worry. We can turn the lights off if necessary."

Danté choked on his saliva, and I bit my lip to keep from laughing.

I laid a hand on his arm. "Everything okay there?"

He finally turned to me. "Yeah. Sometimes I forget you have such dirty humour."

My debatable humour was my most charming trait. At least, I liked to imagine that it was.

"Who said I was joking?"

His smile fell. "This isn't funny."

Danté rubbed the palms of his hands on his faded jeans. A pretty pink crept up his neck and dusted his cheekbones.

"Are you blushing?" I asked, taking his face in my hands.

Was it weird to find him so endearing?

Danté jumped back, holding me at arm's-length. "What? No way!"

I cackled. His face kept getting redder and redder. Unable to help myself, I pinched his cheek, and he batted my hand away.

"You definitely are. Why? You are used to this."

"Not with you, Squirrel."

I froze over, my arms hanging loosely against my sides. It had been clear from the start that I didn't fit his type. Never had Danté brought someone home who looked the slightest bit like me; not the girls who were here for sex, nor the ones he had dated.

"Am I that unattractive that you don't see me as anything other than the silly girl who wore a squirrel onesie?"

His face became serious. "First of all, that onesie is adorable."

And a great contraceptive, apparently. Had I known this,

I wouldn't have worn it in the first place. It made me loathe that stupid nickname.

"And second of all, I'm not going to have sex with you."

Well, wasn't that just great? At least he couldn't be clearer than that. I just couldn't make him see that his words actually felt like a stab wound. I straightened my spine and leaned against my desk for support.

"Woah. I never said I wanted to have sex with you. I just asked you if you found me unattractive. At least now I'm fixed."

As if I were exaggerating, Danté rolled his eyes. Could this moment become even more awkward than it already was? Instead of telling me to shut up, Danté sighed.

"You are anything but unattractive, Evelyn."

"But?"

My fingers tapped nervously against the wood of my desk. A movement that caught Danté's attention. His gaze softened.

"But you are my friend. And I don't do friends with benefits."

That was a nice way of being put in the friend zone, I suppose. I frowned at that. Had I really been the only one to think that after spending the night dancing together, things would change? Apparently.

"Well then, friend, I thank you for bringing back my earrings."

The tone of my voice was sharper than what I had wanted it to be. Danté's eyes widened, but he didn't make a comment.

"I'll see you around, Squirrel."

"Sure."

And then he was gone, leaving my high hopes in shambles.

CHAPTER 15

When we arrived at the College, a bar close to our apartment, I was surprised to find Danté and Alex there. It was always the two of them, just like Jasmine and I were always together. Yet something seemed off. Both men were drinking in silence when I was so used to them being so lively. Jasmine, who was oblivious to the dark cloud hanging over them, pushed me towards the bar. I stumbled to a seat, right next to my neighbour. They both looked at me and the graceless entrance I just made.

"Hello."

Danté greeted me, but he was the only one who did so. I knew that Alex and I weren't friends. It still surprised me to find him so silent. His face was taut, the bags under his green eyes deeper than ever. *Damn you, Jasmine*. I was about to go back to my friend when Alex got up from his bar stool and went outside. He looked straight up terrible.

"You didn't tell me you were coming here tonight," I said,

trying to fill the silence.

"Was I supposed to?"

I bit back a scowl. *Was I supposed to?* What kind of question was that?

"Only if you wanted us to hang out together."

"I didn't think that far. All I wanted to do was get Alex outside."

The person in question lit up a cigarette, smoke drifting in the air. I had never seen the guy do more than drink a beer. Let alone smoke. Judging by the way his hands moved, he had been doing this for a while.

"He falls back into his old habits too easily," Danté said quietly. "I hope that cigarette is the only thing he will take."

My eyebrows shot up at that. Mister Perfect once had a substance problem? I had always seen Alex as confident and maybe a tad bit boring. But then again, we all had skeletons hidden somewhere, didn't we?

"He looks miserable," I admitted.

"He has been feeling miserable for a while now. Alex isn't the kind of person to easily admit that, but I know he's unhappy and scared out of his wits."

Danté didn't have Alex's spidey senses to pick thoughts out of one's head. What he had though was a lot of empathy that also made him rather intuitive. Worry made his forehead crease.

"What happened?"

"You know his girlfriend is in Russia, right?"

I nodded. The mysterious Elena. "I heard something like that, yeah. How did he even date a Russian?"

Danté shook his head. His blonde locks moved to and fro.

"She's from Brussels, just like you. Elena lives there now because she's a ballet dancer."

Damn. That must be an interesting lady. I was very intrigued by the girl who had been able to tame Alex, and who had been able to make him look like a kicked puppy.

"So he misses her."

"He does. It's hard to see him like that, especially because I thought they were soulmates. Now their relationship is getting strained, and I don't know if they are going to make it."

His gaze drifted back towards the window, where Alex softly kicked a stone on the pavement with his Converse, lost in his head. Danté was right, the poor man looked miserable. I couldn't even imagine how distraught he must feel inside. The idea of Danté leaving made me skittish and sad, and we weren't even an item.

"Are you sure they are meant to be together?"

He absentmindedly swirled his drink. "I was. Which makes me wonder if it's really worth it."

"What?"

"Love."

A cold shiver went down my spine. I couldn't muster the courage to ask Danté if there was a chance he liked me too, our last exchange having trampled on the little bit of hope I'd managed to muster. Even if this wasn't about us, I couldn't help but fear what would come out of this.

"Danté…"

"Look at him. If that is what true love does to you, is it worth it? Maybe life will always get in the way."

"I think it's worth it. Maybe I am too optimistic but…"

One of his brows went up in mockery. "You, optimistic?"

I hit him in the stomach. A gesture Danté gave me back without hesitating. We both chuckled.

"Oh shush! I may be a grump, but deep down, I am a softie."

A softie who believed in love. In the many forms it came in. Because if love didn't win, what was even the point?

His gaze turned gentle, less guarded. "I know."

Heat crept up my face and turned it into a furnace. Hopefully he couldn't see my fluster under the dimmed lights of the bar.

I cleared my throat. "Anyway. I like to believe that even though the trials are hard, love will conquer."

Danté took a sip of his beer, his mind lost somewhere inside his head. He let out a long sigh. "I hope you are right. But I don't want all that pain and doubt that he is going through."

I cracked a smile at him as I knocked my elbow against his arm. "Are you saying you'll stay single your whole life?"

"Of course not," he huffed out. "It simply made me realize that I am not able to do long-distance relationships."

In other words, there was no room for me in his life. At least not if he was going abroad for a while. All my hopes I had clung to these few weeks seemed ridiculous now because there had never been a chance. Having my heart broken in a bar before I could even give it away was not how I had envisioned my evening. Not that I could hate Danté for it. Just like I couldn't force him to choose me if he had other dreams. I should've accepted what he meant when he said I was a friend instead of thinking I could convince him we could be more.

I put a hand on his shoulder. "Alex is lucky to have a friend like you."

"Thank you."

"See you later."

Danté opened his mouth to answer, but I slipped away before he could. There was no point in lingering. The message had been clear, and I wasn't sure my heart or sanity would be strong enough to endure even more. When I slid in the booth in front of Jasmine and Theo, I threw a peanut at my best friend.

"How could you push me like that?"

Jasmine shrugged before nibbling on one. "I figured you could use a little help and talk to Danté. You two have unfinished business, if I recall correctly."

"Alex is going through some shit. You chose the worst moment to help me."

Jasmine shot me a sympathetic smile. "I'm sorry, I should've read the room before acting."

I nodded and gulped down one of the tequila shots, then a second one, and a third one. The alcohol burned my throat, but I would need more to wash away the disappointment. It was silly to cling to a man like that. My sister would say there are plenty of fish in the sea. Except that none of them was Danté. Theo brought us more drinks. Before I could gulp even more down, Jasmine put a gentle hand on my wrist.

"You still talked a while with him. Are you sure that it didn't help you?"

Maybe Danté's point of view could still shift. Yet I couldn't muster any more hope, too afraid it would be crushed again.

"I think seeing Alex like that has shaken him up too much."

I would prefer having my toenails pulled out than explaining to her what we had talked about. It wasn't that I hid things from Jasmine. She probably knew me better than I knew myself. Saying out loud that he didn't want to even try long-distance relationships would make it too real, too final. When I looked back at the bar, Alex and Danté were gone. My heart clenched. *Maybe life will always get in the way.*

A movement caught my attention, and my vision focused on Chad and a few of his friends. He smiled shyly, so I nodded. He always seemed so hopeful when I looked at him. Maybe that was what I looked like when Danté was around. A sunflower always hoping for sunshine. Life would have been so much easier if Chad had been the one I had ended up caring about. I downed a few more shots before getting up.

My body jerked awake as my alarm blasted its annoying sound. *Device of the devil.* I stretched until something made me freeze. Something warm touched the skin of my stomach. Not something, *someone*. There was someone in my bed. It was weird that I let someone stay over for the night after sex. No matter how good it was. And all I could remember was how great it had been. Maybe I could give that person my number. As I turned, my heart dropped. Fuck. I really had a talent for making dumb decisions. Chad's eyes fluttered open, and a sleepy smile bloomed on his mouth. Oh, fuck me. This was going to be awkward.

"Hello," he slurred in a raspy voice.

Maybe it was the innocence, or maybe it was the effect of the sleepy voice, but I smiled back. "Hello."

Images from last night came back. Danté at the College, me kissing Chad, Chad holding me close before I fell asleep. I mentally punched myself in the throat and let the smile fall. From all the people I could've taken home, I had to choose the one who I wasn't supposed to touch. I cleared my throat and jumped out of bed when I saw him come too close to kiss me.

"I'm going to the gym. Feel free to take a shower if you want one."

Chad sat up, but I ran towards my bathroom before he could tell me something that would only make the situation even more awkward. I quickly changed into my gym apparel and barely waved to Jasmine who was already studying before escaping the apartment. The cold air made me wince. I hadn't even thought about taking a jacket in my haste. My phone rang. *Jasmine*.

"I've seen you do many walks of shame over the last two years, but this one takes the cake."

I rolled my eyes. She had a point, of course. Jasmine had seen the good, the bad, and especially the ugly.

"I know I should take responsibility, but not now."

She huffed out a laugh before gaining a polite cool. "Oh hey, Chad, how are you?"

Oh gods, if only I could hit myself numb by running into a wall. I heard him say something before our front door clicked shut once more.

"Evelyn Somers," she started.

"I know… I did something bad. I shouldn't have led him on by having sex with him."

"If you know that, then why did you?"

Because my heart had been in shambles yesterday. Having someone care for me in the way that Danté wouldn't seemed a good idea at that time. Selfish too, yes.

Jasmine let out a loud breath. "What did Danté tell you yesterday?"

Was I that obvious? There weren't many people who could make me feel as much as he did, so I guess the options were rather limited. I stopped and looked at my reflection in a puddle. The young woman who once had so many hopes and dreams was now a very sad-looking lass. She was pathetic, especially since she had thought she'd be able to outrun a broken heart.

"That he doesn't want to try long-distance relationships."

There. I said it. The reality of it made my head spin.

"Oh, Evy, I'm so sorry. I wish it could've gone differently."

Yesterday I had been so sure that love would always conquer; I could see the cracks in that belief now. But I guess that Taylor had been right all along. This wasn't a fairy-tale, and it was time for me to accept that maybe Danté wasn't the one to sweep me off my feet like I had dreamed he would.

"Me too."

CHAPTER 16

What had started as an okay day quickly ended up going downhill. I'll admit, it had been immature to avoid Chad during classes. If I had known he would show up at my door, I wouldn't have. Here he was, standing on my porch. I really didn't feel like talking to him. Even if the sex had been rather enjoyable, if a bit sloppy, it had been nice while being drunk. Now that I was completely sober, I knew that was something I wouldn't do again.

"What are you doing here?"

His eyes lit up like a damn Christmas tree as he saw me approaching. "Evy! How are you?"

Things would be better if you didn't show up at my door just because you got laid... Instead of speaking my mind, I plastered a polite smile on my face, which felt forced and unconvincing to me. Yet Chad didn't seem to understand.

"Good. And you?"

"Good."

I waited a whole two seconds to see if he would add anything. Chad flashed me a smile. I'd be lying if I said it wasn't charming. Under other circumstances, it might have given me butterflies. It just wasn't, well, *him*.

I took a deep breath. "So, what are you doing in front of my door?"

Had he been that charming that the concierge let him in?

"Let's go on a date."

I blinked once. *I hate this.* "Why…?"

No, Taylor, karma wasn't a cat purring in my lap. It was a rabid dog made from my bad decisions, ready to bite me in the ass.

"Because we like each other."

For a heartbeat, I was too stunned to speak. How was it not obvious that I didn't care? I wasn't subtle per se about the fact that I wasn't interested. If he was so dense, I felt bad that I was about to break his bubble of hope. My fake smile faltered.

"We do?"

"Would you like to go out with me tonight?"

I looked around the hall. I had to find something. This poor boy was too sweet.

"Oh, you know, I am very busy. I don't think…"

"Well, tomorrow then?"

"No, look, I really don't think…"

How do you tell someone to fuck off without hurting their feelings?

"Babe!"

Babe?! Danté appeared in the hall and sauntered to me. The very reason why I had bothered taking Chad home.

Before I could answer something cohesive, he leaned in and kissed me. From all the fake scenarios I had in my head, this was not one of the ways that I had imagined it would happen. His lips were warm and soft, and he pressed another kiss to my mouth. My traitorous body kissed him back without even hesitating. Then he pulled away ever so slightly.

"Is he bothering you?" he whispered in my ear.

I nodded, breathless. What bothered me the most was that Danté looked fine. Not the slightest bit wound up.

"If you can help me, I'll do anything."

One of his eyebrows shot up. A catlike smile crept up his face. "Anything?"

This was so going to come back to bite me in the ass. That was a problem for future me.

"Yep."

Danté turned back to Chad, his most charming smile in place. He took Chad's hand in his. Danté easily towered ten centimetres over him.

"Hey. I'm Danté."

Chad's face turned beet red. Even more than my own cheeks were.

"Oh, uhm hi."

"Was my girlfriend bothering you?"

My girlfriend. The words were so simple, and fake. They didn't stop my heart from making a flip at how it sounded when Danté said it. Those very same words that made heat spread in my chest were a cold shower for Chad. The poor guy looked so confused I felt bad for him.

"Girlfriend? But we…"

Danté looked back at me. A smug smile appeared on his

lips as he raised an eyebrow. I could practically hear him say "Oooooh, you nasty". My cheeks reddened even more, if that was still possible. Making fun of his sex life was our running joke. Danté doing the same with me was something I hadn't really seen coming, or something I had wanted to see happening either. I already knew that this would follow me until the day I died.

"We're in an open relationship. You can join us anytime you want."

I bit my lip to keep from laughing. How was he so good at this? *Wait.* Was Danté just such a good comedian, or was that something he was truly into? If he was, he could count me in. A threesome had always been on my secret bucket list.

"Uhm, thanks? I am sorry. I didn't know you were dating. If I did, I wouldn't have asked you out."

Chad waved awkwardly and went for the stairs. I let out a sigh of relief, until Chad turned back to me, a puzzled look in his eyes.

"That night, you said you felt lonely and in need of love."

Had I? I could feel Danté laugh quietly while I wanted to disappear underground. What the hell? *Think, Evy!*

"Oh, yeah… He was out of town that week. I tend to feel lonely very easily."

Liar liar, slutty dress on fire! I could almost hear Lucifer yell it to my face. For a brief second, I hesitated between running back inside my apartment or hitting my head against the wall. Chad looked as if he wasn't sure he believed me. Danté saw it too. His arms tightened around my waist, tugging me closer.

"Dude, enough."

His voice dropped so low I barely heard it. Goosebumps made my skin pimple. This time, Chad knew too that Danté's friendliness had reached its limit. Once Chad was finally gone, Danté turned to me.

"You alright?"

"Yeah, it's my fault."

He raised an eyebrow, silently questioning me.

"I never sleep with someone I know. This time I did."

"Why did you do it?"

Danté's heart had a steady beat, and I let my head rest against it. This was nice. He started rubbing soft circles on my back, and my eyes fluttered closed. He was so warm, his smell so soothing.

"Because like he said, I felt lonely that night. And he was there. Isn't that why you bring girls here?"

I didn't mean it as a jab. Sometimes I really wondered why there were so many girls. Did Danté also feel lonely? Did he also try to fill a void with attention and physical contact?

"No, I just do it for sex."

Of course he did. Then the realization hit me. I was still hugging Danté. And he let me cling to him like a monkey. Worse. His arms were still wrapped around my waist. My cheeks heated.

"Oh my gosh!" I stammered as I let him go. "I didn't mean to cling to you like this."

Danté put his hands in his jeans. How could he be so calm about this? He rolled his eyes as if I was being overdramatic. While over here, my heart was beating so fast it felt like it was going to explode.

"Don't take yourself so seriously, Squirrel."

Right. His attitude felt like a sudden, very cold shower.

"Well, I am not you," I snapped. "I usually don't hug and fuck every person I meet."

The words had left my mouth before I had even taken the time to process them. Danté's mouth formed a tight line. I had fucked up. Once again.

"You know, I could just have let you deal with that person on your own, if I bothered you that much."

Then he walked back to his door. I grabbed the back of his t-shirt.

"No please, wait! I didn't mean to snap at you like that."

Danté waited. I breathed in, trying to stomp down my temper. He had not deserved that blow.

"Thank you for helping me. I mean it."

But it wasn't enough.

"Sure."

Danté didn't even look back as he went inside his apartment. Stupid! *Why am I like this?* I groaned and hit my head against the wall, then groaned even louder as pain flashed through my skull. Something clicked behind me. If this wasn't life giving me lemons and squeezing the juice in my self-inflicted wounds.

"Put some ice on that forehead of yours," Danté said. "Or it will bruise."

I sighed, still looking at the wall.

"Great."

Part of me was surprised to see Danté walk inside our café. He had been coming here for years, especially since he got a full-time job and a full-time salary. It shouldn't be a surprise to anyone to see one of our most loyal and regular customers walk in on a Tuesday. But I was. Yes, our coffee was good, and our pastries were awesome too, if I do say so myself, but was it so good that he kept coming back and partaking in the pay check I got at the end of every month even though I was a bitch? He stopped at the counter, and Chloe greeted him without going back to take his order. She just vanished inside the kitchen.

I flashed Danté a bright smile. "Good morning, how are you?"

My too-cheerful voice made me cringe. Danté raised a single inquisitive eyebrow.

"Are you in pain?" he asked instead.

"What do you mean?"

"You're never this happy to see me."

"Of course I am! You're my favourite customer."

He snorted, leaning against the counter. "Is this your way of wanting to make up for being an asshole?"

I gulped. I wasn't used to Danté putting me in my place. My smile wavered, but I accepted the blow. It was fair. I had lashed out because I didn't know how to deal with my feelings.

"You're right," I admitted quietly. "I was awful."

"You were."

"I'm sorry. I didn't mean to."

Danté's eyes bore holes through my skull. He crossed his arms, not believing me. "You didn't mean to say hurtful things?"

My heartbeat was loud in my ears. *Hurtful*. I had hurt the person I wanted. All he had done was help me and I had hurt him. My vision blurred at the edges. I pulled at my ponytail.

"I never mean to say hurtful things, but I always do. I truly am sorry. You didn't deserve that."

I bit my lip to keep from bawling my eyes out. Danté smiled. His somber mood had melted like snow in the sun.

"Stop panicking, Squirrel. We're good."

"We are?"

"We are now."

I breathed out loudly as I felt all the tension leave my body. I felt like Jell-O. My eyes were still prickling, so I blinked rapidly to keep myself from crying. Danté stepped behind the counter and gave me a bear hug.

"I didn't peg you for such a softie, Squirrel."

"I'm sorry."

His hand caressed my hair, making me sniffle. My arms moved on their own, and I found myself hugging him back.

"I know."

Chloe's head peaked out of the door. Her brows scrunched together, but she stayed away. Danté rubbed my back before walking back to where the customers were supposed to stand.

I patted my eyes with a napkin and inhaled deeply before putting on my customer smile. "Can I take your order?"

"A large cappuccino and a blueberry muffin."

That wasn't the same order as usual. Danté snickered as I hesitantly put the order in the computer.

"Are you feeling adventurous today?"

"A bit more sugar to brighten up my day. You should try it."

"I will."

He took his wallet out of the back pocket of his jeans, and I shook my head. I couldn't ask him to pay, not after what just happened.

"It's on me."

Danté opened his mouth to protest, so I glowered at him. He ended up putting his wallet back. "Alright. When is your break?"

Well, if this day wasn't a roller coaster of emotions. I peeked at my watch. "In fifteen minutes."

"Want me to wait for you?"

I kept from yelling yes and nodded instead. I quickly went into the kitchen. Chloe looked up from the dishes she was putting back.

"Can I take my break now?"

"It depends. Is it for Danté?"

"Yes…?"

Her smirk turned catlike. "Then please do!"

She pushed me out of the kitchen and took my place behind the counter. Danté's eyebrows shot up, but if he had a comment, he kept it to himself. We sat down in a booth with two cappuccinos and his blueberry muffin.

"Do you make these?"

"Chloe does. I only make the chocolate cake and the lemon cake."

Kristen baked most of the stuff, but Chloe and I had been given some extra stuff. Since they let me eat my fair share of pastries and drink my weight in tea and coffee, I had accepted without hesitation.

"You're not eating," he simply stated.

"I already ate a piece of cake earlier, so I've had my treat today."

Eating sugar so early on tended to imbalance my mood and food cravings, but I had needed some sweetness to make my guilt more bearable. Had I known that I would spend my break with him, I would've waited. It would've been nice if we could share our pastries.

Danté rolled his eyes. "Of course you did."

"You say that as if it's bad to be reasonable."

"It's certainly not bad. But I think it would do you some good to be anything but reasonable."

That oddly sounded like something Jasmine told me not that long ago. I relaxed in my chair.

"I lash out at people when I feel like it. So that's my balance, I suppose."

"How about you stop lashing out, and enjoy life a bit more?"

Wasn't Danté already the part of my life I couldn't control? That was something I couldn't tell him. He had drawn me into a corner, and he knew it. A knowing smirk tugged at the corners of his lips. I wanted to kiss the smugness off his face.

"Good luck with that."

"Is that a challenge?"

I smirked back. "Maybe."

CHAPTER 17

There was a loud knock on the door, so loud it actually made me jump on the couch. My laptop fell from my knees, landing on the floor with a sad thud. My best friend snickered at my clumsiness. I gave her a middle finger that she gave back without a thought. Jasmine stretched before getting up to open the door.

"Oh, hi Danté. Come in."

My head shot up, only to find our neighbour heading straight to me. It wasn't that I wasn't happy to see him. I always was. The thing that unsettled me was that he had ended up in my place without me dragging him here.

A mischievous smirk played on his lips. "I've come to claim my prize."

I snorted at the corny line before I could even comprehend what he meant. Seeing how determined he looked, I knew something bad was about to fall in my lap.

"What do you mean?"

His grin grew wider. Danté somehow made me think of the Cheshire Cat, always a step ahead and enjoying every minute of it.

"You said you'd do anything I ask as a thank you for getting you out of trouble. Remember?"

Jasmine choked on a laugh while the ground under my feet seemed to disappear. For a second, I found myself back a few days earlier, enveloped in Danté's embrace. I had known it would come back to bite me in the ass. If only his embrace hadn't felt so right. Maybe I would have thought twice before selling my soul to such a handsome devil. Jasmine raised an inquisitive eyebrow as if to say "you forgot to mention something big". I found myself swallowing loudly, which only made Danté laugh. All evil playfulness vanished from his expression.

"Don't worry, Squirrel. I'm not claiming your firstborn."

Part of me wanted to retort that he couldn't claim his own firstborn, just for funsies, but that would probably take the joke too far. I squared my shoulders. Better get this over with.

"What do you need?"

"I need your body," he said in a calm tone.

Oh, fuck me. My face grew hotter than a grill. This wasn't what I had envisioned when he walked in. My best friend was straight out cackling, sprawled on the couch like a queen watching an entertainment. Danté was enjoying my reactions way too much as well. I cleared my throat, then put my hands in the pockets of my hoodie.

"I need foreplay first." I smirked.

Danté hummed, voice low. "I'll keep that in mind for the future."

I did my best to keep my cool. It wasn't a secret to anyone how much I liked him, except for him. But our flirtatious humour wasn't something I liked to broadcast in front of others. Given the way my best friend's eyes widened, she wasn't used to it happening in front of her either. I put away the flirting.

"So, what do you need my body for if it's not for pleasure?"

The fact that he kept standing, straight as a rod, was proof enough that Danté was here to talk business.

"Next week I'll go to a high school to explain my job. I need a body to show some techniques, like cracking a back and trigger point therapy."

That made more sense than what I had hoped for. It didn't matter. I owed him big time for helping me with Chad, who had finally taken the hint and stopped drooling after me.

"When is it?"

"Next Tuesday afternoon. I know you usually go to the gym at that time, but I hope you can spare me an hour or two."

My eyebrows shot up. How did he even know? Danté noticed my surprise; it made him uncomfortable.

"How do you know my schedule?" I asked.

He had always been more observant than what he gave away. For some reason, Danté didn't want people to see how aware and thoughtful he was. That only made me appreciate him more.

"You told me so during one of your shifts."

I whistled at that. "And you remember that?"

The tips of his ears turned a bit red, but he nodded, his

head held high. I bit back a smile.

"Alright. I'll come."

"I didn't tell you the details yet."

The way his eyes still twinkled, I knew I was royally fucked.

"Oh, fuck me," I muttered.

A smug smile tugged at his mouth. That will teach me to accept anything without reading the small print.

"You'll need to wear a spandex bodysuit."

A *what*?

"You're joking, right?"

Danté seemed to pity me. His expression softened. "It's a skin-coloured bodysuit so I can draw on it when necessary. You can still say no."

"Are you going to wear one too?"

The idea alone threatened to make me cry from laughing. I could see us, standing in front of a whole room of bored teenagers, dressed in our bodysuits.

"No, I need the students to take me seriously."

So basically, I'd be the only one ridiculed. That was a sight worth looking forward to.

"Great," I whispered.

"I can find someone else if it makes you too uncomfortable."

It was nice that he insisted on the fact that I could back out if I wanted to. I was pretty sure that Danté wouldn't even be mad if I refused. I shook my head. If he could put himself in awkward situations to help me out, the least I could do was to help him out when he needed someone. Sure, I would look like a dweeb, but that was alright. I could try to make dweebish look cool. Or at least believe it, for the sake of my sanity.

"I said I'd help you. You can count on me."

Something that oddly looked like esteem shined in his eyes. "You sure?"

"Don't let me change my mind, Alighieri."

Danté raked a hand through his blonde locks as if amused by the whole situation. "Then I am thankful. Meet me at my office on Tuesday, and we'll go from there."

"It's a date, then."

I walked him back to the door. Danté hesitated as if he was going to add something. A kiss would have been a rather nice way to seal the deal. A girl can dream, right?

"Thank you, Evy."

"Anytime."

He gave me a wave before disappearing down the hall, probably going back to his workplace. Once the door was locked again, Jasmine sauntered over to me, patting my shoulder.

"You are a smooth one."

I wiggled my brows, making Jasmine cringe. She already knew what was coming.

"Smooth like a smoothie."

"I hate it when you say that."

"I'll stay cringey until the day I die, baby."

Jasmine gave me a hug, then went back to her place at the kitchen table to continue her class preparations. "Go get him, tiger."

It hadn't been the reason why I had accepted to help Danté out. There was just no reason for me to not help him out when he was always the first one to jump to my rescue. It was a nice bonus if I could spend more time with him. Spending an extra day with Danté was always something to look forward to.

"I'm trying."

The medical practice smelled like rubbing alcohol and soap for cleaning floors. The walls were all white, just like I imagined they would be. I didn't feel bad per se when coming inside a hospital or a doctor's practice. It was just always so bare and cold. A sweet receptionist with a messy blonde bun and purple glasses smiled at me.

"Hello, do you have an appointment?"

If you could call the catastrophe that my charisma would undergo an appointment, then sure. I shook my head.

"I'm here for Danté. He asked me to come at two."

"Oh, you are Evelyn! You can go to his office. It's the second door on the right."

I thanked her before knocking on his door. A quiet answer made me enter my head into the room.

Danté looked up from his computer, his face lighting up with a smile. "Hey Squirrel, come in."

Once the door was closed, I scowled at him. "You better not call me that in front of your students, because if you do, I swear you'll never have kids."

He clicked his fingers, pointing at me. "Noted. Just give

me a minute."

Danté was typing away on his keyboard, so I took the opportunity to look around. Unlike the hallway, his office smelled nice. Homey. There was still a hint of rubbing alcohol and soap, and the cocooning vibe of a baby powder scented Yankee candle. Some magnet souvenirs from Spain, Greece, Egypt, and many other places hung on the metal parts of his desk. Had he gotten them when he travelled, or were those presents from his patients? Even the walls had more of a cream colour than the cold white of the halls and the entrance. He took a sip from a coffee cup that had the pun *it's going tibia okay* on it, and I found myself smiling. Danté looked up from his screen, questioning me silently.

"I like your office. It feels very you."

If I had to go to a physiotherapist, then I'd go here. It didn't feel that much like a medical practice room. It had the same warm and calm vibe that Danté had.

Danté got up and grabbed a small bag from his cupboard. "Here is the bodysuit. Do you want to change here or at the school?"

High school bathrooms weren't known for their hygiene, or large space. A shiver ran down my spine.

"I'd rather do it here."

Danté pointed to the light blue folding screen at the back of the room. The object made me think of a beach house with its white stripes. The body suit was the perfect size, which made me wonder how many of those Danté had in his stash. I stuffed my clothes in the bag, and put on my black boots and long black coat. Yeah, style wasn't on my side today. No good girl faith and no tight little skirt. As soon as he saw me,

Danté did his best to stifle a laugh, and failed miserably. So for the sake of it, I did a little twirl on myself. The bodysuit was ridiculous, and so tight. All I needed was a dark pair of shorts, and to walk on my hands and knees, and I'd look like a modern version of Gollum.

In the car, I turned on the radio. It wasn't a surprise that Danté loved Bad Omens, I just wasn't prepared for the song and the volume that would hit me. I yelped and hit the back of my head against the window when "Artificial Suicide" blasted through the vehicle. I could hear Danté cackling next to me while he turned the volume down.

"Sorry."

The smirk on his face told me he wasn't sorry at all.

"Your car is your own little concert hall, huh?"

"Yep. If I blast the music this loud at home, I get annoyed neighbours at my door."

Alright, that little jab was deserved. I shrugged. "Just invite me to the party, and I'll let you blast it as loud as you want."

"Sounds like a plan."

I grabbed his phone to go through the album. Maybe "The Death of Peace of Mind" wasn't the best choice for now, not that I looked very sexy in my new outfit. So I put "Miracle" on. It quickly became clear that that song could also have a place of honour on a sex playlist. Had Danté put it in there?

"Well, damn. The whole album is sexy. Is this one also on your playlist?"

"I removed all Bad Omens songs from that playlist since you like to listen to them."

Oh right. Danté didn't want to bang me. No wonder the songs that I loved would get him out of the mood.

"Are they your favourite band?"

"They're all right."

Right, men. Why was it so hard for them to accept that they were also fans of bands?

I huffed. "They are more than all right if you listen to them weekly."

"Fine. I like them."

"I like the singer. He's very easy on the eyes."

Noah was too charismatic not to be liked. And I wasn't even talking about his voice.

Danté frowned at that. "I didn't know that's the kind of guy you're into."

"I'm not."

It didn't matter how awesome that guy was, he was out of my league. And well, he wasn't blonde. Okay, that detail didn't matter really.

"Didn't you just say he's your type?"

It almost sounded as if Danté didn't like that. If only he knew how many celebrity crushes I had. It was ridiculous. The only thing that I knew for sure was that it didn't matter how many celebrity crushes I had, none of them made my stomach flutter the way Danté did.

"I find him attractive, yes. That doesn't mean he's my type."

"So what is your type then?"

I rolled my eyes as we drove into the parking lot of the school. "The fact that you need to ask this really proves how blind you are."

In the way I could hear him breathe in, there was no denying that he wasn't on the same page as I was.

"I beg your pardon?"

I grabbed my handbag and opened the door. "Danté, look in a mirror. Until then, I'm heading out."

He jumped out of the car to follow me inside the school hallway. "You can't say stuff like that then disappear as if nothing happened."

Damn, I truly was glad that high school was over and I'd never have to go back to it. I could practically smell the awkwardness of being a teenager again. Or was it just sweat?

"Of course I can. Look at me going."

"You don't know where we're supposed to go."

I stopped in my tracks. When I turned back at him, Danté smirked at me, his arms crossed. There went my dramatic exit.

"Fine! Lead the way, o master of us all."

He gave me a little curtsy before looking back at a piece of paper. The part of the building we would have to be in, probably. I followed him in silence until we stood in front of a closed door.

"Thank you again for doing this, Evelyn."

"Glad I can help."

When we entered the classroom, thirty-something pairs of bored eyes landed on us. The teacher presented Danté briefly, who then explained his job and the studies he had done. He hung posters of the human skeleton and the muscles on the blackboard while I stood on the side of the class. I remembered people who came to our school to explain their studies and jobs when I was sixteen so that we could ask them questions to see if what they did was something that could resonate with us. Most people who came were either scientists or teachers. There had been one girl who had brought healthy cupcakes; obviously, she had been the one that had caught my attention. After spending an hour with her, it had become clear that I also wanted to be a dietician.

As I watched the class, I noticed how the girls looked at Danté like he was a model. A part of me wanted to give them a tissue to dab away the drool. The problem was that if I could, I would've sat next to them to admire him too. Danté gave very basic explanations in such a calm but enthusiastic way. It was hard to miss how most of the students were hanging on every word he said.

"This is my lovely assistant, Evelyn," Danté said, pointing at me. "I will show you how to crack some parts without injuring, and how to do trigger point therapy."

He gave me a little sign to get closer. I took off my coat and threw it on an empty desk with my handbag. Now that the bodysuit was visible, some students snickered. I couldn't blame them. I would've laughed at myself too if I didn't need to be professional. Danté motioned me to sit on a stool.

"How do you feel?"

"I'm good."

Danté walked around me, testing the flexibility of my neck.

"Most students have some tension in their shoulders, neck, and back. This is something due to the position in which you study."

"So you're telling us that studying is bad for us?" a student asked, hopeful.

My friend let out a breathy laugh. "Don't tell your parents I said that."

His hands went around my neck. His touch was soft, his skin warm against mine. For some reason, my body tensed. It wasn't the first time Danté would crack my spine, and yet it still felt as intimidating.

"Relax, babe. I need you to breathe."

Babe? I did what he told me and controlled my breathing. Danté tapped my neck and shoulders, then hummed.

"Good. Let your head rest against my hand."

This time, he didn't try to take my attention away by talking. Danté pushed down on my shoulder, and I felt the crack resonate in my whole spine. A girl yelled at the sudden sound.

"Holy shit!" I squeaked.

Danté put his arms under my armpits and lifted me up. My body continued cracking, without ever hurting. Some students watched us with fascination, others with disgust. When he was done, Danté levelled his head to mine. His eyes searched mine, making sure I was alright.

"Is everything alright, love?"

The students ooh'ed and aah'ed, and I did my best to not blush at the sudden attention. Or the pet name. It would have been unprofessional to call me Squirrel in front of a whole class and its teacher. But love? I nodded, keeping silent. If Danté hadn't realized the way his words had affected me, I wouldn't react upon it.

"What do you feel?"

"I feel like Jell-O. A pressure I didn't know I had was lifted from my shoulders."

"Perfect."

His hand lingered on my neck while he explained a few techniques. It took everything in me to not lean into the touch. The next hour went by in a blur, one where I just let Danté order me around, and quietly enjoyed the physical contact between us.

Danté grabbed a marker from his bag and started drawing some trigger points on my shoulder. He was so close I could see the small beauty mark under his right eye. His breath fanned over my cheeks, and I did my best to keep from shivering. Danté noticed my stare.

"You're blushing, love," he whispered.

Fucking hell. I sucked in air and pretended to look outside. But when I looked back at my friend, there was also a bit of pink tinting his cheeks.

The trigger points were awful. It had taken all my strength to not push Danté away when he squeezed. And even then, Danté kept checking on me.

As we walked back to the car, I was skipping. Maybe I could bribe my lovely neighbour into being my private physiotherapist with cake.

"How are you feeling?" he asked, fishing for his car keys.

"Great. It almost feels as good as sex."

Danté chuckled, the low sound of it warming my tummy. I put my hand in the crook of his elbow. Maybe it was in my head, but he seemed to enjoy the touch.

"I didn't know you were such a flirt around an audience."

Not that I would complain about it. I couldn't help but

feel special when he looked at me the way he did in that classroom. Like he would've undressed me hadn't there been anyone else in the room. And I would probably have let him do anything he wanted if he asked for it.

"Generally, I am not."

"Then why were you now?"

"Because the boys were looking at you hungrily."

I squeezed his bicep playfully. "Oh, please, don't tell me you felt threatened by a bunch of kids?"

"I didn't."

I raised an eyebrow, not convinced. Danté approached, getting so close to me until I was pressed against his car. There was a smug smile playing on his lips. One I would've loved to kiss away, leaving him breathless instead. His hot breath fanned over my cheek, and goosebumps erupted on my skin under the Spandex.

"The bodysuit you are wearing leaves little to the imagination of your anatomy. I've been like them, so I know exactly what some of them were thinking about when looking at you. What some of them would've said out loud without any shame. No one would've made a comment about your body because they thought you were with me."

I swallowed but tried my best to not look too flustered. It was a failure, if Danté's smug expression was any indication. His eyes followed the bob of my throat.

I smirked back. "Next time, just grab my ass. It will be just as effective, and a lot quicker."

He touched my nose ever so lightly. His smile turned toothy, and his dimples appeared. "Trust me, I wanted to. Not just for the show."

I just stood there, unable to say something smart back. Danté leaned even closer, and the rhythm of my heart picked up its speed. Was he finally going to kiss me? There was a click, then he opened the door to the passenger seat for me. I did my best to not let the disappointment show. Before he stepped back, Danté brushed a soft kiss on my temple.

"Maybe I should wear this bodysuit more often," I whispered.

He put a strand of curls behind my ear. "Maybe you should."

I climbed in the car, unable to keep the idiotic smile in check. When I looked at Danté, his grin was just as big as mine. This outfit was so going home with me.

CHAPTER 18

"What are you doing for Christmas?" Jasmine asked, not looking up from her weekly preparations.

Christmas was in less than two weeks, and I had been putting it off. I still hadn't opened the message my mother had sent me to ask if I would join them. One thing was sure. If I refused to go, I would feel guilty about it, and Eleanor would end up here to smack me. Something I probably deserved. If I went, I'd feel uncomfortable, just like I had the last time. It hadn't been worth it.

"I haven't decided yet. I think I'll just visit my grandmother."

That, at least, would be a cosy time where I didn't need to plaster a polite smile on my face and hide most of my days inside a bedroom that no longer felt like my own.

"You won't go to your parents?"

I looked back at the vegetables that I was cutting. This whole ordeal was making me so tired. Christmas was supposed to be jolly, so why was it that thinking about it made me feel so empty?

"I don't want to go, honestly. Does that make me a bad daughter?"

It had been years, and every year I felt the same dread. Just like I had the same questions. And I hated it. I hated being like this: too afraid to just tell my parents how I felt about them. Jasmine put down her pencil and focused on me.

"Oh, Eves, I don't know. I think you need to put in more efforts with them because they are trying. But I also understand why you don't want to go."

Yeah, I was a rubbish daughter. I had known it for quite a while. It had been clear when they finally came home and wanted to spend a night with me, and it had felt like they intruded on my life after I had to be on my own for years. It still felt like that when I saw them.

"So I should go?"

Merry Christmas. Your gifts will be uneasiness and guilt.

Jasmine stood next to me. "I didn't say that."

"I am a horrible daughter."

My hands started trembling. She took the knife from my grip and pushed me towards the kitchen table.

"You aren't. They let you down when you needed them. Feeling the way you do is valid. If you don't want to be there for Christmas, that's your right. But I do believe that you should call them a bit more often."

Small steps. I could do that, right? Then why did the idea alone give me anxiety? I breathed in deeply. That was a problem for future me.

"You're right."

"You're always welcome at my house. My parents absolutely love you."

I refrained from immediately accepting. I wanted to say yes. After all, I had spent several Christmas Eves at their house, as well as New Year's Eves. And unlike Jasmine, I loved cooking, so it had always been a fun moment between her mom, her aunties, and me. There was one detail that kept me from accepting.

"Isn't Theo coming?"

"He is."

That was reason enough to not go. Aswaa and Nadim were basically my adoptive parents. Back in high school, her dad even accompanied me to a teacher meeting because mine forgot to come. Uncle Nadim even scolded me for talking back to my teacher, then gave me a bear hug as I bawled my eyes out because I was the only kid without her parents. But times had once again changed. Jasmine was with Theo now, and if he was going there for their first Christmas together as a couple, I couldn't be there. Jasmine included me in everything she could, which I was grateful for. I also knew that Theo wanted her for himself, and I was always in the way.

So I smiled reassuringly, shaking my head. "I'll stay here."

"Are you sure?"

I'd have to ask if I could pick up a few extra shifts at the café, otherwise I would be crushed by loneliness. Just the idea of Jasmine being away and the apartment being empty made me sad.

"Positive."

"Is this because of Theo?" she asked warily.

"It's not."

She hit me with a kitchen towel. Why had I picked out a best friend who showed her concern by physically attacking people? Theo hadn't asked for me not to come. He would never say something to hurt me. If anything, Theo and Jasmine often saw me as the fragile friend who was two seconds away from having a mental breakdown. Christmas always made me feel anxious ever since my parents were present again. It didn't mean I couldn't take a hint.

"Yes, it is! Don't say no because you feel like you have to. Theo loves you!"

Apparently, I wasn't the only one who had to take a hint. Jasmine and I had always been attached at the hip. I wasn't sure she realized how often she included me in her plans before thinking about Theo.

"I don't doubt that. But I am not his girlfriend."

I had made a point. Jasmine opened her mouth to protest, but no retort came. Her eyes grew sad, and even if I wanted to accept, I couldn't. Soon they would live together. Maybe it was time for us to learn how to spend time apart.

"I'll accept it if you promise to be there for Christmas next year."

A tear fell down when I laughed. Jasmine was my guardian angel. She had always been, and once again, she proved to me why she had become my family.

"I promise."

Jasmine hugged me from behind, her arms tight around my neck and shoulders. There was dampness on her face as she pressed her cheek against mine.

"I love you, Evy."

"I love you too."

My phone rang. One look at the name that appeared on the screen and my heart fell to the floor. There were only so many times I could ignore her before it became too obvious.

"Hi, Mom."

My too-cheerful voice made me cringe. My mom didn't seem to notice.

"Hi, darling, how are you?"

"Good, how are you?"

"Good."

My mom chatted away for a few minutes, and I let her, barely hearing anything over how loud the rushing of my blood sounded in my ears. It was ridiculous how anxious these moments made me. Not that I could help it. Then came the painful subject.

"What would you like to eat when you come home for the holidays?"

My palms were so sweaty that my phone kept slipping in my grip. This was going to be a disaster. I took a deep breath to steel my nerves, then jumped up from my desk to pace the room. *There we go*.

"I'm not coming home this year."

I had to use the word, no matter how wrong it tasted. If I also told my mother that her home wasn't mine anymore, things would truly escalate. Things would already escalate as it was. There was the sound of a chair scraping against the floor on her side of the call, which probably meant that she sat down.

"What do you mean?" she asked calmly.

Too calm. Her composure made me queasy.

"I have a lot of preparations to do for my upcoming exams, and I promised Kristen that I would take some shifts during the holiday, since most students go home."

Technically, I had begged her to give me a few shifts so that I had an excuse to not go. I could say a lot of things about my parents, except that they didn't care about keeping promises. That would've been a lie.

"But we were supposed to celebrate Christmas together."

My father said something in the background that I couldn't hear. From the way he sounded, he wasn't too pleased by the announcement either. Well, too bad.

"I know, I'm sorry."

I was sorry to disappoint her. I really was. Just not enough to change my plans. I had a choice to make between being a good daughter, and sanity. And just this once, I chose sanity. No matter how selfish that might be.

"You should've told us sooner."

She did her best not to sound too upset. I had to give her credit where it was due.

"I know. I'm sorry," I said again.

"Alright. Try to not overwork yourself."

"I'll do my best."

And as if there was nothing positive left to be said, my mom bid me farewell. Once the call from hell was finally over, I let out a breath. A little voice in my head whispered that this would probably bite me in the ass later, but I told her to shut up. I had just scored two weeks of peace of mind. It was worth it.

CHAPTER 19

Jasmine was running through the apartment like a mad woman. Or at least, that was how Theo and I saw her. She was going to her parents for a few days only, and yet she was fretting like she was leaving for months. It probably had to do with all the presents she had found for her family.

When she went back to her room, Theo turned to me. "Thank you."

"What for?"

"For stepping back and allowing me to merge into her family."

In other words: thank you for not coming. Of course, Theo had known Aswaa and Nadim as long as I had. Jasmine just hadn't bothered telling her parents that she and Theo were a thing until recently. That was probably the less-than-fun part of having a sometimes overbearing and overprotective father who hadn't been ready for his little girl to be a woman. Now it was pretty much clear that they would stay together, and that they wanted a future together after college. I didn't fit inside this scenario. It was alright. I would have many more opportunities to see Aswaa and Nadim.

I nodded. "Enjoy the holiday for me."

"I'm sorry you have to spend Christmas alone because of me."

"Don't worry. I'll be fine."

We loaded Jasmine's little car with their bags and presents. I was already dreading the empty home once I went back inside.

Jasmine gave me a tight hug. "You can still change your mind and come with us."

I eyed the back seats full of bags and boxes. Unless they put me on the roof or buried me under the presents, that would be a tad bit complicated.

I shook my head. "Give them a big hug for me."

"I will," she promised.

Back inside, I let out a long sigh. Well, this was it then. Suddenly it was too silent. Too empty.

"Alright Evelyn, we can make this night work."

I put myself to work and lit all the candles I could find. Jasmine and I never went big with Christmas decorations. All we had was a tiny, overdecorated Christmas tree that still smelled like plastic after three years of use. I even put on Taylor's Version of *1989* and poured myself a drink. Still, I couldn't shake the emptiness away. Christmas was so overrated. There was no point in doing it if there was no one to celebrate it with.

My stomach grumbled, so I grabbed some carrots and a cauliflower from the fridge. At least I could make myself an aperitif, right? If I was going to be sad, I could at least be sad but fancy.

Snow was falling on the city. The snow and the Christmas lights gave the city a magical hue. Even from here, I could hear the Christmas songs playing on the speakers outside. I took a big gulp of my Passoa. Maybe I should study. That way, at least, I wouldn't be wasting my time. A loud knock on the door made me jump from my chair. *Please, let it not be a choir.* As I opened the door, I found Danté outside. He showed me a dark bottle.

"Got room for one more?"

Danté gave me a little smile, and I found myself nodding.

"Uhm, I have. Please come in."

His hair was wet from the snow, and some melted snowflakes clung to his lashes. The cold had also given his cheeks a cute rosy colour. As I stepped aside, Danté went straight to my kitchen.

"Where are the glasses?"

"Most right upper shelf. But we don't own champagne glasses."

Jasmine and I were cocktail girls. And students. We always drank our booze in regular glasses. Or little shot glasses that Theo had once brought here. I watched Danté move around my kitchen, unsure of what was happening to me. Why was he here? Had the skies heard my silent prayer and sent me an angel? Danté hummed with "Style" as he filled two mustard glasses with sparkling wine, and I was surprised to hear how soothing his voice was. Or that he even knew the tune of the song. When he gave me my drink, I felt the corners of my mouth tilt.

"Thank you."

"You can smile, Squirrel. Christmas is made for you to be happy."

"Christmas is a day like any other."

Both of us were dressed in all black. Could we be any more festive? And yet, I liked the fact that our outfits were coordinated, even if it hadn't been on purpose. He clanked his Pua glass against my Iron Man one.

"Maybe it is, but it is also meant to spend it with people you care about."

"And yet you are here."

"And yet I am here," he agreed.

So I gave him a smile – a real, toothy one. Danté dropped a kiss on my forehead. The gesture was so sweet I found my cheeks hurting from smiling so hard. His eyes were as gentle as ever, and I thanked the skies for sending him to my doorstep. Danté looked at the plate full of pieces of raw carrot and cauliflower I had left untouched.

"Were you about to eat?"

"I was. I'm afraid I didn't calculate for two people, but I have some instant ramen."

It was absolutely pathetic. Who would want to eat instant noodles today? And yet, Danté smiled, as if he was truly having a good time.

"That sounds like the perfect Christmas Eve meal, doesn't it?"

I could kiss him for being so positive. The loneliness I had felt earlier vanished. Now there was only him. Danté grabbed the plate with the veggies and went back to the living room. I followed him dumbly.

"We should watch a movie."

I hummed in agreement. "Now that sounds divine. Do you have anything in mind?"

"How about a horror movie?"

I paused. He was joking, right? "Do you want me dead?"

He rolled his eyes. "Please don't tell me you are team Christmas movies."

I made a gagging noise. Never had I liked Christmas movies. For someone who loved clichés, Christmas movies hadn't been a genre I had learned to appreciate.

"I don't like either one. I prefer romcoms."

Although Jasmine often said I was the real-life version of the Grinch because of my prickly personality.

Danté plopped down on the couch before showing me a smirk. "How surprising."

Yeah, there was nothing surprising about me. I knew that. I was also fine with that knowledge. The unsurprising, curly-haired Grinch. Seemed rather fitting.

"What's wrong with that? I like light-hearted stuff. If we watch a horror movie, I won't be able to sleep for a week, and I'll jump at every sound that I hear."

"At least it would distract you from the gloomy mood you were in."

He was rather good at convincing people to do what he wanted. I had no doubt about that.

"You have a point there," I admitted.

"So…"

I sighed loudly as I let myself fall on the couch, just to spill some of my drink on my shirt. "I can't believe I am agreeing to this!"

Who knew that he could cackle like an evil witch?

I pointed at him. "Just know that if I have nightmares, you're going to keep me company at night."

Danté swatted my pointy finger away, looking at me in fake shock. "Naughty Squirrel! Is that your way of asking me to spend the night?"

"I was going to tell you to sleep on the floor." I shrugged.

I would've actually asked him to join me under the covers. Not that I would give him the satisfaction of knowing that.

"Cold-hearted woman."

What was meant as a mere joke on his part felt like an arrow shot straight into my core. It struck so deep that I couldn't even pretend to laugh. Tears blurred the outer part of my vision.

"You really think so?"

All traces of humour left him. Before anything could happen, he took the glass from my hands to put it aside. Danté wrapped his arms around my shoulders and pulled me closer.

"No Evelyn, I don't think you are cold at all. If anything, you hide how sensitive you are behind biting comments and faked nonchalance."

Then the dam behind my eyes broke down. My whole body shook as I cried, and I was unable to stop the flow of tears. Danté rubbed my back softly, cradling me even closer. If this wasn't a jolly Christmas, then I don't know what could possibly take the cake. When the tears finally subdued, I tried to pull away, but Danté just held me tight. I patted my cheeks dry with the sleeve of my shirt.

"I am fine. You can let me go."

If I was completely honest, I didn't want him to let me go. It was nice to be held like this, like there was no one else in the world but us. Or as if there was nowhere else he'd rather be. Danté didn't move.

"You're not. Tell me what's hurting you."

Instead of trying to pull away a second time, I just let myself enjoy the feeling. Danté's heart had a slow, steady beat, and his smell was divine. Fresh laundry, and a hint of rubbing alcohol. I closed my eyes, and everything tumbled out of my mouth. At no point did he let me go.

"What are you so afraid of?" he asked, his voice soft like velvet.

The question echoed in my head, making me dizzy. My head rolled back against his shoulder when I looked up. Worry made him frown. I didn't even want to think how I looked, yet it didn't seem to matter to him. Danté pushed some hair strands from my forehead, his fingers lingering on my temple. I forced myself to ponder over the question. My stomach churned.

"That I find out that I can't forgive them for abandoning me. It's so selfish, and I hate myself for it, but I can't help feeling this way."

Bile burned the back of my throat once the words were out. I ran for the toilet just in time as I vomited the contents of my stomach. Acid tears burned my eyes while I retched. If only this would stop. There was a noise behind me, but I couldn't register what it was until a hand squeezed my shoulder.

"Evy, let go."

I blinked against the tears and saw that I was holding the

toilet for dear life. I let myself fall back as Danté flushed the toilet for me. He dabbed my face with a wet cloth. I had had many lows in my life, but this had to be the lowest point I could possibly reach.

"Sorry," I croaked. "This is probably the worst Christmas you could ask for."

One of the corners of his mouth went up. "It sure is an eventful night."

I could feel my lips tremble from guilt.

"I don't regret being here. Please don't cry because of me." Danté wiped my eyes with the cloth ever so gently. "There is nothing selfish about wanting your parents to be there for you, especially if they weren't there for years. I think you should give them a chance to prove that they are here now, just like you should give yourself the chance to forgive them. But if you find out that you can't, that is your right."

Was it though? I felt torn between being ungrateful and being ready to give up. Danté offered me a hand. I looked at it, unable to know what he wanted. He was smiling patiently.

"The floor is cold. Let's go back to the living room."

I nodded and let him help me up. Once I had brushed my teeth, I left the bathroom. Danté was already scrolling on Netflix, searching for a movie. I plopped down on the couch, not even pretending to have any grace left. If a guy had seen me puke, there was no going back from there. Danté kept seeing the worst sides of me, and I appreciated the fact that he was around after everything. There was a can of Coke on the low table. I smiled at the attention.

"Thank you," I said before taking a sip of the soda. "I swear I don't get mental breakdowns like these very often."

"I'm just glad you weren't alone."

That made me think.

"How did you know I was going to be here tonight? I don't recall telling you I wouldn't go anywhere."

"Jasmine told me."

The smile fell from my face. He was here because Jasmine had asked him to babysit me? Danté looked back at me when I didn't respond.

"She didn't ask me to be here, if that is what you are wondering. We just talked about it a few days ago."

"Then *why* are you here?"

"I worked today, and I didn't have anything planned."

I raised an eyebrow, and Danté silently laughed. He pushed on my forehead with his pointer finger until I stopped making that face. I pouted instead.

"You don't believe me, do you?"

"Not quite."

"Can you accept the fact that I might just want to spend the evening with you?"

I couldn't stop the stupid smile from blooming on my face. Danté's face relaxed. It didn't really matter what had pushed him to me tonight. He was here, and that was more than I could've wished for.

"You should've just said that."

He was studying me, kind of as if he couldn't believe what was in front of him.

I shifted in my seat under his scrutiny. "Why are you looking at me like that?"

It was a miracle that after everything he had seen tonight, he was still here, and still smiling.

"It's interesting to see who you are on the inside."

"My inner self is a mess. I hope you won't see her again."

"Most of us are a mess but are too afraid to show others what makes us human. You shouldn't be afraid to show that side of you."

"Stop talking, or I might start crying again."

In the end, we ended up watching *The Conjuring*. That was apparently a scary movie that "wasn't so bad". Or so Danté said. The lights were off, and even though the movie had barely begun, I found myself staring at Danté every now and then. It was weird that we sat next to each other with enough space for an extra person between us. What had happened earlier didn't mean anything. He was still Danté, and I was just Squirrel, the weird neighbour. If only I could go back to earlier, when his arms were around me and I could listen to his heartbeat.

Danté slightly turned his head, and he grinned. Of course he had caught me staring. "Are you scared already?"

"No," I lied.

Like the scaredy cat I was, I jumped when the hands clapped behind the lady. Danté chuckled, and I felt my cheeks grow hot. What a dumb idea to agree to watch a scary movie when I couldn't even handle action movies with lots of violence. He motioned me to come closer, so without thinking it over, I nestled against him. I quickly put the soft blanket over us both before resting my head against his torso. Danté put his arm over my shoulders and pulled me closer, just like he had done earlier. And with his heartbeat being the main sound, the movie wasn't so atrocious anymore. Danté's watch lit up at one point, and he looked down at me.

"Merry Christmas, Evy."

And in its own, twisted way, this Christmas Eve had been perfect. All thanks to the man sitting next to me. I beamed at him.

"Merry Christmas, Danté."

The first thing I noticed was the amount of light around me. Had I forgotten to close the curtains? The other thing that was out of place was the unusual warmth that surrounded me. Yet my mind felt completely at ease. I cracked an eye open, only to find a sleeping Danté under me. How had I even landed on top of him? He was everywhere. The sight. The smell. His body. Our legs were intertwined, and his arm was draped over my shoulders. How long had we been lying like this? A soft, tingling heat spread through my body. His hair was messy, a few strands on his forehead. Danté seemed so peaceful, almost youthful in the winter sunshine. All I had to do was move my head forward a few centimetres for my lips to touch his. I found myself smiling. Now this was a sight I would love to wake up to every day. I reached my hand out towards his face but hesitated mid-air. What now?

"Enjoying the view?" he rasped.

I froze on the spot. Had he been awake all this time? I meekly let my hand fall back. Here I had been staring at him like a creep. The worst part? It hadn't gone unnoticed.

Danté's eyes fluttered open, his blue eyes locking with mine.

"Hi," I tried.

"Hi."

His voice was raspy from sleep, and gods, it did something to me. A little smile played on his mouth. He didn't look away. I breathed in deeply. I have no idea what gave me the courage to move. Was it his smell that was intoxicating me, or the feeling of our bodies pressed together? I finally reached forward and removed the blonde strands from his forehead. They were soft against my fingers. I waited for Danté to tell me to move. He didn't. His arm moved before he let his hand rest on the small of my back.

"What are your plans today?" he asked.

"I'm going to visit my grandmother. Other than that, I think I'll just study."

He hummed in response.

"What will you do?"

"I don't have any plans."

"You don't want to see your parents?" I wondered.

"I see them all the time."

I should move. Going to Grandma's house would take a little while. I didn't want to move. Part of me wanted to stay here with Danté, in this bubble that had become our own. I let my head rest back on his chest. The bubble would pop eventually. I just wanted a moment longer before I had to let him go.

"Where does your grandmother live?"

"Not that far if you have a car."

Which I didn't. I didn't even have a driver's license. Just the idea of sitting behind a steering wheel gave me anxiety, so I hadn't bothered trying. Jasmine had once pointed out that my anxiety came from my need for control.

"Can I come with you?"

My head shot back up. "You want to see my grandma?"

"Sure."

"You… want to see my grandma," I repeated, as if saying it out loud would give more sense to his words.

Danté shrugged. His face was neutral, but his eyes never left mine. I poked him in the ribs.

"If you want to spend the day with me, you can just say so."

He huffed but didn't contradict me. That warm feeling spread further. He turned his head away, and I found myself laughing. It was unlike him to not be vocal about his thoughts.

"Fine. Let's spend the day together."

"There you go."

I sighed before finally getting up. The list of things to do unfolded in my head. Shower, breakfast, makeup. I shook my head. No need to be on a tight schedule on Christmas Day. Danté stretched, and it was then that I noticed that his legs were too long for the couch. That must've been a rather uncomfortable night. Yet seeing him lying on my couch like he owned the place did things to my heart. Danté jumped up, ready to move. I giggled. That made him stop in his tracks.

"What is it?"

"You have antennas."

I smoothed his hair back in its original position. Danté shook his head, and his hair was again all ruffled up.

"I need to shower anyway, so it doesn't matter."

"Alright. You can take my key, so you can come back in if I am still in the shower."

Danté hesitated.

I knew it was because of the key, but I couldn't help but smirk. "What are you waiting for? Wanna watch me undress?"

He let out a breathy laugh. Once he had my key in his pocket and was about to leave, he turned back. "You wouldn't walk out of this apartment today if I did."

My mouth dropped open, but no sound came out. Danté winked before going out. This would be a very long, cold shower.

Danté was already in our kitchen when I emerged from the bathroom, still towelling my hair dry. He had swapped his all-black outfit for a lighter blue jean and a cream-coloured knitted sweater. The colours gave him a soft vibe. A devil's grin appeared on his angel-like face, and all the softness vanished. Part of me wanted to throw an apple at his face to wipe that evil smile off his mouth, the other part wanted to kiss it away. The way his smile turned daring, he probably knew where my thoughts were at. I steeled myself and went for the fridge. Though the thought of us spending the whole day under the covers, exploring each other's bodies, was more than alluring, I wanted more. We would have that conversation sooner than later. I saw it coming;

Danté probably saw it too. But it would have to wait a bit more. If the bubble had to pop, I wanted to enjoy being inside of it as long as possible. Danté was my Christmas present, and I would cherish him, no matter what would happen once the illusion was over.

I made a pumpkin spice latte – yes, pumpkin spice had its place in my diet, even during Christmas – and pushed my mug towards him. Danté shot me a worried glance but sipped anyway. His expression stayed blank, so I waited for him to react. He ended up pushing the mug back to me without commenting. He'd be excellent at poker.

"So?" I asked.

"That's pumpkin spice, I suppose?"

"Yes. Homemade."

He was trying to find something nice to say about it. The attention was kind. I raised an amused eyebrow. Danté cleared his throat.

"It's… bearable."

I shook my head. That was going to be as positive as it could get.

"Do you want me to make you a regular coffee?"

The playful gleam in his eyes meant something was coming my way.

"I'd rather not. It's bad for my cortisol levels."

My smile fell. I looked back at my latte. The coffee inside it was mocking me just as hard as he was.

"Touché," I sighed, then something hit me. "Wait, you remember that?"

"Of course. Why wouldn't I?"

I truly could've kissed him then and there. I was used to

talking about such subjects without people caring. Except for Jasmine, no one really listened. Even Eleanor wasn't able to do more than pretend like it was interesting.

"I am just surprised that you listened."

Danté scrunched his brows, a muscle in his jaw twitching. I had said something wrong, hadn't I?

"That's rather insulting."

I grabbed my mug with both hands to keep them occupied. "I didn't mean that you're not someone who listens. I am just surprised that you cared about my food facts. Most people don't."

"I am not most people."

"I know. I'm sorry."

"And most people don't care about you the way that I do."

My head snapped back up. Danté got up and placed himself in front of me. His gaze was so gentle and so open I couldn't hold it. I wanted to tell him what I felt. Those feelings were so big and beautiful, but especially terrifying. Icy panic rushed through my system, making it hard to breathe. What would happen if I said them? Did he care enough to want to give a chance to long-distance? Did he even want me that way? Danté's gaze turned worried, and I had to force myself to snap out of it.

I didn't know what the future held, just like I didn't know if his feelings were of the same magnitude as mine were. One thing was sure, however. Danté cared. A lot. Because he was here, now, while there were hundreds of other places he could've been instead.

"I know," I admitted.

Danté put his forehead against mine. I inhaled his scent, which was becoming the theme of my holiday. It was easier to spend time together without putting a label on it. That label could change too much too fast. That conversation would have to wait a few more days; I wasn't ready to put my heart on the line.

"Thank you."

His eyes went wide. "What for?"

"For caring."

I couldn't complain. I had never been alone, not really – some people had always cared for me. It didn't change the fact that when it came to Danté, him caring for me the way he did made me feel like I could move mountains.

Danté looked like he wanted to comment, but smiled instead. "Are you ready to move?"

I nodded before grabbing the box of Ferrero Rocher I had bought for Grandma. I still felt silly for always buying her nothing but chocolate. I also knew that if I didn't get her those, she would smack me with her ten-pound handbag. When I was a kid, it had been all I could afford. So for years, I had given her a box of chocolates. Even though it was just that, Grandma always acted like it was the best gift one could hope for. The day I finally had more than twenty euros in my pocket, I had offered her jewellery. I thought she would be happy with something else, something better. Instead, she had asked me why I had stopped with the chocolates because that was the only gift she looked forward to every year. The Ferrero Rocher had become our little tradition.

Once we were in the car, reality downed on me. Danté was coming with me to see Grandma, and I hadn't warned her that he was coming. Gods. I didn't even know what I was supposed to tell her. Panic began to set in. It was unlike me to do something without thinking about the consequences. *Breathe, Evy.* It was too late now. Danté was coming. The only thing I knew for sure was that she would adore him. I smiled at the idea. The panic vanished as quickly as it had appeared. This could be fun.

"Red" came on the radio, and I bobbed my head to the beat. It wasn't the first Taylor Swift song that had come up since we got in the car. When the song switched, and it was another one of her tracks, I knew.

"You put her *Red* album on."

Not just the album. *Taylor's Version*.

"I did," he answered without taking his attention off the traffic.

It was the first time that I saw him listening to something other than metal, or the darker beats that were on his sex playlist.

"You like it?"

He had hummed to one of her albums yesterday. Maybe he was also a Swiftie?

"Not particularly."

First of all, *ouch*. Taylor was my queen, and a beacon of light when I was sad. *Most people don't care about you the way that I do*. This was too sweet. Danté was playing a dangerous game, but so was I.

"You're setting the bar too high."

His hand found its place on my thigh. He squeezed gently.

"Good."

CHAPTER 20

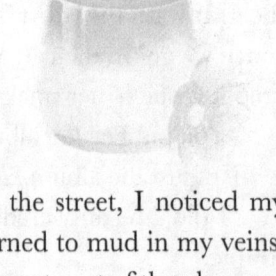

The moment Danté pulled up the street, I noticed my parents' car. *Fuck me.* My blood turned to mud in my veins, panic rising to the surface. This was not part of the plan, nor was this something I had prepared myself for. Danté said something, but it didn't register in my brain. Until he waved a hand in front of me and snapped me out of it.

"What's happening?"

"My parents are here."

Most of the time, they spent Christmas with my father's parents, not with Grandma.

"You want to go back?"

Yes. No. Maybe? I steeled myself.

"Let's go. I promised I'd come to see her."

My heart picked up its rate. Nothing would happen to me. I knew that. Then why was my anxiety flaring up? Probably because I wouldn't be able to ignore the disappointment. It was easy to let someone down when there were miles between us and not feel a thing. Danté lifted his hand to push on the doorbell; instead, I just opened the door. Voices came from the living room. When we entered, all the heads turned. Grandma jumped up from her one-person seat.

"Oh, darling, you're early." She opened her arms and took me in for an embrace. She smelled like freshly baked cookies.

"Hi, Grandma. Merry Christmas."

"Merry Christmas, Evy."

My parents and sister got up from the couch. My father's expression was neutral, my mom's a bit less. Eleanor was glaring. Until Danté reached out his hand.

"Hello. I am Danté."

They all shook his hand and presented themselves politely. My sister's eyes went from mad to shocked. It hadn't been that long ago that she thirsted after him. And today he was mine. Even if it was only for a few hours. Then my mother ticked.

"I thought you were too busy."

"I am too busy to leave for a whole week, not for a few hours."

"It sounds like an excuse to not come home," she quipped back.

I couldn't answer back. My mom never responded, not to me. Now that she did, I didn't know what to tell her. Not only did it sound like an excuse, it *was* an excuse. Shame was gnawing at my sanity, and I found myself unable to even look at her.

Danté put a reassuring hand on the small of my back. "She's been studying very hard. She'll visit when she can."

My head shot up. Had he just taken my defence even though I was the one to blame? I could kiss him right then and there. Danté noticed me staring and gave me a warm smile. When he was with me, I truly felt like I could rattle the world. From the corner of my eyes, I noticed Eleanor assessing the whole situation like a cat in a tree would. Nothing went unnoticed by her.

Grandma cleared her throat before hugging me again. "Welcome home, darling."

My father's brows furrowed at the words. *Home*. The place his house was supposed to be to me. Luckily, he stayed silent. Me on the other hand, I felt warm and fuzzy inside when she said it.

Grandma winked at me. "I hope you brought my chocolates."

"Even better. I have the regular box, but I also found a huge one."

I grabbed the candies and gave them to her. The grand Ferrero was bigger than a snowball.

She clasped her hands together. "Marvellous."

Grandma ushered us to the kitchen, and when the adults – well, the more adult adults than us – went back to their discussion, I stole a cookie from the counter. Danté pretended to be shocked.

"You filthy thief!" he scream-whispered.

"Shush! She doesn't like it when people take them before she says so."

I took a bite of the goods and sighed from contentment. An evil twinkle appeared in my friend's eyes.

He placed his arm over my shoulders and whispered in

my ear, "It would be such a shame if she saw that, then, wouldn't it?"

"Fine! I'll trade you half of the cookie if you keep silent."

"Perfect."

I didn't get to break his part off; Danté took a bite and almost the whole cookie was gone. I rolled my eyes.

"If that was what you planned, I would've given you a new one," I said as I put what was left of it in my mouth.

At that moment, Grandma and my parents looked in our direction. My crime had been discovered. I swallowed as Danté laughed quietly next to me. They were all expecting something. Had someone asked me something while I had been chatting with Danté?

"What is it?"

"How are the cookies?" Grandma asked, smiling mischievously.

I let out a nervous giggle as I rubbed my forearm. "They're amazing."

She patted my cheek in such a sweet, loving way that the gesture almost made me tear up. "Good."

Eleanor took that as a cue to take one herself. Grandma tsked, and my sister dropped it.

"Don't eat them all now. It's for after we open the presents."

Eleanor opened her mouth to protest. I wasn't the favourite, but I was the one Grandma knew the best. I could get away with way more than my sister or my cousins. Grandma raised a single eyebrow, and Eleanor plopped down on a kitchen chair, sighing.

"Your mom asked when your internship starts," Dad said.

Oh right, so they had asked me something. That piqued Danté's interest.

"The first week of February."

I was so ready for it. And if I was lucky, I could walk out of that internship with a job. *The* job.

"Where will it be?" my mom asked.

If she was trying, so could I. I opened my mouth to answer, but Grandma was faster.

"At the medical practice near her apartment. They might even offer her a job."

Except that her excitement didn't help my case.

"How do you know that?"

Mom's disappointment shone through now. Hadn't I told her that?

Grandma beamed, not noticing that her daughter had lost all her colour. "She told me when she got the internship. A position that would be deserved. A hard-working girl, that one."

My sister looked down. One of our uncles once said that Eleanor was the pretty sister, and I the smart one. In both cases, it has been insulting. After having spent years in and out of the hospital, Eleanor's academic career had been heavily delayed. Where I was almost graduating, she still had more than a year of college to go through. I shot a glance at Danté, biting down on my lip. He stood closer to me, our arms touching. I was waiting for my mom to explode. She was the one I got my horrible temper and sharp tongue from – a bad personality trait Eleanor also had inherited. So imagine the shitshow if the three of us lost our marbles at the same time.

"It looks like you know more about our daughter than we do," she snapped.

Eleanor and I winced. *There we go.*

Mom tried to regain her cool. "The way you keep pushing us away is not fair, Evelyn. We are your parents."

"Your mother is right," Dad added. "We let you do what you want, but you should tell us those kinds of things."

A snort escaped me. Danté bumped his shoulder against mine, grounding me. *Breathe, Evy.* I hadn't come here to create drama.

"Can't you see that we are trying to be part of your life?" Mom insisted.

"Well, maybe I don't need you to be present in every aspect of my life."

I had blurted the words out before I could even think them through. Grandma's eyes went wide at the sudden shift in the atmosphere. She knew how bad my outbursts could be. My mom, however, hadn't seen it coming. Because even though I had the same bad temper as she had, I had never lashed out at her. It was too late now. My words were in the open. And I meant every part of it. Danté laid a hand on my shoulder. When I looked up at him, he shook his head. I swallowed back my anger.

"Why do you have to be so cold? This family loves you. We *need* you."

I saw red. Danté let out a long breath. My brain short-circuited, and the little common sense I had left broke down.

"You weren't there when *I* needed you," I yelled, "and I waited for years. So stop pretending like we are a united family. Because we are *not*."

My whole body was trembling, and the nausea came back. My mother left the kitchen, my father and sister rushing after her. Grandma looked back at me, her hands twitching. The disappointment on their faces meant nothing compared to the sadness on hers.

"Grandma, I'm so sorry," I started before a sob came out of my mouth. "I'm so sorry."

Then another sob came out, and another one, until guilt made it hard to breathe. How could I spiral out of control like that?

Grandma gave me an embrace. "Oh darling, I know."

"I'm sorry."

My fears had been true – I was a rubbish daughter. Then why did it feel like a huge weight had been lifted off my chest? I didn't feel sorry for saying those horrible words; I was sorry because I meant them. Grandma stroked my back until I stopped hiccupping. She made a tissue appear out of her apron and dabbed my cheeks dry.

"I ruined your Christmas."

"No love, you didn't. This has been coming for a very long time." She let go of me and turned to Danté. "Please take her home. They all need to cool down."

Danté nodded. She gave him a tight hug before kissing my cheek. Danté grabbed my stuff in the living room where my parents were while Grandma pushed me outside.

"Take the time you need to clear your head, but don't let things deteriorate, alright?"

It was easier to not think about the future, or that I would have to face my parents again after today. But she was right. I couldn't let things deteriorate. I just couldn't do it today.

Probably not tomorrow either.

"Yes, Grandma."

Danté came back with my jacket and my handbag. "I'll wait in the car."

He greeted Grandma with a kiss, and she beamed at him. Once he was out of hearing, her smile turned cheeky.

"What a handsome man you have."

My cheeks reddened. "Oh, Danté is not my man."

"You don't believe he's just a friend, do you?"

There was no point in pretending like he was. Not today. If anything, Danté had been the strength I needed.

"One thing is for sure; I don't want him to be."

"Good. I'll see you soon."

"I'll call you."

"I'm counting on it."

The ride back home was over in the blink of an eye. At least, that was how it felt for me. At one point, I recall Danté saying something I hadn't been able to focus on. If anything, I felt drunk. Empty. I let my body use its muscle memory to take me upstairs. What now? In less than ten minutes, I had been able to make my family hate me. If I had had any chance to mend the relationship I had with my parents, I had just watched it burn. Worse, I had lit those chances aflame with my anger and bitterness, and I hated how good it felt.

Danté put my stuff on the low table in the living room,

keeping his distance. "Do you want to talk about it?"

"What is there to talk about? You saw everything."

He should never have seen any of this. So why didn't I care that he had? I couldn't even muster the energy to feel ashamed anymore. I let myself fall on the couch and turned the TV on. Maybe it was better to not feel anything in the moment. Once the haze was over, I wouldn't feel so calm anymore.

"Evelyn, if you need to cry or vent, please do so."

"I feel empty."

"Do you want me to leave?"

"Do you want to leave?"

"That's not what I'm asking."

The cold settled in my body. Gods, I was so tired. Danté dropped to his knees in front of me, putting the back of his hand against my forehead. His skin felt warm against mine. The features of his face were taut with worry. Maybe that was why I couldn't lie.

"I never want you to leave."

"Alright."

He went to the kitchen. I could hear the doors of the cupboard open and close, and cutlery clink. Danté came back a few minutes later with a mug. From what I could smell, it was chai. He gave me the cup, and the heat of it made my body regain some of its sensations. The tea wasn't strong enough for my liking, nor was it sweet enough. The gesture was the sweetest though. Danté plopped down next to me and took the remote.

"I won't be able to convince you to watch a horror movie tonight, huh?"

"Can we watch *Strong Girl Bong Soon* instead?"

Humour and pretty boys were the only things that could make this day a bit less shitty. Danté put the drama on without complaining. Once the first ten minutes were over, I scootched over, half draping myself over him. I was probably overstepping boundaries by doing so, but if I was, Danté ignored them too. Because for the rest of the night, he held me close until I fell asleep.

CHAPTER 21

Eleanor: *you fucked up.*

The words danced before my eyes. It felt like my insides became hollow, and my hands started trembling. It was so unlike Eleanor to be this cold through message. I guess I deserved it after what happened yesterday.

Evy: *I know*

I waited a minute, then two minutes. When I finally let the phone fall back on my bed, certain there would be no answer, the screen lit up again. My hands turned clammy.

Eleanor: *You better plan a great apology because Mom's inconsolable*

What had I expected? Of course they would scold me for

my behaviour. It was silly to hope that my sister would understand. The three dots on the screen went up and down.

Eleanor: *Are you going to reply? I know you read my message*
Evy: *I don't know what to do*
Eleanor: *Are you okay?*
Evy: *No...*
Eleanor: *Do you wanna talk?*

It was selfish, but I knew that talking to Eleanor would only make me feel worse. As long as I didn't apologize, she would still be mad at me. Perhaps it was also better for her to not be stuck between me and our parents.

Evy: *Not right now*
Eleanor: *Fine. Call Mom when you've calmed down.*

I rubbed my cheeks dry and took a deep breath. They would have to wait a bit longer because I was not ready to make that call just yet. This time, I would call the shots, even if that meant I would go to hell.

The following days went by in a blur, mostly. Things were weird, and not at the same time. I spent most of my days studying, whether it was at mine or Danté's place. He had given me his key, even when he went to work. At first, it felt intrusive to be here, especially since he also had a roommate. And even more since my own place was only on the other side of the hall. Luckily, Jared wasn't here for the holidays, which gave me all the space one could need and more. It felt nice to be outside of my own apartment, which had started to feel stuffy after my little mental breakdown on Christmas Eve. That was how I had ended up on Danté's couch with all my books, summaries, and my laptop. Staying the night was where we had both drawn the line, not that we ever spoke about it. Spending days together and falling asleep on the couch in each other's arms was one thing, sharing a bed was another. Neither of us was ready to go there.

The door opened, and Danté went to put his coat on the hanger. When he turned, he seemed surprised to find me here. I had been here for the last three days, and yet he always seemed taken aback to find me roaming around the place. He had been the one to give me a spare key, so no take-backsies.

"Honey, I'm home."

I grinned as he walked to the couch. Instead of simply removing my stuff, he looked at the course I was studying. Danté always seemed intrigued by what I was doing. He sat down on the coffee table in front of me.

"I can make space for you, you know."

"S'alright. Keep studying."

"I'm done for now."

"Do you want me to interrogate you?"

I blinked at him before making a face. I expected him to say it as a joke, but he was dead serious. That was oddly endearing.

"I've been studying by myself since I was fourteen. There's no need."

"Are you sure? I don't have anything better to do."

I often forgot that he had been a student not that long ago. A student who had gotten two master's degrees. I kind of liked the fact that he wanted to test me. Which was why I handed him the papers.

Half an hour later, he handed me back my course with some attention points written on it. I scowled at my summary.

Danté gave me an encouraging smile. "You still have plenty of time. Most students don't start studying that early."

"I know. I just don't like it when it's not perfect."

"I noticed."

Obviously, everyone noticed that. Maybe Jasmine was right and I was a control freak. His stomach grumbled.

"Let's make you something to eat," I offered.

We switched apartments since the only spices I could find in their pantry were salt, pepper, and paprika. Danté poured us both some rosé wine. Although it wasn't my beverage of choice, it gave spending the night together a cosy feeling. I chopped some sweet potatoes to make oven fries while Danté kept interrogating me. He fell quiet when I made the dipping sauce. When I looked up, Danté was watching the chopping board suspiciously.

"What's wrong?" I asked.

"That's a whole lot of garlic."

Garlic needed some time to infuse when it wasn't cooked. I held back the comment, or he would call me a know-it-all. So I shrugged.

"It's not like I'm going to kiss anyone today, or

tomorrow."

"You're still going to stink," he shot back.

I smiled wickedly at him. Danté raised a single brow.

"But so are you, so we'll be stinky together."

"What if I was planning on kissing someone?" he asked, falsely offended.

"Well, now you can't, unless you're planning on kissing me."

I winked to give some more effect to my words. I wanted him to kiss me, but having him unable to kiss anyone else was a good enough start. Not that I was letting him leave me tonight. Did that make me psycho? Oh well. Danté leaned forward, letting his elbows rest on the kitchen island between us.

"When are you finally going to admit that you're trying to sabotage my love life?"

"I can't divulge to you all my plans. Otherwise, they won't work."

He raised his glass before taking a sip. Seeing Danté drink wine in my home was a sight I loved too much for it to be sane. As he smiled at me, I knew I wouldn't walk out of this unscathed. Cheers to that.

CHAPTER 22

I was changing in my bedroom when I heard the front door open. It was the shriek that made me hurry back to the living room before I had the time to even put my shirt on.

"Who are you, and what are you doing in my daughters' apartment?"

Oh, fuck me. I could hear Danté answer, without understanding what he was saying. When I got there, they all stared at me with wide eyes. Danté's eyes went from my head to my bra. He quickly turned away, and I felt my face heat up. I quickly put the shirt on before running towards them. I hugged Nadim before jumping towards his wife.

"Auntie Aswaa!"

Jasmine's mom gave me three kisses – one kiss on one cheek, and two on the other – before giving me a tight hug. She smelled so nice. It was the same roses and bergamot perfume I've always associated with her, and it made me tear up. The smell was comforting. She held me at arm's length and watched me. She cupped my cheek, smiling brightly.

"Merry Christmas, *Amirti*. You look good. How was your holiday?"

Chaotic. Nerve-wracking. Out of control. A myriad of words came to mind, yet I couldn't bring myself to say them out loud. I searched Danté, not knowing what to say. He stepped closer, something that didn't go unnoticed by Aswaa and Nadim. Both raised a brow. Aswaa joined her hands.

"We met your neighbour. Is there something you want to tell us, *Amirti*?"

I gulped. I hadn't really cared when I had introduced Robert to my parents. It wasn't like I'd seen us as something that would last long. It was the same reason I hadn't bothered introducing him to Jasmine's parents. No one had really been fond of us being together, and I didn't want them to disapprove or to be disappointed in me. They had known about Robert. No more, no less. Now they both looked at Danté who was standing too close to be a mere acquaintance or a simple friend. It hit me how badly I wanted them to know him. Except that I couldn't tell them what I wanted. I eyed Danté, only to find him waiting expectantly, his head ever so tilted to the side. My stomach twisted.

"I fought with my parents on Christmas Day," I admitted, letting my head fall down. "Danté has been my rock these last few days."

The shame still had a bitter-sour taste on my tongue, yet I hadn't found the courage nor the will to call my parents to apologize. I knew I had to do it. The wound would only fester the longer I waited. I also knew that right now I wouldn't mean the apology. And lying somehow felt just as bad, if not worse.

"Evelyn, what happened?" Uncle Nadim asked in a gentle voice, trying not to spook me.

Breathing became difficult, and it seemed like no matter how much air I sucked in, it wasn't enough. A warm hand touched my back, then I could smell fresh laundry. I swallowed back the tears.

"I said things I shouldn't have said."

Aswaa and Nadim glanced at each other, their expressions sad but not surprised. It had been a long time coming.

"You should come home and we'll talk about it," Auntie offered without pushing.

That had always been the way they handled me. Auntie would make couscous or chicken with olives, and we would talk about all my worries around fresh mint tea. Once I had bawled my eyes out, they consoled me with food and their presence. It had always worked like a charm. Not because the only way to handle me was by feeding me – which was always a nice bonus – but because they understood how much it meant to have a parental figure who would devote their evening to my emotional well-being.

I nodded. "I'd love to."

Jasmine and Theo walked in, and my best friend rushed to me to give me a hug. She squeezed me, and I squeezed back.

"Oh gosh, I missed you," I whispered.

Less than a week had gone by, yet it felt like Jasmine had been gone for weeks.

"I missed you too, Eves."

When she looked up, her brows shot up as Danté greeted her with a nod. Jasmine questioned me silently.

"I'll fill you in later."

Having all these people in our small home seemed to be the cue for Danté to go back to his own place. When he said goodbye, Nadim and Theo seemed to be relieved to see him go. Aswaa on the other hand, analysed everything, undisturbed and completely aware of everything that was left unsaid. Once we were in the hall, and the chatter of my family had picked up, I let myself breathe.

"It's time that I give back your key."

Before I could take his key from my key ring, Danté shook his head.

"I'd rather you keep it."

"Why?"

"In case you might need it someday."

My insides turned hot. It had been nice to be allowed to walk in and out of his home, a bit as if Danté had given me a key to his life. Keeping it made me too cheerful. I tried to hide it.

"That sounds a bit like a marriage proposal."

Danté let out a breathy laugh. I didn't want him to leave. I was also aware that I had to let him go at some point. Danté had been the best thing that could've happened to me these last few days. It didn't mean I could keep him forever. Life would have to go on again.

"Well, you already know how good I look in a tux."

The fucker knew how much I had appreciated seeing him wearing one, didn't he? His attention on my face was unsettling, kind of like he knew what I was thinking inside that skull of mine. There was no point in lying.

I nodded. "I can't argue with you on that one."

Danté turned back to his own door.

"Thank you for having my back. I don't know how I could ever repay you, but…"

"I don't want you to repay me, Evelyn. I'll always be there if you need me."

This time I couldn't keep the smile at bay. Had Danté chosen to be the person who would always fight my corner?

"Then I am grateful."

Before he could leave, I went over to hug him. His arms found their way around my shoulders, and I let myself enjoy the moment. When he finally let me go, it didn't feel that hard to see him go anymore. Danté pressed a kiss against my temple.

"I'll see you around."

Once his door was closed, I let out a shaky breath. It was time to break the bubble and to ask Danté out.

My nerves were eating me alive, so much so that I was afraid I would collapse from dizziness. In the distance, Alex waved as he walked over to us, Danté's roommate and two girls with him. A blondie and a brunette. The blonde girl didn't pay us much mind, but the brunette did. She looked at my friends with interest. She was absolutely gorgeous with piercing dark eyes and high cheekbones, and man was she tall. Though it was freezing out here, her caramel-coloured skin was glowing. How she did it, I had no idea, but I would love to know her skincare routine. Was she Alex's girlfriend? As soon as Alex greeted us, the girl flung herself at Danté, arms around his neck. The way his arms tightened around her and his eyes crinkled from smiling, my heart dropped. There was no way she was Alex's girlfriend. No one would be fine with his girlfriend hugging and kissing another guy. Jasmine and Theo shot me worried glances, so I put on a reassuring smile, even if on the inside, I didn't feel reassured at all. This was not going according to plan. When she finally let Danté go, she looked at us. She grabbed my hand. Even her hands were warm in this weather.

"Hi, I am Manal."

"Evelyn."

Her eyes widened comically. "Oh! You're the squirrel girl!"

Now it became harder to keep my smile in place. *Squirrel girl?* That's how Danté talked about me? I inhaled loudly.

"For you, it's Evelyn."

The conversation around us stopped, and all eyes weighed on me. Had they really thought I'd enjoy being called *squirrel girl* by a stranger? Danté's jaw tightened. I squared my shoulders, my smile never faltering. Manal's brows shot up, and she let go of my hand like my touch had burned her. The atmosphere became heavy and awkward.

"Let's go," I said.

Without looking if anyone had gotten rid of their stupor, I started walking. The fairy lights and jolly music only made me feel more out of touch with the rest of the world. There had been nothing merry about this Christmas. The only thing that I waited for now was New Year. I wasn't a huge fan of making resolutions. It never seemed like something people did genuinely or made happen. New Year's resolutions were practically made to be forgotten after a few days, or a few weeks. I hoped that next year would be a little bit gentler; a year where dreams could become true, even if they were small ones.

I stopped at a jenever stand. The carefree chatter of my friends and the others had returned, but I didn't have the energy to mingle. Jasmine had insisted on us going so that I would leave the apartment, and see other faces. It would've been better if I had stayed at home. They ordered several shots, so I did the same. Everyone clanked their plastic shot glasses, all smiles. I couldn't even look at their happy faces without feeling myself grow cold inside. I downed a shot of apple and cherry jenever, then I downed all my shots. Danté looked at me with worry, but it was easier to ignore him.

The group moved again, and I ended up walking behind. It was easier to stay silent when no one was next to me. Every now and then, Jasmine searched for me. She knew me well enough to leave me alone as long as there would be an audience around us. I wanted to tell her to not worry about me and to enjoy the evening; no sound came out.

Manal grabbed Danté's arm, hugging it as they walked farther. Conversation and smiles were so easy between them, unlike how they were between us most of the time. I was way over my head, wasn't I? I had been a fool for thinking these last few days meant anything. If sweet, kind girls like Manal existed and made him smile, the messed-up ones like me had no place here.

Alex, who had been with Jasmine a few moments earlier, adapted his pace to mine.

"Are you okay, Little One?"

I scowled at him. "Just because you're tall doesn't mean you get to call me little."

White clouds left his mouth when he huffed. We walked in silence for a few more seconds, until Alex put his hand on my wrist.

"I'm serious. What's going on?"

I opened my mouth to tell him to fuck off, that I was fine. It would've been a lie, and Alex was too good at reading character to buy any of my lies. My eyes stopped on Manal who was feeding Danté a steaming, sugar-loaded beignet from one of the little stands. They both laughed when she accidentally smeared powdered sugar on his face. Alex followed my gaze, his brows scrunching together.

"I wanted to ask him out tonight," I admitted softly. "Do you think I waited too long?"

Alex clucked his tongue in annoyance, still watching his friend. When he turned back to me, his expression softened. "I don't know. He's giving me mixed signals too."

My breath hitched in my throat. If only I could go back home and pretend like tonight had never happened.

I looked at the Ferris wheel and the coloured lights that lit it up. As a kid, I loved these. It felt freeing to be so high up, and to see as far as one could. I couldn't remember the last time I had gone in one, or if I had enjoyed it enough. I wasn't sure I would enjoy it as much now. Seeing the world from a distance might give me some perspective, just like seeing the world as one glowing, happy painting might make me feel more out of touch with the world I couldn't connect with.

"Do you want to take a ride?"

I startled, only to find Danté standing next to me. Everyone else stood a few feet farther, everyone including Manal. The fairy lights gave him a golden glow. In another world, Danté could've been an angel who walked out of a fairy-tale. In this one, he was the one who could make my heart beat faster, just like he could make it stop beating altogether. That thought alone made me numb. Children were laughing in the queue of the Ferris wheel. If only I could have their carefree mind. If only I could stop living in my own fucked-up head that had to fuck up everything.

"Evy, are you alright?" he asked as I hadn't answered. "You've been aloof this whole evening."

"I'm fine."

Jasmine walked over and positioned herself next to me. "Let's go on the Ferris wheel! You love those."

I appreciated the fact that she tried to make me feel better. I found myself nodding, the last bit of my energy being crushed when Manal arrived and put her elbow on Jasmine's shoulder like they had been friends for a while. How long had I stopped seeing what was happening around me?

"Awesome! Danté, let's go!"

"I'm going with Evelyn."

Manal looked in my direction with bright eyes. I wasn't being fair, so I mustered the last bit of courage I had and attempted a smile.

"You can go together. I'll go with Jasmine."

We all queued for the ride. Alex and his friends went in

the first cabin, then it was Danté and Manal's turn. She tugged him inside, and he almost tripped over his feet when he lost his balance.

I turned to Jasmine and Theo. "I'm going home."

My best friend's face turned sad. I felt bad for her.

"I can go with you," she offered.

I shook my head. Unlike me, Christmas was important for her, and she loved Christmas markets. It would be better if she could enjoy the evening without my sadness tainting it.

"I don't want to ruin your night, but I can't stay here. Please."

Jasmine gave me a tight hug before stepping inside the cabin with her boyfriend. Once they were all in the Ferris Wheel, I went home. Far away from the music, the laughter, or the happiness of others that just couldn't become my own today.

When I grabbed the key to my apartment, my eyes stopped on the key of the door behind me. I opened Danté's apartment and looked at the place. It seemed like just the two of us being here had been a lifetime ago when it had only been yesterday. I laid the key down on the low table. It was better like this than to live in a world of pretence and false realities. Then I returned to the darkness of my own bedroom and let myself fall in a slumber.

CHAPTER 23

Incense, fresh mint, and spices created a rather overwhelming mix for the olfactory senses for those who weren't used to it. To me, it smelled like home. The familiar scent of Aswaa and Nadim's house made my shoulders relax a bit. During the whole ride here, I couldn't stop fidgeting in my seat. I hadn't been able to talk back every time Jasmine tried to start a conversation. Gods bless her, she didn't take it personally.

Jasmine dropped her bag at the door with her luggage, and we both swapped our shoes for babouche slippers. Isam lifted his eyes from his phone and flashed us a toothy smile. He still had a lot of baby fat in his cheeks, but as he stood to greet us, he towered over both his sister and me. Jasmine merely patted his arm before going to the kitchen.

"'Sup, Little One."

His grin only widened before he hugged me. Isam tilted me up, and my feet were lifted off the ground. Maybe Little One was a nickname that would have to go.

"I see you're still as ugly as always," Isam shot back without any hesitation.

Oh, to be sixteen again. I whacked him on the back of his head now that I could reach there.

"Isam! Where are your manners?"

Isam hid behind me to avoid the babouche that his mom threw his way. The slipper hit me in the stomach. Auntie Aswaa put her babouche back on before giving me a tight hug.

"Oh dear, I'm sorry, *Amirti*."

She flicked her son on the forehead. Isam at least had the common sense to pretend like he felt scolded. Aswaa's hand pressed my shoulder and tutted.

"There's no need to be so tense, Evelyn. You're safe here."

"I know."

I pulled her closer for another hug, and she gently threaded her fingers through my hair. I followed her to the kitchen and grabbed the glass with my name engraved on it. They had offered me a mug and a glass when I arrived here seven years ago, because everyone had their own mug and glass, and they didn't want me to feel like a stranger at home. Nadim and Jasmine were already chatting at the kitchen table when I plopped down next to him. He pressed a kiss to my temple before continuing his conversation with his daughter. Aswaa took a round wooden tray and put the tea glasses and the Moroccan teapot on it. Her eyes met mine. Even though I knew nothing would happen to me, my heart rate spiked, and I had trouble swallowing.

We all settled down in the Moroccan sitting corner,

except for Isam, who took this as his cue to leave Jasmine and me with the adults. Auntie Aswaa poured everyone a cup of mint tea, before sitting down next to me. As always, she kept her demeanour open and inviting, her gaze kind.

"How have you been, *Amirti*?"

I took a sip of the delicious tea, readying myself for the next hour.

"I'm alright," I started.

"She's not alright at all," Jasmine interjected. "She's been hiding in her bedroom for two whole days, barely eating."

I glared at my best friend, who glared back right away. She knew I would not talk if she didn't throw me under the bus. I didn't even know where to start, or what to say. This whole week had been a disaster, and a blur. At this point, I couldn't say what hurt the most. Or maybe I could, and that was so much worse.

"I didn't go to my parents for Christmas. I told them I had to study and work at the café, but I didn't think I'd see them at my grandma's house when I went to visit her."

I grabbed a pillow to hide behind. Aswaa gently squeezed my knee, motioning for me to continue. So I told them everything that happened. What I said to my parents. How Danté had stayed with me through the tears and the outburst. Jasmine's eyes lit up at the mention of our neighbour, unlike her father's, whose were shooting lightning in my direction. If only he knew that Theo spent most of his time at our place, and what happened behind closed doors in Jasmine's bedroom. Danté and I sleeping on the couch was probably the most innocent thing that happened in our apartment when a guy came over. And yes, sure, I had taken home my fair share of men, but it wasn't because I didn't commit that Jasmine was more innocent than I was. The handcuffs inside her nightstand told a whole story, and she wasn't the one wearing them.

Auntie Aswaa took her slipper off and hit Jasmine on the forearm.

"I told you to bring Evy home for Christmas!"

Jasmine yelped in surprise. My best friend grabbed the babouche before Aswaa could strike again. "I invited her! She's the one who refused to come."

Aswaa turned to me, her eyes clouded with anger. She hit my thigh with her palm.

"Why did you refuse?" she shrieked.

I rubbed my leg, keeping my gaze low. Jasmine hated it when I said she was exactly like her mom. Somehow moments like these kept proving my case.

"So Theo could ease into the family without me being in the way," I mumbled.

This time Aswaa flicked me on the forehead.

"Nonsense. You're our daughter. You are never in the way."

"I appreciate the thought," Jasmine added, "but Mom's right. Next time, you'll stay with us."

"*Amirti*, you are going to talk to your parents, right?" Uncle Nadim asked.

I let my chin rest on my knees, scratching at the denim with my nail. "I know I have to apologize, but I don't mean it."

"Then don't," Aswaa shot back matter-of-factly.

Nadim shook his head, clearly disagreeing with his wife.

"She should talk it out."

"Of course she should talk it out. But Evelyn shouldn't apologize and pretend like she's fine when she's not."

My eyes burned at how strongly Aswaa stood behind me. Nadim nodded, staying quiet.

Auntie turned back to face me. "Call your parents and tell them what you need."

"And if I need time? How can I tell them I don't want them around?"

Both Nadim and Aswaa looked at each other, silently agreeing on what to say next. I, too, wanted to find the kind of relationship where my partner and I could understand each other without having to talk aloud.

"Then just say so. They let you wait for years; you can tell them to wait until you are ready. But they need to know."

Okay. I could do that. I swirled the tea inside my glass. This was going to be such a messy conversation, but I could do this. It was the least I could do. My parents deserved the truth, no matter what it would be, just like I deserved the peace of mind of being honest for once.

Jasmine cleared her throat. "What about Danté? I know there is more that you're not telling us."

Traitor. I knew that once I said out loud what happened, I wouldn't be able to pretend like nothing happened anymore. Not like I had been very good at pretending, but that's beside the point. I bit my lip.

"Danté stayed with me these last five days."

Uncle's eyes darkened. I ignored his reaction and continued. My heart squeezed painfully while talking about Danté, and about the few days we had spent together. Like I had said before, he had been my rock. He had taken my defence in front of my parents and held me close afterwards. Something I hadn't expected him to do. There weren't enough words to describe the gratitude I felt towards him. But even this wasn't enough. The closer we became, the more I wanted him. Yet I kept being reminded all the time that we were not meant to be. And that hurt so much more than anything else. I loved Danté. That was the sad reality. Like a pathetic little girl, I waited and kept praying that he would love me too. I stopped talking, sniffling, and doing my best to keep my tears at bay. In vain.

"I don't like this," Nadim stated.

The contrary would've been a shock for everyone in this room.

"We are not a thing, Uncle. There's no need to worry."

"He slept with you."

My cheeks heated up at the image that flashed in my mind. Dirty, *dirty* mind. "In a non-sexual way."

Uncle Nadim sputtered his tea out while his neck and cheeks grew red. I pressed my lips together. That was the type of conversation I wasn't going to have with them. They weren't ready.

"But you want him," Aswaa interjected.

"I do."

I wanted it all: the good, the bad, the ugly. I wanted the laughter, the fights, no matter how explosive or silly they could be, like bickering over who ate the last piece of cake. The trust and knowledge that we would always have each other's corner, no matter what would come our way. Uncle's brows went down to create a deep frown on his face.

I let out a wet laugh. "I also meant that in a non-sexual way."

Jasmine cackled, and her father's head went up in horror.

"Though I'll admit that he looks more than fine without a shirt on."

"*Amirti!*"

"Sorry Baba, but she's right. Danté is a snack."

"And very well mannered," Auntie Aswaa added.

Yes, Danté checked all the boxes. Kind, funny, considerate. He was a total sweetheart. That was what made it so hard not to love him. A tear rolled down my cheek. Aswaa took my hands in hers.

"It seems like you care about that young man a lot," Aswaa tried.

Especially since it was the first time I told them about a guy.

"I love him, Mom."

"Then why are you crying?"

"Love is supposed to be wonderful. But every time I think we can make it, and be more than friends, he slips through my fingers. I don't know what to do."

After all, I was just me: the weird, grumpy squirrel girl with her life planned out, and Danté was everything I was not. I didn't stand a chance next to a sunshine like Manal.

"You need to stop running, Evelyn. There is a chance that he loves you too."

"But…"

"And if he can't see the kind girl that you are, he doesn't deserve you. So talk to him, because you need to know."

Just the idea of talking to him made my stomach churn,

an acid taste burning the back of my mouth. I shook my head. This was going to be a total disaster. It was better to have Danté in my life, even if it meant watching him from the sidelines while he was happy with someone else.

"I can't."

Aswaa clicked her tongue, disappointed in my reaction. "*Amirti*, you can't keep pretending like everything is fine. Be honest."

Deep down, I knew I had to be honest at some point. Right now, it felt like I was drowning, but the thought of going back to the surface was scaring me.

"Can I at least pretend tonight?"

Her gaze softened. "Just tonight then."

CHAPTER 24

It was rather obvious that most people were home for the holidays. A good amount of our customers were students. Now that they weren't on campus or near college, the café was mostly empty. Some retirees came for a hot cup of coffee and some social interaction. Other than that, it was too calm. That was how Chloe and I had ended up in a booth, where she was helping me study toxicology. I had a hard time focusing, so when she asked me to explain the courses to her, it gave me enough motivation to do it right. She asked me in-depth questions, and when I answered right, she gave me a freshly baked oat cookie. Every now and then, Kristen appeared in the doorway to the kitchen to see if we were still there. At one point, she even put a fresh pot of hot lemon tea on our table and some cucumber sandwiches.

"How is the studying going?" she asked.

"Evy will do just fine, like always," Chloe told her as she poured three cups of tea.

I packed mine with a whole lot of sugar, which wasn't great. Especially if I was going to preach to patients later that too much sugar was bad. But hey, I was only human. I let out a satisfied hum as I took a sip.

"You know you can ask for a few days off if you need to study at home," Kristen told me.

She had always been such a chill and understanding boss. I would miss working for her, and this café. Chloe and Kristen had been a great supportive system during the two and a half years I had been here. The bell chimed, and Danté walked inside. *Shit*. I had forgotten we were Tuesday, and Danté never skipped coming by on Tuesday. My shoulders slumped. I hadn't seen him or heard from him again since I had abandoned them at the Ferris wheel. After having let myself cry and wallow in self-pity for a day because of how much I hated myself these last few days, I had picked myself up and focused on my upcoming exams. It had been enough to keep my mind off all the rest. Until now. Chloe shot me a questioning look, and I sighed before walking over to the counter. I put on my charming customer smile.

"Hello. What can I get you?"

Danté stayed silent for a while. He watched my every move when my fingers started tapping nervously against the wood of the counter, his expression carefully blank. My stomach churned under the intensity of his attention. Chloe and Kristen were both watching us, ready to jump in if necessary. He finally moved, only to drop a key on the counter. My breath hitched in my throat. He wasn't here just for coffee then.

"You gave me back my key," he stated.

"I did."

"Didn't I ask you to keep it?"

Great. Now I felt like an asshole. I let go of the smile.

"You did."

"Then may I ask why you gave it back anyway?"

Unable to keep eye contact any longer, I looked away. That numbness that I had felt at the market came back. Only this time, it didn't drown out the sadness. I just felt cold and alone.

"It felt too heavy to keep."

His head dropped to the side, as he was unable to understand where I was going. Danté opened his mouth to answer, so I cut him off.

"I don't want to have it. So please stop talking about it."

I couldn't have that key. It felt like too much for the little that we'd had together. Being reminded constantly that I would never be anything else but the prickly squirrel girl in a world where the kind ones like Manal existed only made it harder.

"Squirrel, what happened that night?"

My heart felt like a hand grenade that had been thrown after the pin had been removed. I exploded in tears and anger. "You really ought to stop calling me that!"

Heads shot up at my outburst, and I fled to the kitchen. Danté followed me. He took a step towards me, and I took one back. His eyes turned worried.

"Evelyn, what is going on? Did I do something wrong?"

Had he done something, or was it just me? I pulled at my hair as more tears fell down. Danté took me in his arms, even when I struggled. He held me close, and let me sniffle against his sweatshirt.

"Talk to me."

Except that being this close only hurt more. His hands rubbed invisible circles on my back.

"I need you to stop being so nice to me."

"Are you hating yourself so much that you don't want me to be nice to you?"

Maybe I did. But it wasn't just that. I didn't want him to be just nice if that was all he could be to me. It had been too clear that Danté was just nice. I didn't want it if that was all he had to offer me. I let myself bask in his clean smell a second longer before I pushed him back, rubbing my eyes with my sleeve.

"I don't want your kindness if that's all it is. And I don't need your pity."

"What? Evelyn, I don't pity you."

"Look, I am grateful that you were there for me last week. You didn't have to, but you were there. But I am not a kid you need to watch over or someone you have to take care of. So please, just keep that key."

A muscle in his jaw twitched. I had hoped Danté would drop it now, but he stepped closer, so close until I was pressed against the fridge.

"Is that how you see me? Like I watch over you like a kid because I have to?"

"How could I not? She called me Squirrel Girl!"

"Evy, there was nothing insulting in what she said."

I knew that. Of course I did. That didn't change the fact that it still hurt.

"Danté, don't you see it? Can you really be so dense?"

He didn't answer. I inhaled loudly through my nose. My vision blurred again, so I just closed my eyes.

"I am smart. More than that, I am at the top of my class. I work hard for everything I need or want, and yet the only thing that someone remembers from what *you* told her is that I am that ridiculous girl wearing a squirrel onesie. Can't you see I am more than that?"

There was silence. All I could hear was the blood rushing through my head. When I opened my eyes again, Danté stood closer than before. The right corner of his lips was uptilted. He brushed some of my unruly curls from my face, his fingers grazing my forehead ever so slightly.

"I see you, Evelyn Somers. Not just as a funny girl, or as a brilliant woman. I see all of you. I am sorry I made you feel like I didn't take you seriously."

I could feel my lip wobble. "You do?"

"I do."

He cupped the back of my neck and held me closer. This time, I didn't fight him. This time, I just let myself enjoy the embrace.

"Next time, instead of bottling up your feelings, please just tell me. You know I'd never hurt you on purpose."

"Sorry. It's been a rough week."

"I know," he murmured without letting me go. "I know."

Danté patted my arms before letting me go. He handed me a tissue that I took to blow my nose.

"Do you always have a stash of tissues in your pockets?" I asked, cleaning my glasses that were all smeared with half-dried tears.

"I figured you need them quite often."

This should probably have irked me. At this point, he had seen me puking and all snotty, and there was nothing I could do about it anymore. It didn't matter. One thing was certain. There was nothing left for me to impress him with. That knowledge was liberating somehow, because I could be the worst version of myself, and Danté would still stand by me.

"Better?"

I nodded. "I guess I just needed to explode."

His eyes crinkled as he smiled. My insides grew warm at the sight. My peace was short-lived. When we went back to the front of the café, Manal was chatting with Chloe at the counter. I stopped in my tracks at the sight of her. Why did she have to be everywhere? Her eyes lit up as she saw us.

"Hello, Evelyn."

She emphasized my name before giggling sweetly like it was a private joke between the both of us. It wasn't. I couldn't hate her for it, no matter how much I wanted to. If Danté had golden retriever energy, Manal had the demeanour of an overexcited puppy. Danté went to her, and she hugged him like she had done that night. Chloe shot me a confused glance. Instead of letting him go afterward, her arm stayed around his middle. I had thought Danté was single all this time. Had I been so mistaken? She said something I didn't hear. Chloe stepped forward, apparently to take their orders. I forced myself back into motion and looked at the order so I could help prepare it. When I put their take-out coffees in front of them, they were chatting and laughing, still wrapped in each other like lovers in their honeymoon phase would.

"Enjoy your coffee."

Danté grabbed the key that was still on the counter and

their drinks. He gave me a questioning look, so I faked a smile. I was good at those these days. I wouldn't destroy his happiness just because my heart couldn't stop feeling. They both waved, not a cloud in their sky, unlike in mine. When he walked away, arm in arm with her, my heart cracked even further.

CHAPTER 25

A stranger was caressing my breasts through the sheer fabric of my nightgown, while his too-wet lips trailed kisses on my neck and collarbones. I waited for my body to wake up, to react to the touch. It never did. Until he pinched my nipple so hard that I hissed from the pain. This was not what I had envisioned when I had picked him up at the bar. If anything, I'd liked his confidence and witty humour.

"I'm so sorry," he stammered.

You better be. What was he trying to accomplish? Tearing my boobs off? I gave him a little laugh, and he went back to his ministrations, albeit a bit softer. His fingers went south, gliding between my legs. Yet my body still didn't react to him. Gosh, I was so bored. As if it were a sign from the heavens, my phone rang. I almost pushed the guy off me to grab the device. *Take out the trash.* How could I be so happy to see such a stupid reminder? I jumped out of the bed.

"What…" he started.

"I... need to do something very important. It will only take a few minutes."

Before I left the room, I looked back at him. A tiny part of me still hoped that this night would not be a total blunder.

"While I'm gone, why don't you think about all the things you want to do to me?" I asked in a sultry tone. "I love surprises."

That seemed to bring back some light to his pupils. When the door was closed, I let myself sigh. Why was it so hard to find a good one-night stand these days? I had even put on a very short nightgown! It seemed like all the men I had taken home hadn't been able to make me feel a thing.

I put on my dino slippers, grabbed the bin bags, and went downstairs to the back of our building. From here I could still hear the traffic: honking cars and trams. It was far enough that the noise seemed distant. I looked at my bags and let out a sigh. I would have to go back upstairs, and something told me it would be a total waste of time. I threw the trash away and readied myself.

"Squirrel, what the fuck?!"

I yelped in surprise only to find Danté storming at me. Before I could even register anything, he draped his sweater over my shoulders.

"What are you...?"

He cut me off. "I could see your underwear."

Mortification made me silent. My cheeks became hotter than the sun under his stern gaze. I quickly closed the zipper of his sweater to hide my body. Danté let out a sigh, running a hand through his damp hair. He was only wearing sports shorts, now that I was wearing his sweater. A thin layer of sweat covered his toned torso, and I found myself unable to look away. Was it gross to want to touch his sweaty bare skin? I mentally hit myself with a frying pan in the head. A guy was waiting for me, and here I was lusting after my neighbour once again.

"Stop looking at me like that."

"Like what?" I wondered.

"Like you want to eat me."

"Oh my gosh…"

I had been staring at him like a starved girl in front of a free dessert buffet. Danté made a sign for me to follow him towards the staircase. Most people used the elevator. The both of us being in the medical field, stairs had always been our first choice.

"Why are you dressed like that? Are all your funky pyjamas due for laundry?"

"I don't wear my "funky" pyjamas when I have someone over."

His eyes went wide. "Then what are you doing here?"

"He wasn't getting me in the mood, so I told him to think about what he wanted to do to me while I went outside."

A silent laugh shook his shoulders. "I always forget how honest you are."

I found myself staring at his back while we went up, and how his muscles moved. Danté caught me staring. "Like what you see?"

I cleared my throat, cheeks only getting redder and redder. He had caught me twice in less than two minutes. Lying would be dumb.

"Obviously."

He stopped between two levels. Suddenly he was unable to hold my gaze. "You really have to stop looking at me like that."

"Or what?" I asked softly.

When Danté finally turned back to me, I could see his dilated pupils, his eyes now more black than blue. I had to refrain from walking over to him. Danté seemed to get my thoughts. A second later, he had me pressed against the wall.

"You make this very difficult, Squirrel."

"I didn't do anything. Yet."

His smile grew, and he leaned in. I could smell the shampoo in his hair and the soft tang of sweat on his skin, and it made my head grow fuzzy. Before I could think, I found myself tracing the muscles of his chest. Goosebumps made the hair on his arms rise. Danté leaned in, his hot breath against my neck. His lips made heat spread in my blood as they trailed kisses towards my shoulder. His hand found my thigh, and I felt goosebumps spread on my own skin. He had barely done anything, and I was ready to follow him anywhere, ready to take everything he would give me. His cool fingers stopped at the band of my underwear, then he hesitated.

"Evy..."

Instead of going back down, his fingers caressed the lowest part of my stomach. I felt my knees getting weak.

"Oh, fuck me."

I clasped my hands on my mouth as the words left me.

A low laugh shook him. "Be careful what you wish for."

This was taking too long. I wrapped my arms around his neck, and our mouths finally collided. I pulled back when

Danté hesitated. Had he not wanted this? His eyes glided over my face, then fell back on my mouth. If there had been any restraint in him before, it was gone now. He lifted me up and pressed me harder against the wall when his lips finally found mine again. A satisfied sigh escaped me as I kissed him back. My legs circled his waist, his toned body pressed against all the soft curves of mine. His tongue slipped inside my mouth, and I let him deepen the kiss. There was heat building up in my chest. My fingers found his back, and as I slightly scratched his skin, his breath hitched. There was now a hardness in his shorts that was pressing against my most sensitive area. My body responded on its own, and I rolled my hips. Pleasure shot through me; we both gasped at the friction. As I did it again, Danté stopped kissing me, his full attention now on my face. Then he moved too. For a mere second, I thought about asking him to take me to his place. Those thoughts were crushed like glass under a boot when we heard steps coming up the stairs. Danté put me down and we ran towards our own level, laughing. By the time we stood at our doors, we were both out of breath. It had been easy to believe that I could have followed him inside. But now the moment was over. There was still a bulge in his black shorts, and I couldn't help but feel pride at the sight. Danté watched my door warily, his jaw clenched.

"Think of me when he fucks you," he said in a clipped tone.

Was he mad? Oh, fuck me. Like I could ever forget what had just happened.

"Wait, before you go," I shot back.

I unzipped his sweater and took it off, taking my sweet

time. Dante's eyes darted over my neck, my cleavage, and where the sheer material was barely covering my breasts. My skin felt hot under his attention. I wasn't the only one feeling it. He looked like a dream with his flushed cheeks and kiss-swollen lips. And he looked like he wanted to get back at it again.

"Don't forget your sweater." I gave him the piece of cloth, that he numbly accepted. I flashed him my sweetest smile. "I'll be thinking of you. Goodnight."

I slipped inside and waited behind the door. There was a loud sigh on the other side, then finally, his door clicked shut. I bit my lips to keep from giggling. I ran towards my room, my body buzzing with newfound excitement. It had to get out of me. Now.

Jasmine looked at me over her cup of mint tea as I did my walk of shame. I pretended to not notice and filled a glass with water. Jasmine stayed silent, but I knew she had questions. She always did. At first, she had disapproved of me bringing guys home. Unlike me, Theo and Jasmine were more than old news. He was her first serious boyfriend, her first time, and apparently the one. I, on the other hand, had become like Danté after Robert and I had broken up. Having sex with strangers or almost strangers was fun when you actually found someone who was on the same wavelength. It became less and less fun the more Danté added himself to the formula.

"Let's go grocery shopping," she said in a too-calm voice.

Did she know something? I gulped my water down, the sound of it too loud in the silent apartment. She couldn't possibly know what had happened yesterday, right? Most of the time, I didn't mind sharing all the saucy details with my best friend. This time, things were different. Gods, I couldn't even bring myself to think about what had happened yesterday, and what could've happened.

Jasmine grabbed two boxes of tampons from the shelves. It was the perfect moment to also make sure my condom supply was restocked. I could feel Jasmine's eyes burning holes in my skull. The only thing I couldn't pinpoint was if she was so inquisitive because I was so awkward, or because she knew. But I'd rather die than discover what it was right now. When we entered the building, the person who had been on my mind all night walked down the stairs. Did he ever work? Why was this guy everywhere when I needed him to be far away? I grabbed Jasmine's arm and went for the elevator. Fuck physical condition.

"Hey Squirrel, where are you running to like that?"

Gods bless Jasmine who didn't fight me and just followed.

"Gotta go!"

As if he didn't just come from upstairs, Danté followed us to the elevator.

"You know, if I didn't know any better, I'd think you're avoiding me."

"I *am* actually avoiding you. So if you noticed, be a darling, and let me avoid you!"

"Is there something I should know?" Jasmine asked. She

stopped in her tracks before we could reach the elevator.

"No!" I yelled, tugging harder at my best friend's arm.

Jasmine didn't bulge, her attention fixed on Danté. Danté patted my head like one would with a child. I pulled back, scowling. His shoulders shook from silent laughter.

"I saw her in her underwear. Stop panicking, Squirrel, I've seen more revealing lace than that."

My whole face and neck turned red. I smacked him on the chest, but Danté just laughed it off.

"I also heard someone leave your place a few minutes after we met."

Fucking hell. No wonder he was so smug.

"Not helping!"

"What?" asked Jasmine, her face contorted by shock and laughter.

My best friend was too big a fan of tea to follow me back to our level. *Traitor.*

"Don't worry, Jasmine. I didn't do anything to her."

Jasmine relaxed at that.

"Nothing she didn't like, anyway."

Oh, if only the floor could open and swallow me whole. The bastard knew he had just thrown me under the bus. Satisfied with himself, Danté squeezed my shoulder before leaving us.

Jasmine tried not to laugh. "You forgot to tell me something?"

I did my best to not look at her and finally pushed on the button to call the elevator.

"I had someone over last night," I started.

"I am aware. He tried to sneak out in front of me while I

was eating cereal."

I bit back the comment on how it's bad to eat those sugars at night. Now was not the time.

"But I had to take out the trash, so I told him to wait a few minutes, and to imagine what he would want to do to me."

Jasmine shrugged, not even phased. "What happened?"

"While he was waiting for me to return, I was outside of the apartment… And Danté had his tongue in my mouth."

And his hand under my nightdress, which I didn't tell her. I had no idea how to face Danté after what we'd done. How do you go back from that? Had he asked, I would have followed him inside. I would've given him anything he wanted without even hesitating. And that was fucked up. So perhaps it had been a good thing that we had been interrupted.

"Waw, two guys in one night? Your life really is a drama, huh?"

I hid my face with my hands. "This is so embarrassing."

Especially trying to get myself in the mood with that guy after meeting Danté outside. Which was why I had sent him away. I had been up for a wild night. A very long, wild night. The problem was that after that kiss, it had been clear there was only one person I wanted to spend the night with. And that person had taken a step back when we had been breathless. During the whole night, I could still feel all the places where Danté had touched me. Which had made me wonder all night if kissing him had been a mistake. A kiss here and a caress there weren't enough.

"I'm so fucked," I muttered, tugging at my hair.

Jasmine snorted. "For once, I disagree. You actually need

to get fucked. So get your shit together and talk to him. And get laid!"

I looked back at my best friend, unable to keep from laughing.

"What?" she asked defensively. "I live with you. Of course I'll end up talking like you!"

I hugged her as we walked out of the elevator.

"It only took you two years to get there," I teased.

Like the adult that she was, Jasmine hit me on the back of my head. "I'm serious, Eves. You love him. You can't pretend anymore."

She opened the door, and when we were finally back inside our safe place, I asked the question I had been running away from.

"What if he loves Manal?"

To move on, I knew I had to know if he loved her or not. Or more importantly, I needed to know if he felt the same way that I did. Not loving Manal wasn't good enough.

"Well, does he? He had his tongue in your mouth, and if I take your red cheeks into account, he probably had his hands somewhere else too. Where was Manal then?"

She had a point. I coughed from embarrassment. It wasn't awkward to talk about sex when it was about sex with strangers. But then, I hadn't felt this giddy and hormone-fuelled around other guys like I did with Danté. Jasmine showed me a cheeky grin, proud that she had been able to make me tongue-tied. When the cheekiness dissipated, Jasmine sobered up.

"You promised you'd talk to him. Stop being a coward and do it."

In the way that my gut clenched and churned, I knew I had run out of time. The time where I could hide my feelings and pretend like they didn't exist was officially over.

CHAPTER 26

My hands were shaking as I brought the cup of chamomile to my lips. And as I took a sip, I burned my tongue and lips.

"Oh, fuck me."

Jasmine eyed me over her own cup of tea. I had been trying – with an emphasis on trying – to steel my nerves. I wasn't doing a very good job at soothing anything. Jasmine opened her mouth to say something, so I held a palm up.

"Don't say anything. I know I'm a coward."

It was a truth I could no longer ignore. I was a coward, and a liar. It had to stop today. At least on one front. I couldn't fight every battle in one day.

"I was actually going to tell you that Alex invited us to go bowling this weekend."

I raised an eyebrow. Now that sounded rather fishy. Sure, I didn't despise the guy anymore, but inviting me to go bowling seemed like a stretch. We didn't like each other *that* much.

Jasmine let her chin rest in the palm of her hand. "What is it now?"

"I have a hard time believing that Alex invited us just to go bowling. And by us, I mean me."

"Danté is coming."

"Of course he is," I grumbled.

It was becoming quite clear that Jasmine and Alex both tried to meddle in our business, or lack of business. I hadn't seen Danté again. That was probably for the better. I couldn't muster the courage to see him these days. Jasmine was still waiting for my reply. This whole situation was getting preposterous, so I nodded. Perhaps it would help soothe my nerves to have a friend's night out before I actually told Danté that I was in love with him.

"Now if you'll excuse me, I have to call my mom."

I downed the rest of my now lukewarm chamomile tea and went for my room. *You can do this, Evy. Things cannot get worse than they already are anyway.* I dialled her number before I could give myself the time to chicken out. Every beep of the line made my heart rate spike up. My hands grew so slick with sweat that I feared I'd let my phone drop. Every second felt like an eternity. Gods, I hated this. Finally, unfortunately, she picked up.

"Evelyn?"

No hello, no nothing. I swallowed hard.

"Hi, Mom. How are you?"

She hesitated, probably thinking about how to keep this conversation under control. "I'm okay. How are you?"

"I'm hanging in there."

We both stayed silent for a while. For once, I hadn't rehearsed what I needed to tell her, so I had no idea what to say.

"So," she started.

"About the Christmas fiasco," I said at the same time.

"Yes?"

I hated myself at how hopeful she sounded. Here I was, about to step on her feelings. Aswaa was right. I had to be honest. It was better for all of us if I told her what was really on my mind. What had been on my mind for years.

"I am not going to apologize for what I said because I meant it. I'm just sorry that it came out that way."

"Evelyn, that's not fair. You know we are trying."

My eyes prickled with tears. Gosh, I was such an asshole, wasn't I?

"I know you are. I'm just not able to pretend like I'm fine anymore."

"Then what do you expect of us?"

This was it: my mother's outstretched hand. My heart was beating painfully in my throat, and my vision blurred. My knees were getting so weak I had to lean against my desk. Still, I felt too nervous to sit down.

"I need time. Time to know what I need and to know how to get better. I hope you can give me that."

Her breathing trembled. I knew she was doing her best not to cry.

"Evy, you know we never wanted to leave you behind, right?"

A tear rolled down my cheek, and I was glad that my mom couldn't see me now. I quickly wiped it away.

"I know. It doesn't change the fact that your absence hurt me. And I know there are a lot of things we need to talk about, but I'm not ready."

When a soft sob escaped her lips, I could feel my heart break. Things would get better for all of us one day. They had to.

"I guess you won't come back home then?"

"I won't, no."

I also remembered that Danté and Jasmine had both told me to give them a chance. So I reached a hand out as well. It was the least I could do. She was still my mother.

"Let's maybe go out for a coffee in a few weeks?"

So that the dust could settle, and I could try to get my shit together until then. Mom sniffled on the other side of the phone.

"Yes, that sounds lovely."

"Thank you."

"Alright, we'll talk later. Take care."

"Bye, Mom."

She hung up faster than she ever had. Probably to bawl her eyes out. Though I felt like crying and pulling my hair out myself, I couldn't ignore the amount of weight that lifted from my shoulders. Jasmine's head snapped up, her eyebrows drawn together in concern when I got back to the kitchen. She got up slowly, trying not to spook me.

"So, how did it go?"

I opened my mouth to answer, but all that came out was a sob. Then another one, and another one, until I was a crying mess on the floor.

Jasmine hugged me, rubbing my back. "Did it go that

bad?"

I shook my head. Once the sobs calmed down, I let myself lean against the wall. "No, it went surprisingly well."

"Then why are you crying?"

"I hurt her. And no matter how much I've resented them, I never wanted to hurt them."

"It's better this way, Eves. They were also hurting before. Now at least they know why."

Jasmine and I stayed on the floor in silence. The impatient drivers honking and tram bells ringing outside were oddly comforting. Life would get back to normal. Things would get fine. Just not today, and not tomorrow.

"How about a drink?" I asked.

"That's probably the smartest thing you've said all week."

"Asshole."

Jasmine hit me on the arm before getting up. Then she offered her hand. For a small girl, she had more strength than she let on. Jasmine lifted me as if I weighed nothing. Once I was back on my feet, she gave me a satisfied smile.

"An asshole you cannot live without."

"Damn right you are."

Days had gone by in a blur. My exams were mostly over, and to be honest, I'd rather go out for a drink than for a few hours of bowling. But a promise was a promise, so I picked out a dark red velvet dress and put on my black biker boots.

And for once, I made my septum visible. If anything, I looked quite like a badass. The gods knew I needed to feel like one because my sanity was tearing apart at the seams. I had survived my mom, so I would survive confronting Danté as well. That didn't make it easier though. Jasmine and Theo were waiting for me in the living room. Jasmine whistled, so I turned to show them the whole outfit.

"Damn girl," Theo said, "you sure do clean up nicely."

"Jasmine told me I need to get laid. Hopefully, this will do the trick."

Theo looked at his girlfriend in shock; she just winked back at him. I wasn't going to tell him I had corrupted her.

When we arrived at the bowling alley, Danté and Alex were already at the bar, both drinking a beer. Was it the anxiety or the fact that I was happy to see him that made my heart speed up? Alex greeted us. By the way his smile turned cat-like, it was clear that Alex knew what my plans were. Luckily for me, he at least had the decency to stay silent on the matter. Danté, on the other hand, was not so quiet.

"Waw, Squirrel. Who are you trying to impress?"

I kept from scowling at the nickname. My friends snickered at how oblivious he was, so I did my best to keep an impassive face. His eyes lingered a few seconds on my legs, then on my piercing. One of the corners of my mouth lifted.

"Does it look like I am trying?"

Jasmine gave me a thumbs-up, and I bit my lip to keep from laughing. Danté looked to the others, who all did a terrible job at staying neutral. Especially Theo. I rolled my eyes at how obvious they were. Alex, gods bless him, cleared his throat.

"Alright, we're all ready to start the game?"

My friends and I agreed; only Danté shook his head.

"Manal will be here a bit later, but I guess we can already start."

My stomach dropped to the floor. What the fuck! Manal was going to be here? What was even the point then? Alex shot me a worried glance, so apparently, he hadn't known of her presence here either. Danté seemed confused at the sudden silence of the group.

"What's going on?"

Except for the fact that both our best friends had been working together so that I could confess, and that Danté had invited his friend (or more?) to the night out, everything was fine. Oh, how I loved it when things didn't go according to plan. It seemed like no amount of planning would save me tonight.

Alex regained his composure. "I just didn't know she would come tonight."

"Well, you said it was a friends night out."

It was too late to turn back now. I followed the group to the alley. Alex did his best to make the teams. He tried to put Jasmine with Danté and me, but no matter how hard he tried, Danté didn't see why he wouldn't have Manal on his team. And Alex didn't want me to be in another team than Danté's. So once Manal was here, she would join Danté and me. In other terms: this evening was doomed. At least for now, she wasn't here. Danté started the game with a spare.

I grabbed a pink ball that wasn't too heavy and threw it away, only to go straight in the gutter. I liked to think that I was a girl of many talents. Bowling, however, wasn't one of them. On the second try, I scored two pins. Pathetic. Danté gave me an encouraging smile. It didn't make me feel better. This game would be a disaster, then the rest of the evening would be a disaster. Call me a pessimist, but I knew which battles I could win. Tonight wasn't one of them.

At one point, Danté took pity on me. "Alright Evy, do you need some help?"

"I don't want you to score for me, if that is what you're suggesting."

It was a fool's pride, but I'd rather go down trying than let someone else win for me. He gave me a smirk and stalked over to where I stood.

"Get in position. Bend your knees a bit more."

I did as he told me.

"Good. Now look at the arrows on the floor. You've been trying to aim for the middle, but try to aim for the one right to the centre."

Danté gave a sign for me to try again. I took a deep breath and threw the ball again. For the first time in ten minutes, I didn't have a gutter ball during the first try. Granted, I only got four pins. It was still four more than I had been able to get before. I looked up at Danté, proud of my small victory.

"Did you see that?"

"I did. Try again."

The second time, I was able to take another four pins down. That was probably the first time in my life that I had been able to get an eight. Danté lifted his hand, and I gave him a high five.

"Thank you for the tip. Maybe I'll still be able to beat you."

His eyes turned into crescent moons as he laughed. "I'd like to see you try."

A dark tornado came between us. Manal gave Danté a bear hug before engulfing me in another one. My brain barely registered what was happening, so I dumbly patted her shoulder until she released me. *Someone ought to tell that girl to not hug every stranger she meets.*

"I'm sorry I'm late!"

Like always, I plastered a polite but fake smile on my face. This was where the evening stopped for me. Immediately, Danté and Manal started talking animatedly about life, about work, about their common friends. So this was what it felt like to be a third wheel. Spending years with Jasmine and Theo should've prepared me. It hadn't. Manal joined the ongoing game and quickly scored more than what I had. And petty and competitive as I was, I wanted to do better.

When it was my turn again, I blocked out the surroundings and focused on the arrows on the floor. Spare! I turned back to Danté to see if he had seen it, only to find him still talking to her, holding her hand. My breath hitched in my throat. This really was a fight I wasn't going to win. Might as well let it go. I pushed the disappointment that threatened to crush me and plopped down next to them. One of them said something to me; I just couldn't register who said it, or what they said. It took all my concentration to keep from breaking down in this stupid place.

Once the first game was over, I went to the bar. Let them do another game if they wanted to. I had seen enough of it. I was surprised to see Danté sit next to me. The silence was awkward. It felt like he wanted me to break it. I just didn't know how to. Danté bumped his knee against mine.

"So, what ruffled your feathers this time?"

This time? Like it happened that often. Maybe it did, but that wasn't the point.

"I beg your pardon?" I asked in a clipped tone that proved him right.

"One second, you're fine, then you're moody. What happened?"

The damper I kept on my emotions lifted, and a tsunami of sadness and anger drowned me. There was no light there where I was headed.

"You lied to me."

He almost knocked over his soda as he turned to me. "What?"

Danté looked at me as if I had hit him. The way he looked was the way I felt. I felt played, and stupid for having been blind all this time.

"Well, how is she then?" I asked. "From one to ten?"

The question was out before I could think about whether or not it would be wise to voice it aloud.

"Evy, what are you talking about?"

I stared at the bubbles rising to the surface of my glass of tango. It was easier to not look at him anymore. If he wasn't going to be honest, I would be. I was tired of him walking all over my heart and my peace of mind. It ended tonight.

"You said once that you never sleep with your friends. You should've just told me you don't like me instead of lying straight to my face."

He let out a long sigh, which only meant he was battling the annoyance he felt because of me. "Where is this coming from?"

I faced him. Danté's expression was grim; he knew things would go south from here.

"Who acts with their "friends" the way you and Manal act together?"

A muscle in his jaw ticked, a sign that showed I had probably gone too far. "What the fuck is your problem?"

There was no turning back now.

"So you expect me to believe nothing ever happened?"

"Yes!" he exploded. "Not that it is any of your business, but yes."

Tears blurred my sight; I quickly blinked them away. He was right. It was none of my business. It was time for me to go home.

"Well, I don't. I'm tired, and I don't want to see you right now."

I grabbed my bag and jacket. I had barely made two steps when Danté grabbed my wrist. His skin was searing against mine. I tried to free myself from his grip in vain. He was seething, and it made me want to crawl under the bar.

"Who do you think you are to say things like that?" he asked in a tone that was so cold and low it gave me shivers.

I had seen Danté being annoyed because of me on several occasions. It was the first time that I saw him actually get mad. Tonight, he wasn't the only furious one, so I clung to that rage.

"If you hadn't toyed with me the way you did, I wouldn't have to say anything. Now let me go."

That took him by surprise. Just not enough for him to release his grip on my arm. "Toyed with you?"

I started tugging harder at my wrist, but Danté didn't bulge. He put his face closer to mine.

"We're not done here."

"If you don't let me go, I will scream."

We stared each other down. Danté was wondering if I was bluffing. I wasn't, and he realized it too because he immediately let me go. His expression turned sad. Disappointed. My fury only grew bigger and bigger.

"Good night," I spat before disappearing into the night.

CHAPTER 27

Grandma was shuffling around the kitchen preparing her specialty: grilled tomato and basil soup. Like always, she tutted me away when I offered to help, so I watched her while sipping some tea. I had needed a break from my own head to be able to concentrate on my exams. It was also the perfect excuse to visit her. It was nice to be back here without my parents or my sister, where it was just the two of us.

"How is your friend doing?"

"Jasmine's doing great. Her exams are going well."

Grandma hummed but didn't respond. When I looked up from my agenda, she was watching me, her eyes full of laughter. My insides clenched.

"You meant Danté."

"I did. But I'm glad Jasmine's well."

I didn't know what to tell her. So many things had gone south these days, and I was well aware that I was being an ostrich about it. Telling her about it was too much.

Grandma cleared her throat. "So?"

"We're not really on speaking terms at the moment."

"What did you do?"

I scowled at her over my cup of tea. Grandma had seen me scowl and scream and do so much more for years. Me scowling now wasn't bothering her.

"Why are you assuming I did something wrong?"

She stirred her soup before resting her hip against the counter, hands clasped together. "I'm not assuming you did something wrong. But I know you and your terrible tendencies to pretend to be fine and then explode. So, did you?"

"I might have said some things," I grumbled.

"Darling…"

"I know, Grandma. I hate myself for it."

She handed me a bowl of steaming soup, smiling brightly. "You'll do better next time."

"How can you be so sure?" I asked, swallowing back my tears.

If anything, I had proved time and time again that I made the same mistakes without getting better.

Grandma's palm was soft against my cheek. "Because I believe in you. You should too."

Unlike me, Jasmine had finished all her exams. Which meant she could start going out and meeting her friends again. Lucky bastard. Not that I was in the mood to go out or anything. I had spent the last days wallowing in self-hatred. Though I couldn't really pinpoint what exactly made me hate myself the most anymore. Did I loathe my mere existence because of what I had said to Danté, or because I truly had felt like there could be a future for us where he liked me too? Not only did I hate myself, I had also accepted the fact that I probably was the biggest fool on this planet. I had been delusional and had seen what I wanted to see instead of taking the hint like most people would have. But no, stupid Evy was in love with Danté, the guy who would never give her the love she hoped to receive from him. If only it were so easy to stop loving him.

After the disaster that had been the bowling night, I had locked myself in my room and put in earplugs. It was the only way to ignore my friends on the other side of the room while I bawled my eyes and heart out until I fell asleep. I had felt guilty for exploding in Danté's face the way I did. But no matter how much I looked back at that terrible moment, I couldn't help but feel misled. Because never had Danté been with me the way he was with Manal, just like he had never given a real sign that he cared for me when she was around. And that hurt.

Jasmine closed my textbook, and I jumped at the sudden gesture. I looked back up at her and glowered. Just because she was done with her exams didn't mean she could to meddle with my schedule. She was not impressed.

"You've been staring at the same page for over twenty minutes. I think you should accept the fact that you need a break."

"Alright, o wise one, what do you suggest?"

Jasmine clicked her tongue and whacked me on the head. When I tried to hit her back, she took a step back.

"Don't go sassy on me, you bitch. Let's go to the College."

"I'm not sure that's reasonable. I still need to study."

"Evelyn, you need a break. If you don't want to drink or drink much, then don't. Staying here and staring at a page and not being able to read because you cannot focus is not going to work."

I hated it when she was right. I also had to admit that studying was more of a formality, because I wanted to have the best scores on the exams. I already knew what was in those books enough to nail the tests as it was. I ended up agreeing.

"Fine, let's go out for an hour."

Since this night out wasn't supposed to end up any other way than me getting back home early enough to get a good night of sleep, I didn't bother with a fancy outfit or a lot of makeup. Mascara was more than enough. I quickly put on a black knitted jumper and a wide pair of jeans and called it a day.

Theo met us outside of our building, and we walked to the bar. My friends were talking, but I let them. I didn't have the energy to really participate in the conversation. I just felt drained. The first thing I saw when we arrived at the College was Danté sitting at the bar. It was time to accept that I was a magnet for doomed evenings. I stopped in my tracks and hesitated if I should go back home. Jasmine, who was completely oblivious to my internal turmoil, pushed me inside. Luckily, the space was rather crowded. The chances that Danté saw me were reduced by at least thirty percent.

We hadn't seen each other since the bowling night. Me snapping at him and regretting it later was an ongoing theme. I hated myself for always exploding like that. I just couldn't help the bitterness and the sadness that always followed me when Danté and Manal were nearby. I darted to one of the booths near the back. If Jasmine or Theo suspected what was going on, neither of them said anything. Theo went to the bar to get us drinks. Jasmine leaned over the table.

"Why are you panicking like this?"

As if on cue, my leg started bouncing. "Danté is here."

Had I known that he would be here too, I wouldn't have come. Call me a coward. I already knew that.

"So?"

"Remember what happened last time I saw him?"

"You can't keep avoiding him. You guys should talk it out."

I wanted to. Gods, I had to make it up. But how? When I lifted my head in his direction, Danté's eyes locked with mine. The golden retriever energy that I was so used to with him was nowhere to be found. He was mad. I could practically taste his anger from across the room.

Theo came back, and I downed three shots before they could say anything. This night was going to be a disaster. There was no way things would go smoothly. I might as well get as much liquid courage in my system, even though I tended to be a rather sad drunk whenever Danté was involved. I could still feel his attention weighing on me, so I downed two more shots of tequila. When I finally gathered the courage to look back up, he wasn't alone anymore. I recognized the blonde girl. How could I not? It was the very same one I had seen the first night at our apartment, and many more nights afterwards. And she was about to kiss him. My heart clenched, and I shot up, unable to stay in the same room as Danté and Blondie. Both Jasmine and Theo stopped mid-conversation.

"Evy, are you alright?"

"Yes," I lied. "I just need to get some air. I'll be right back."

I practically ran outside. The air was chilly, just what I needed. I leaned back against the wall and listened to the music when the song changed. "The Death of Peace of Mind". Of fucking course. The song set the theme. A second later, the door opened. I didn't need to open my eyes to know who stood there.

"How long are you going to do this?"

I blinked at him. Danté was clenching his jaw. It was the first time that his demeanour seemed so dangerous. I swallowed.

"Doing what?"

Although I had an idea of where he was going.

"You don't get to comment on my actions the way you do."

He walked over to me. Every step he took resonated in my bones. Danté leaned down until our noses almost touched. I tried to pull my head back, which only worked so well with the wall in my way. My pulse sped up to the point I could feel my heartbeat in my throat.

"I'll ask you only once more. What is your problem?"

"My problem?" I squeaked.

The corners of his mouth twitched, but he kept his dark gaze locked on mine. So this was what a mouse must feel like when a cat was about to devour it.

"With the women I take home. Why does it bother you so much?"

He was going to take her home? My breath got caught in my throat, and the edges of my sight blurred. This was getting way out of hand. Panic fluttered in my veins as my breath quickened.

"They're not me," I whispered.

I clamped a hand over my mouth. That was not what I had wanted to say. Danté's eyes went wide at the confession. His shock quickly gave way to a satisfied smirk.

"Oh Evelyn, you should've just said so."

He came even closer. So close that I could smell the alcohol on his breath and the soap on his skin. I found myself leaning my head towards him. Danté pressed me against the wall and his hands found their way to my waist. A shiver ran down my spine when he brushed his nose against the column of my neck. His teeth grazed against the sensitive skin. I let a gasp out when he bit me. Danté let out a breathy laugh at my reaction.

"Tell me what you want, Evelyn."

Him. Wasn't that obvious? I wanted all of him. Not just the sex, not just the banter. Everything.

"Do you want me to kiss you?"

I opened my mouth to say yes. Danté waited, his mouth so close to mine I could feel his breath on my lips. His pupils were wide, his hair slightly tousled.

"Not if a kiss is all you can give me."

Danté opened his mouth, but before any sound came out, the door opened again.

"Danté, what are you doing…"

The voice stopped mid-sentence. We both turned our heads to Blondie. My cheeks burned red. Her eyes narrowed. I tried to free myself, but Danté didn't move. Nothing had happened, and it still felt like we were caught. Not being able to stomach both of them any longer, I pushed him away.

"Evy, wait."

I ignored him and fled back inside. We all knew what would happen if I let him kiss me. Except that there would be no coming back from that.

My morning shift at the café had lasted longer than it should. The sudden rush of customers thirty minutes before I was finished for the day had been a bad surprise. I couldn't leave Chloe alone in such a situation. But that left me with twenty minutes to take a shower and get to the campus to arrive in time for the exam. As I was running to my door, Danté walked out of his. *Oh, fuck me.* I skidded to a stop, out of breath, fishing my keys out of my backpack.

"I think we ought to have a talk," he said instead of greeting me.

There was no light in his eyes. If anything, Danté looked rather grim. The last time I had seen him, he had me pressed against a wall, and his sex friend had been glaring at us. If I had been able to avoid him for two whole days, my luck had finally run out. He was right. It was time to talk it out. We should've done that months ago, rather than going in circles the way we did. I looked at my watch. I was running late.

"Not now. I need to go to school."

"Evelyn, when will you stop running away? We need to talk."

"I am not trying to run away. I really need to go."

I bit my lip; this day was not going according to plan. It didn't seem like I had a choice but to go with the flow somehow. To hell with the shower.

"What is it?" I asked without looking at him.

From my peripheral vision I could see him leaning against the wall, arms crossed. His fingers were tapping nervously against his elbow.

"You know what it is."

"I don't have time for this," I pressed. "Just say what you have to say."

"Tell me what you want!"

I looked around the hall. Luckily there was no one around. I also hoped that the other neighbours didn't hear us. Making a scene with witnesses wasn't particularly high on my bucket list.

"You can't keep nagging at me about my life, my friends, or my choices and refuse to be upfront about what you're expecting."

"I don't expect anything from you."

Not anymore, at least. Danté pulled at his hair in frustration. The anger that had seeped from him when we were at the bar was now gone. Instead of anger, there was nothing but apprehensiveness.

"Then tell me why you are acting like that. You dated that lame guy for a year, and take others home, which I've never held against you. So why do you care so much when I do it?"

Had he watched me that closely all this time? Unable to stand still any longer, Danté started pacing.

"Alright," I said, finally facing him. "It does bother me when you take all those girls home. But you already knew that."

His brows shot up in surprise. "So why is it acceptable if you do it, and yet not when I see people?"

I took the blow. I deserved that one. I let my head fall back and took a deep breath. *There we go.*

"I only do it because you do it," I admitted quietly.

I was tired of running away, just like I was tired of fighting with him. Danté and I had been in a vicious circle since the day we met; and granted, it had been my fault. I dated Robert because he had been ready to give me what Danté hadn't even considered. All the fight that he had inside him seemed to leave his body. Danté looked like I had slapped him in the face.

"What do you mean?"

I glanced at my watch. I had to move now. "You never asked me out."

Then I slipped inside my apartment. My heart was beating so loudly it felt like I would throw up, yet I couldn't finish that conversation now. Not that there was much left to add.

It was the first time in my life that I had gone to an exam being all sweaty and breathless. Even Professor Leloux had looked at me with wide eyes as I barged into her classroom to take the exam. Fucking Danté and his bad timing. I glanced at my watch. I had barely made it. The teacher made a sign to take a seat in front of her. *Let's go.*

From the kitchen, Theo and I could hear Jasmine sing along to Ariana Grande while she was showering. When I had gotten home, the first thing Jasmine had said was "Now that your exams are finally done, let's get drunk." Later she'd asked if I had nailed it. Obviously, I had.

Every now and then, Theo glanced at me, then pretended to look back at his phone every time I caught him staring. I sighed at the third time.

"What is it?"

"What are your plans tonight?"

For once, my planning was rather simple: shower, get drunk, have a hangover, and spend the whole next day sleeping. A few months ago, getting laid would also have been on that list. I didn't see that in the cards for me right now or in the near future. There was still a dark cloud hanging above my head, and I didn't feel like having a stranger putting his hands all over me as long as Danté and I hadn't talked it out. Really talked it out, that is. So I just shrugged.

"Get drunk and sleep. Why?"

"Oh, nothing."

Nothing, my ass. I wasn't blind, so of course I saw his shoulders sag from hidden disappointment. Theo had been my friend for years. We weren't as close anymore since he and Jasmine had begun dating. Being a third wheel did that to a friendship, even if they did their best to include me in their plans. I was still able to read him like an open book, just like I had been able to do for the past ten years. There was no denying that Theo wanted Jasmine for himself every now and then. It seemed that my evening plans were not what he had hoped for.

I toyed with my piercing as I asked him, "So, why do you want me out of the house?"

Theo's spine straightened. "I don't want you out of the house. This is your place."

It was. Regardless, there was something he wasn't telling me.

"So do you want to go out without me?"

It wouldn't be the first time. Theo shook his head, also remembering how that went last time. I could stay at home if he needed tonight to be a date.

"No, I want you to come."

And his smile was sincere, so what was he not telling me? I crossed my arms.

"Out with it."

He let out a sigh, his long, slim body turning into an

overcooked noodle. Theo slid in his chair until only his head was still visible.

"Jasmine and I haven't done it in weeks because of the exams. I had hoped that we could tonight."

A sudden laugh escaped my lips, and Theo gave me the middle finger. Well, at least some of us would have a glorious night.

"Sorry, buddy. There is no other bed available for me tonight. Getting dicked down is not where I am headed."

He let out a strangled noise, which only made me cackle louder. I patted his head.

"Don't worry, I can put my earplugs in if that's what's bothering you."

"If you also don't mind staying in your room."

"Whatever. As long as you don't fuck on my kitchen counter."

Pink dusted his sharp cheeks. What?!

"You guys fucked on my kitchen counter?!"

"It might have happened once or twice."

I couldn't help but gag at that. Now it was Theo's turn to cackle like a witch. Tomorrow, this whole kitchen would be sanitized. Twice! Jasmine walked back inside the kitchen, her hair wrapped in a blue towel. Her cheeks were a lovely shade of red thanks to the hot water.

"Your turn," she said.

I shot them both a glare as I got up.

"Fine, but don't fuck on my counter while I'm showering."

Jasmine silently questioned Theo, who only snickered in response as I went for the bathroom. *What a bunch of perves.*

CHAPTER 28

Danté

Jasmine: *Come and get your girlfriend, please. She's whining*

Danté huffed out a laugh. What was going on? Jasmine never sent him messages. Had Evy told her something? Not that there was much to say. The last time he had seen her, which was only a few hours earlier, she hadn't been keen on talking to him. The truth was, Evelyn had been able to knock the air out of his lungs with no more than five words. *You never asked me out.* He couldn't help but smile. That piece of work of a girl had been able to get under his skin until she had become the only thing he could think about.

Danté: *Where are you?*
Jasmine: *At the College*

By the time he got there, Evelyn was alone at the bar. Jasmine was talking to her boyfriend and Alex. It shouldn't have been a surprise; Alex and Jasmine got along too well for his sake. Evy was staring at the wall, absentmindedly swirling her drink, her face sad. Danté sat down next to her.

"Hey, Squirrel. Are you ready to talk now?"

Evelyn stayed silent. She just looked at him with her bright eyes as if she couldn't believe he was here. It was hard to concentrate under her heavy gaze, or the tight black dress she was wearing.

Very well. Danté cleared his throat. "You can't say those things and then run away as if they mean nothing."

Her attention went back to her drink. It was so unlike Evy to be quiet. Where had her inner fire gone? An uneasy feeling tugged at his heart. What if she was preparing herself to run away again? Or worse?

"Evelyn, can you please answer? I can't keep doing this."

A tear fell down her pretty face.

Alex appeared on her other side. "I hope you're not trying to have a rational conversation with her. She's drunk."

She glowered at his friend.

"Evy, are you alright?" Danté asked.

More tears rolled down her cheeks.

"Why won't you love me?" she slurred.

Alex let out a surprised laugh at her bluntness. She wasn't just drunk; she was completely wasted. And Evy was known to be a sad drunk.

"Let's get some air," Danté offered.

The girl gulped down the rest of her drink then followed him outside on high heels and wonky legs. Hopefully, the fresh air would sober her up a bit. Goosebumps appeared on her naked arms. The dress was even shorter and more revealing now that she was standing. Danté cursed, but quickly gave her his jacket.

"What's going on?"

"My head feels fuzzy. I think I'm drunk."

"You are."

Evy hid in the too-large jacket like she would with a blanket. When she finally looked up, her glazed eyes were wet.

"Why don't you love me?" she asked again.

How could she even believe that he didn't?

"What makes you think I don't?"

"I've tried to catch your attention for years."

He could feel himself smile. Evy was a sad drunk, but also an honest drunk.

"You should've just asked me out."

You never asked me out.

"I tried, but you had all those girls come over every time. I never stood a chance."

"I am sorry, Squirrel."

"Stop calling me Squirrel!" she yelled, stomping her foot and almost losing her balance.

Danté bit his lip to keep from laughing. It would only make her madder if she believed he didn't take her seriously.

"Stop seeing me as that pathetic girl. And stop leading me on."

New tears were forming in her huge eyes, and his heart squeezed at the sight. It was no use to talk about it now. The chances that she couldn't remember tomorrow were high.

Still, he couldn't help but say, "I never led you on. You kept pushing me away."

She seemed to sober up rather fast. "How could I not? They were always around!"

"When?"

"At the bar, at the Christmas market. What did you expect?"

She thought that Manal had been one of those girls? No wonder she had lost her marbles.

"Evy, this is not what you think."

Not giving himself the time to change his mind, he kissed her. She tasted like sweet cocktails and tears. She didn't kiss him back.

"I love you," he whispered. "I do."

Her whole body trembled. "You do?"

As he nodded, she threw her arms around his neck and kissed him back. Her kisses were clumsy and wet and perfect in their own way. He could feel her smile against his mouth. Danté wrapped his arms around her waist and pulled her closer. Why had he waited so long? Had he known those were the thoughts she had been with, he wouldn't have. Evelyn kept trembling.

"Let's go back inside."

"You'll stay with me?"

"I will."

Before he could stop her, she went for the bar and ordered another cocktail.

"I am not sure that's reasonable."

She flashed him a cheeky grin, her worries long forgotten. She downed half of the drink in one go. "I didn't come here to be reasonable."

Jasmine sat down next to her. She was way less drunk than her friend was. Her brows furrowed when she noticed the puffy eyes.

"What happened to you?"

Evelyn jumped from her bar stool, almost knocking it over. She made Jasmine jump with her. Her looking almost sober outside had been nothing but an illusion. Evy leaned towards Jasmine's ear, though the bar was loud and crowded, and she had to talk loudly for her friend to hear her.

"Danté told me he liked me. But don't let him know I told you."

Love. Not liked. Jasmine looked at him over Evy's shoulder, her eyes full of laughter. He shook his head, unable to keep a straight face. Evelyn looked at her with pleading eyes.

"I promise, I won't say anything," she just said.

Evelyn clung to her best friend like a koala.

"I'll take her home," she offered.

Evelyn let go, shaking her head so violently that he feared she would end up on the floor. "You're not taking me hoooome!"

"You're drunk."

"I don't care. Theo wants to bang you, a looooot," she slurred.

Then she giggled, her lower face hidden behind her hands. Jasmine's ears and cheeks turned so red that Danté felt bad for her.

"Don't worry. I'll watch after her. You're free to…" He hesitated, but that only made Jasmine turn redder. That had been the wrong way to start the sentence. He cleared his throat while Evy kept on cackling. "Free to do whatever you please."

"I'm telling you, their night will be HOT! I'm so jealous. Hey, do you wanna bang too? I scrubbed and put on nice lange... lounge..."

Now it was his turn to feel the blush creep up his neck and face. Inebriated Evy was a dangerous woman, and she wasn't even aware of it. She pinched the bridge of her nose in frustration.

"Lingerie, you mean," he offered calmly.

"Yes. Come, I'll show you!"

Jasmine patted his arm. "Good luck. It seems like your night will be far wilder than mine. Just, don't do something you might regret tomorrow."

"Nothing will happen."

Evy wrapped her arms around his middle. "I love him. Do you think he knows?"

Jasmine offered him a sorry smile. "If he still doesn't know now, he's probably stupid."

"Exactly!"

Alex was laughing so hard he almost fell off his bar stool, and Danté could feel his face burn from the attention. Jasmine had been right; this night was going to be intense. Jasmine handed them Evy's jacket and purse.

"Let's go?"

"Where?" she asked.

Her large eyes were unfocused. It didn't matter. She was more beautiful than ever when she looked at him.

"Home."

A shy smile appeared on her pink mouth. She nodded and grabbed his arm.

"Have fun, brother," Alex said.

Danté showed him his middle finger before he took Evy out of the bar. The walk towards their block was slow, her steps unsteady because of the alcohol and the shoes. He lost count of the times she tripped over her feet. She hummed a Taylor Swift song as they walked inside his apartment. He didn't know if Jasmine had gone to Theo's place, or if they stayed here. One thing was certain, he didn't want to walk in on them. Evy was so far gone that she might find the whole walking-in on her best friend hilarious.

"Where is your roommate?" she asked, throwing her purse and jacket on the couch like she owned the place.

"At his boyfriend's house."

She hummed appreciatively. Her voice became low and sultry. "So we have the apartment to ourselves?"

"Yes, but…"

Evy had stopped listening. She went down the hall and entered his bedroom, full of confidence he had never seen her have. Gone was the shy and buttoned-up girl. This was a side of her he had seen in glimpses. Once the door was closed, Evy took a few slow steps towards him until his knees hit the bed. She didn't hesitate and pushed him down before straddling his lap.

"Woah. What do you think you're doing?"

A cat-like smile twisted her pretty mouth, and all he wanted to do was kiss her until she was out of breath. Evy sensed it and kissed him. Her movements were more controlled than they had been at the bar. His good resolve thinned when her whole body pressed against him. Her perfume smelled divine on her skin.

"What does it look like I am doing?"

Her tongue stroked his, leisurely. Her hands roamed over his chest and started unbuttoning his shirt. Goosebumps erected on the skin where she touched him. There was no hesitation when she reached his belt.

"Undress," she ordered.

If he didn't know better, Danté would've listened and done everything she wanted. A voice in his head screamed how wrong this was.

"Evy, let's not."

He grabbed her hands before she could open his pants. This was going to be complicated. Her hot breath fanned over his mouth, and he found himself kissing her.

"I want you," Evy whispered.

She pushed him down before taking off the dress. She had been right about the lingerie. The black material was so sheer it left little to the imagination. Everything about her was enticing. The warmth or the softness of her bare skin, the shapes of her curves. Her taste. He wanted to feel it all. Taste it all. When she kissed him again, her hands had found their mark. His blood heated, and his whole body reacted to her. Danté pushed her off and jumped from the bed, inhaling deeply. This night was getting out of control; he didn't stand a chance against her. Especially if he didn't stop her now. When he looked back, she sat on his comforter, in her almost translucent underwear, with sad, lost eyes.

"I thought you said you loved me."

His heart broke at the words. He fell down on his knees

before her. Danté grabbed her chin, forcing her to look up.

"I love you. And I want you. All of you."

The flame in her eyes came back to life. "Then why won't you have sex with me?"

"I want you sober, and fully conscious."

The alcohol in her system made her slow to understand. She ended up nodding her head.

"Does that mean I can't touch you?"

"Not like that."

She let out a long, loud sigh. "Party pooper."

"You can still kiss me."

A smirk appeared on her harmonious face. He leaned forward, and she put a finger on his lips to push him back.

"No sex, no kisses."

"I am pretty sure you're saying that so there would be sex."

A cute giggle escaped her, and Danté couldn't help but grin back.

"That obvious?"

"Just a bit."

He offered her an old T-shirt. His heart made a flip when she put it on. She looked almost as hot with nothing but her lacy underwear and his shirt. When they were both under the covers, Evy intertwined her legs with his.

"Please be there when I wake up," she whispered.

"I'm not going anywhere."

CHAPTER 29

When my consciousness came back, I felt hot. The feeling of having someone holding me in bed was nice. I sighed from contentment. Until it clicked in my mind that I had no idea who was holding me. My eyes flew open. This wasn't my room!

"Oh my gods."

The place was clean, tidy, and the walls had the same creamy colour as mine. My blood turned to ice. Oh, fuck me. This couldn't be true. As I tried to get up, the arms around me tightened their grip.

"Stop moving. It's early."

Oh no. Oh no no no. *What have I done?* Of all the places I could've landed, this was the only one I should have avoided at all costs. I jumped from the bed, but the dizziness from the hangover caught me fast. I grabbed the desk to steady myself.

"Evy, stop fretting so much."

How could he be so calm about it? Danté finally sat up,

with nothing but his pyjama pants on. The sun gave his naked torso a soft golden glow. A weird part of me wanted to mark his skin. If those were my thoughts while being sober, I was afraid to imagine what I had done a few hours ago. I couldn't even remember meeting him at the College. I gulped down some air. *Here we go.*

"Have we…?"

My voice died down. No matter how hard I tried, I couldn't get the words out. Danté sensed my distress. He stayed silent a few seconds too long, enough to make my anxiety creep up and make me nauseous. *Bastard.*

He huffed out a laugh. "No."

"Oh, thank goodness."

The icy panic in my limbs went down, and I fell back against the desk. Except that by doing so, I gave him a full view of my ass, and the little black panties I wore couldn't hide much. I straightened and tugged at the faded blue t-shirt. I wanted to burn that piece of fabric.

Danté smirked, an evil twinkle in his beautiful eyes. "Though you were very insistent on trying to get in my pants. I almost had to tie you to a chair."

I should have been relieved that he stopped me. I would have been even more mortified if I had to face him after we had actually slept together. Except that I couldn't stop the disappointment from blooming inside my chest. And embarrassment. So much embarrassment.

"Someone kill me, please."

"Don't worry. You were completely wasted."

"That never stopped you before."

The words left my mouth before I could think. Danté

crossed his arms over his abs, which I tried to ignore as best as I could. He had brought so many drunk girls here. Why would I be the exception? I waited for him to bite back, but he didn't. I just grabbed my clothes that were folded on the nightstand.

"I am sorry for the inconvenience. This must have been as mortifying for you last night as it is for me now."

All I wanted to do was go back to my own room and wallow in self-pity for as long as I could. A little smile played on his lips. Had I kissed him? If I did, I wish I could remember. I wanted more memories than a few stolen kisses in a half-lit staircase. Because now my chances were over. Stupid little Evy with her stupid puppy crush on her neighbour.

"Evelyn, please calm down. You look like you'll combust any time soon. I don't mind."

I don't mind. Just great.

"Because I'm not your type. I know."

Danté sighed but kept his cool. How he did it, I had no clue. I would hit my own head against the wall if it wasn't already pounding.

"You are my type. I already said so."

"Stop joking. I'm standing in your bedroom with nothing on but see-through underwear and a shirt every single one of your one-night stands has worn. This really isn't funny."

"Why would I be joking?"

I let myself lean against his desk, holding my black dress against my stomach like armour. Like that piece of cloth would be able to keep me standing once I had to walk out of that door. The words tumbled out of my mouth. "Because

I've had the biggest crush on you since we met, and you pity me."

He flashed me his toothy smile, where his eyes disappeared in crescent moons. That was the man I had liked from the start. The one that actually smiled at people and was very kind and compassionate. Not the one whose anger was cold and terrifying, albeit very hot.

"You are adorable."

"See? You're pitying me!"

He threw one of the pillows at me. I had a hard time catching it, my limbs heavy. I was preparing myself mentally for what would follow. Danté laughed. Why was he so happy?

"Oh, Evelyn, shut up. You literally live on the other side of the hall. If I didn't like you, I would have put you in your own bed."

That was a rather good point. Hope fluttered in the organ hidden under my ribs. I just hoped he wouldn't break it.

"Really?"

"Of course."

I bit my lip, a gesture that didn't go unnoticed. His eyes dropped to my mouth.

"Then why did you stop me last night?"

Danté snapped his head back up. There was no judgement in his eyes. "Because I don't want you to be a drunk one-night stand."

"Huh, but... I am very confused right now."

I tilted my head to the side. Drunk one-night stands were our thing. Danté got up and made the bed. His muscles moved under his smooth skin. Skin I could've scratched and marked if he had let me.

"I'm not. Get dressed, and we'll talk about it around breakfast."

"Do you mind if I change at my own place? I don't feel like getting breakfast in high heels."

Or in a tight black dress that smelled like alcohol and cigarettes.

"Please do. But don't forget to give me my shirt back."

My cheeks heated. Could this morning be even weirder?

"Oh, right," I stammered.

He had seen most of what was underneath it anyway, I supposed. As I started tugging at the shirt, Danté grabbed my wrists.

"I didn't say right here and now! Go back to your apartment!"

"Right…"

I could hear Danté snicker as I grabbed my pumps and handbag before opening the front door. I shot a quick glance in the hall; luckily no one was around. I quickly opened my own apartment. Jasmine and Theo were sitting at our kitchen table, eating a breakfast made of cereal and orange juice out of a box. Both turned to meet me. Theo's attention fell on the t-shirt that was clearly not mine, that barely covered my intimate parts.

"Well, someone had a rough night," he said, all smiles.

Not as rough as my morning had been.

"I'll quickly take a shower."

Jasmine followed me inside the bathroom. She crossed her arms while I waited for the water to warm.

"So, how was your night?"

"Honestly, I am relieved to not remember anything. Danté said I almost tore his clothes off."

I shivered. Yeah, I really didn't want to remember that. Maybe having been that drunk was a good thing. I shook my head.

"Good, he kept his promise then."

Wait. She knew?

Jasmine blinked once. "You told Danté Theo wanted to 'bang a loooot', if I recall it correctly. So Danté refused to let me take you home."

He had babysat me, basically. Moments like these should convince me to stop drinking so much if that was what I got afterward, except they never did.

I made a face. "Well, I hope you banged a lot, then."

Jasmine laughed. "We did. Are you going out?"

"He wants to talk."

She nodded. "Please be honest with him. You know you can't continue the way you do."

My heartbeat sped up. In the heat of the moment, I hadn't really thought about what our talk would look like. One thing was sure, this was the talk we were supposed to have months ago. The one that would determine what would happen to us. Even though I felt nervous, things didn't seem as grim as I had been eyeing them all these months.

I sighed. "I'll be honest."

"Good."

I didn't waste time with makeup like I normally did. If there was a chance I would walk out of the café with red, puffy eyes, there was no need to add smudged mascara to the lot.

Danté was already sitting at our booth when I walked inside Hot Stuff. The familiar sound of the bell calmed my nerves ever so slightly. His hair was still damp from the shower.

"So, what are you getting? A healthy smoothie? Lots of protein?"

I rolled my eyes at the jab. How could I believe for a mere second that Danté would stop teasing me? Most of my panic went up in smoke.

"First of all, rude. How dare you stereotype me like this? I want to help people in their relationship with food, and keeping them from eating stuff they like or crave is just the fastest road to failure. So no, I am going to indulge myself with a big plate of pancakes. And secondly, juices aren't good actually. It increases the blood sugar levels."

Now it was his turn to roll his eyes. If this was supposed to be a sort of date, things between us felt as comfortable as they had always been. Well, before I blew everything up, that is.

"Alright, Miss Knows It All. Understood."

"Are you mocking me?"

I grabbed the menu and hit him in the arm. Danté showed the palms of his hands in surrender. I dropped my makeshift weapon.

"I would never."

"Of course you wouldn't. What will you get?"

Danté put a theatrical hand on his chest. "A sweet coffee,

eggs, and toast with lots of butter."

The sweet drink and unholy amount of butter did sound amazing.

"Good."

My stomach grumbled as if it agreed. Pancakes it was. And a hot chocolate milk with speculoos and lots of whipped cream. Chloe appeared with her little notebook to take our orders. Every now and then, she shot me a questioning look, but ended up grinning before going back to the kitchen. I danced on my chair. This breakfast was making me excited. Danté stared at me, and I stopped moving. Him being so serious could only mean one thing.

"I'll get to the point since you're not going to talk first," he started.

Danté clasped his hands together on the table. I found myself fidgeting under his intense gaze. This was it. My palms grew sweaty.

"I care about you. More than a friend should."

His gaze was so intense that I couldn't hold it, so I looked at my hands instead. The sound of blood rushing through my veins was so loud that I could barely hear my surroundings anymore.

"You shouldn't say things like this."

"Why not, if I mean them?"

My hands held the edge of the table until my joints turned white. It was time to be upfront. "Because you never commit. Pretty words leave your mouth all the time, but you never commit. So tell me what you want, because I can't do this anymore."

All this going back and forth between us was tiring, and

heartbreaking in its own way. I wanted him. Since the day we met, he had become the person I wanted to share my life with. I couldn't keep sharing my life with him if he wasn't going to be serious.

Danté leaned over the table and kissed me in front of the whole café. I found myself too stunned to react.

"You. I want you. Is that clear enough?"

I could feel a dumb smile creep up my face as I looked away. I nodded. "I think so."

Chloe put our orders on the table, and I bit my tongue to not tell her to fuck off, in a loving way. She had seen everything. Oh gods, so things were real now? I took a bite of my fluffy pancake to let it sink in.

"Does that mean you and I are, like, a thing?"

"There is no "like". We *are* a thing."

There was still a shadow looming over us, one that kept me from jumping from my chair and doing a happy dance. It would be easier to just be an ostrich like I always was. Being an ostrich wouldn't help me out now. If anything, it would only give me anxiety in the long run.

"What about Manal?" I asked, doing my best to keep the uncertainty out of my voice.

"What about her?" Danté asked back, sipping from his drink. How could he not see?

"Is she family?"

"No."

His cool and his obliviousness made me want to hit some sense into him. I gulped some air down.

"Is she gay?"

Danté's eyebrows went up. "No, she's not. Why do you

even ask?"

"I need to know if I have to keep my eyes open whenever she's around."

More like I needed to know if there had been any reason for me to be so afraid of her in the first place. Danté was here with me; it had to count for something. Danté scrutinized my face. I wasn't sure of what he found there. When he offered his hand across the table, I took it and held on tight. His touch was soothing.

"She's one of my closest friends, so she'll be around plenty of the time. But no, there's no reason to be afraid of our friendship. It's just that: friendship."

This was what I needed to hear. I nodded, suddenly feeling lightheaded. Maybe Manal and I could be friends then, if there were no ambiguous feelings between her and Danté.

"Shouldn't you ask me out then? In an official way."

There was a short silence. One that didn't prepare me for what he was about to unleash.

"I didn't know that was still required after you did a striptease and tried to get in my pants."

I choked on my chocolate milk and splashed whipped cream over the table. My cheeks became hotter than a furnace. I didn't know what would be better: to hit myself unconscious against the tabletop or to smack Danté senseless. The mischievous smirk on his lips told me how much he enjoyed embarrassing me.

I wiped my mouth with a napkin before cleaning the mess I made on the table. "Oh my God! Can you not bring that up?"

"No," he simply said. "I'll bring this up many, many times."

I let my head fall in my hands. This was so embarrassing. He gently patted my forearm.

"Alright, Squirrel. Let's date. How about that?"

I smiled. Embarrassed or not, this was what I wanted. He was the one that I wanted.

"I thought you'd never ask."

When we were back in front of our doors, I didn't know what to do. It was strange to go from friends to more. Was I supposed to kiss him or ask him to come inside? Let's be honest. I was bad at relationships. Robert had been the only person I ever dated, and when he started to see us as something too serious for my liking, I had called things off.

Danté let go of my hand to fish his key out of his pocket. There was a happy glow on his cheeks. When he looked back at me, I hesitated.

"Everything alright?"

"Yes!" I almost yelled.

Danté raised a humoured brow, and I let myself fall back against the wall. There was no point in pretending with him, nor was there any point in wanting to impress him. Danté had seen me at my lowest, my worst, my best, my most awkward, and my horniest. And he was still here. And he had still asked me out. I sighed.

"I'm not so good with relationships. I don't know what to do," I admitted quietly.

"Just be yourself. That's how you got me."

I felt myself grin at that. I still couldn't wrap my head around the fact that Danté was my boyfriend. A part of me wanted to open a window and sing and yodel my heart out. Luckily for others, I couldn't yodel.

"I guess I did."

He leaned down to press a sweet kiss to my lips. As he pulled back, I grabbed him by his sweater.

"Not so fast."

The corners of his mouth tilted upwards. "Yes, milady?"

"You can't just give me a simple kiss and disappear afterward."

His little smile turned toothy, and his dimples appeared. Gods, how was he so beautiful? Then he kissed me again, ever so softly. Again, and again, without tongue or teeth. It was perfect. His mouth was smooth and warm, and it tasted like coffee. And it was mine now. My hand crumpled the fabric of his sweater.

When we were both breathless, Danté pulled back. "There you go."

"Can I ask you to stay?"

"Naughty Squirrel, are you trying to get in my pants again?"

I let out an outraged gasp and poked him in the ribs. Except that Danté poked me back, and once he started to tickle me, I had to surrender.

"No sex. I need to patch up my bruised ego first. And build up the tension again."

Danté laughed, his head falling back. I had no doubt that sex with him would be wild. Just like it would take me a long time to get used to him. Danté hadn't wanted us to be a drunk one-night stand. I wanted us to have something solid before sex would be involved. Never had I expected us to stand where we stood today. I could wait.

"Don't worry, Squirrel, we have all the time in the world."

We did. The idea alone made me giddy.

I pouted. "Shouldn't you stop calling me Squirrel now?"

"Do I have to? I like it."

"You really don't want to call me babe or love?"

It would be weird to hear him say it at first. At the same time, my heart was beating a bit faster at the idea alone.

"You are a babe, and you are lovely. But you're the only one I call Squirrel."

I almost cooed at how adorable that was. Was that why he always gave me that ridiculous nickname? An evil idea appeared in my head.

"Then I can keep calling you Alighieri?"

His smile fell. "Fine! I'll stop calling you Squirrel."

I hugged his middle. Danté hugged me back.

"Call me whatever you want. If you like it, I like it."

"Now now, Squirrel, don't get all mushy on me."

"You know my love for romcoms. Of course I am mushy."

He tousled my hair before opening his door. My heart fell to the floor. Was this it?

Danté turned back to me. "I have some paperwork to do. How about you stay at mine instead?"

I looped my arm with his. "If you insist."

CHAPTER 30

I waited for my boyfriend in front of his door. Though I had to admit that I was pondering if yes or no I still wanted Danté to be my boyfriend. *Let's spend the morning together* had been a text message that made me squeal in delight, until he had sent another text.

Danté: *wanna go for a run?*

No Miss Ma'am's, I didn't want to go for a run. Being weak, I had accepted. His door finally opened, and Danté sauntered to me in his black gym shorts and black t-shirt. Maybe if he took off his shirt, I would be more inclined to run outside. Danté gave me a quick kiss before lacing his fingers through mine and pulling me outside. We walked in a comfortable silence for a while to warm up, then Danté set the pace. I was sure that he had taken a slower pace to fit mine. Except that it didn't. There was just no way for me to keep up with his pace longer than thirteen minutes. I stopped in my tracks and let myself fall against a wall, huffing and puffing like I had never done a workout in my life.

"When you said you wanted to spend time together," I wheezed, "this was *not* what I had envisioned."

The sweat was running down my back and between my boobs. I took pride in my ability to be able to jog for thirty minutes without a break if I followed my own rhythm. Danté was still jogging. His face had gone red, but other than that, he looked fine.

"Oh, come on. A couple that works out together, stays together."

I snorted. "Bullshit."

He finally stopped. "Don't tell me you are breaking up with me now? It's too late for that."

"Damn it."

At this very moment, the idea was tempting. Kissing him was even more so.

"Come on, Squirrel. Is this all you can do?"

Or throttling him. That sounded rather nice too. I glared at him, but Danté just tousled my hair in response. I swatted his hand away.

"Stop provoking me! I am dying here."

"I thought you had more stamina than that."

I hummed in response. "Trust me, I have a LOT of stamina for certain things."

His laugh made my toes curl inside my sneakers. Alright. He was still cute.

"I'm sure you do."

"I look like a garden gnome next to a courgette like you!

This was never fair to begin with."

He took off his black cap to rake his long fingers through his blonde locks. I wanted to do that too.

"A courgette? How is a courgette tall?"

"Well, a courgette is way taller than a tangerine. If you compare sizes."

"What kind of fruit do you think you are?"

We started walking again. He nudged me to run again. The pain in my ribs was indication enough that I wouldn't be running again today.

"An apple. An apple a day keeps the doctor away."

At least, if you throw the apple hard enough. Wasn't that what they say?

Danté rolled his eyes, a small smile on his pretty mouth. "Of course that's your choice."

As he mocked me, he tripped over… I forced a laugh back down.

"Did you just trip over nothing?"

"I trip over nothing and choke on everything, if you must know."

I coughed. That was a sight I had not seen coming.

Danté gently flicked me on the forehead. "Naughty Squirrel! I meant choking on water and other beverages."

"Oh. Right."

"You know I'm straight, right?"

I had never doubted his love for women. I just had never asked if he liked more than just women. That could make things rather interesting if he did.

"You could've been bi."

"Have you ever seen me flirt with any guy the way I flirt

with you?" he asked, arms crossed.

"You're flirting with me?"

Danté blinked once, apparently done with my bullshit. "I have for the past year, but thank you for not even noticing."

Heat bubbled under my skin, and I found myself smiling at that. "You should've just said so from the start."

"I would've, had I known how oblivious you are," he shot back.

I guess we both were too oblivious for our own good. We walked back to our doors. My sweat had dried, and now I felt so sticky. Once I had fished my key back out of my pocket, I looked up at my boyfriend. It was still surreal to be able to say that he was now my boyfriend. Like what?

"I am going to take a very hot shower," I announced. "Under other circumstances, I would've asked you to join me, but my legs feel like Jell-O."

His pupils grew darker as his gaze felt heavier, warmer. "I could carry you."

It took all of my self-control to not drag him inside and make him act upon his word. I was pretty sure that I would find enough stamina to follow him. I shook my head.

"Even though I'd love nothing more, I want us to wait."

A neighbour walked past us, and I waited for him to be out of hearing. We hadn't talked about it yet. Danté leaned against my door, patiently waiting for me to say what I wanted.

"You said you didn't want us to be a drunk one-night stand, and I don't want our relationship to be based merely on sex."

A cheeky smile bloomed on his mouth. Now I really

wanted to kiss him breathless and to take him to the bathroom for a shower.

"The lady is demanding. Very well, Evy. What are your rules?"

It was nice that he was open to following my rhythm without any objection. I had wanted to have sex with Danté for a long while. It probably would've happened a few days ago if he hadn't made me stop, or if we hadn't been interrupted. Things were different now. Danté liked me, and he wanted me. There was no reason to rush things.

"I don't have rules," I admitted. "I just want us to be able to take our time, and to enjoy getting to know each other as a couple."

"Does that mean I can take you on a date?"

I giggled. Dates could be just as fun. I nodded, biting my lip to keep from laughing like a mad woman. "Obviously."

"Then I'll see you later."

He dropped a sweet kiss on my mouth before going to his own door. Danté looked over his shoulder one last time. "Enjoy your shower, and try not to think too much about me."

My cheeks turned beet red. I wasn't going to, until now. He winked, and then he was gone.

CHAPTER 31

It was funny how Danté found his own place in my life in just a few days. It was as if there had always been a space waiting to be filled up by him, in a non-sexual way. Changes were small but apparent. Most of the evenings, he ate with us. During the evenings and weekends, Danté did his paperwork or watched sports on TV while I finished studying for my last weeks of classes. In a few weeks, I would finally start my internship, so there were still papers and projects that needed to be wrapped up before.

Since it had also become quite clear that he and I could not go for a run together – that's just how things were when two people had too different heights – he went to the gym with me. He never stopped complaining about how it was boring to run on a treadmill. In the end, Danté was the one to drag me there.

The lines we still hadn't crossed were sleeping in the same bed, and sex. It was an unspoken rule between us. If Danté was in my bed and ready for me, how could I resist? I wasn't that strong. It didn't mean I didn't miss him at night. I just hadn't expected everything to feel so natural. Except for the extra kissing and snuggling, we were still bickering and annoying each other like we did before. It was a relief that we were still just Evy and Danté, and not just a mushy couple that suddenly didn't have an identity outside of its bubble anymore.

I was typing away on my computer, lost in my homework, when Danté poked me in the ribs. I startled and almost chucked my laptop at his face. Every time I wanted to get back to my paper, he found another way to bug me. The first two times, I had laughed it off. It wasn't just that he was trying to annoy me. The constant fussing like a mother hen like "Are you drinking enough water?" kept distracting me. The third time he went to poke me, I snapped.

"Can you not? I'm trying to work."

My voice sounded much louder than what I had meant it to be. The cutting tone took Danté by surprise. His eyebrows went up, and he showed me his palms. I almost expected him to tell me to chill the fuck down or to call me a drama queen. He never did. Danté gave me space, and I could finally focus again.

Danté was on the couch, looking outside, face blank and shoulders stiff. I closed my laptop before padding over to him. The sky had gone dark outside. He was so lost in his own thoughts that he didn't hear me approach. I draped myself over his shoulders, gluing my cheek against his. His spine stiffened even more as he startled, but he never relaxed.

"Are you alright, babe?"

He hummed, his posture getting a tad bit rigid. That was a first.

"How is the paper coming along?" he asked in a tone that sounded light-hearted. It also sounded fake.

"Slowly but surely. I hate writing papers."

Finally, a little smile bloomed on his face, though he still looked worried. "I'm sure you'll nail it anyway."

"Of course I will."

I flashed him a cheeky grin, which he returned. Danté got up and went for the door. I followed him to let him out.

"I need to get a few things from the store. Do you need anything?"

"Some coconut ice cream if you find any."

Danté nodded without adding anything. For a second, it looked like he hesitated on what he should do. He ended up waving before going back to his own door. There definitely was something wrong.

"Not so fast, Ortega."

Just like we had for years, we stared at each other from our apartment fronts.

"Why do I get the feeling that you're running away from me?"

It wasn't like him to not answer. Danté always knew what he had to say, whether it was something I wanted to hear or not. His silence was answer enough, and it made me anxious.

"What's the matter?"

"Everything is fine."

Still, he didn't look my way. What was going on?

"Then why didn't you kiss me before leaving?"

The silence stretched. I went over to his side of the

hallway and wrapped my arms around his middle. Just like before, his muscles hardened under my touch. So I was right. I was the problem, in a non-antihero sort of way.

"Tell me what's troubling you. You stiffen when I touch you."

"You told me to stop."

My head shot up as realization hit me. "Is this because I asked you to stop teasing me?"

His gaze lingered a few moments on me before falling to the carpeted floor. I sighed. His love language had always been touching, and like a bitch, I had walked all over his feelings without even noticing.

"I am sorry I snapped at you. I didn't think you'd be hurt by it."

"It's not just you."

And yet, he still couldn't look at me.

"Then tell me what it is."

He finally lifted his head, looking me straight in the eye. There was a vulnerability I hadn't seen there before. "Do you find me too clingy?"

My anxiety made my hands sweaty. What had I done?

"Where is this coming from?" I asked slowly.

"Two of my exes told me I was too clingy, too present. I need to know if that's how you feel too."

Oh, just great. Not only had I been rude, but I had also made him doubt himself. It was unsettling to see Danté without his usual confidence. Or his usual carefree self.

"What if I did?"

"Then I guess I'd have to do something about it."

My heart broke at the resolve in his voice. I appreciated

that he wanted to do his best for me, just like I felt sad he even thought he needed to change for me at all.

"Please don't. I know how important it is for you to have physical contact."

"But you..."

"I wanted you to stop *teasing* me," I said, giving him a reassuring smile, "because I needed to focus. I didn't mean that you couldn't touch me."

Hopefully, this would make him relax a bit. It didn't. He nervously rocked on his feet.

"You'll tell me if I become too much?"

"I already knew you were like this, and I liked you anyway."

"Evelyn, promise me," he insisted.

Whatever had happened in his previous relationships, I couldn't let that happen again.

"I promise I'll always be honest with you. Now please stop looking so sad. I like the fact that you are a human koala."

The tension in his body seeped away. His dimpled smile was contagious. I opened my arms, and without hesitating, Danté lifted me up, making me twirl like a princess. He pressed a kiss to my temple.

"You're the best."

I didn't like serious moments like these.

"I know. Now go get my ice cream."

Danté let out an exaggerated sigh. Yeah, I know, I had ruined the moment. That had been the whole point.

"Only you would think about food at times like these."

"Food is the love of my life."

"Ouch."

"Don't worry, babe, you're a close second."

His eyebrows shot up, and I pressed my lips together. That was not how I had envisioned talking about love with him. My palms became slick as panic invaded my system.

Danté's eyes disappeared when his smile grew wider. He put me on the floor ever so gently. "Why don't we go out for ice cream instead?"

Catastrophe averted.

"I'd love that."

As we went out for our date, he never let me go, and that was perfect.

CHAPTER 32

The lady at the front desk smiled sweetly when I walked inside the practice. I did my best to reciprocate her smile.

"Hello, I have an appointment with Elijah."

"You must be Evelyn Somers, then."

I gave her a nod. She tapped a number in her phone with a pencil, and I took the opportunity to take a deep gulp of air before she put the phone down.

"He'll be here in a minute. Can I get you a coffee?"

"I'm too nervous, so I'm not sure that would be wise."

Not that I would've had the time to finish the drink. Elijah appeared in the lobby, wearing a white coat like the doctors did in Grey's Anatomy. Would I also get one? How cool would that be! He grabbed my hand and almost crushed it with his firm grip.

"Evelyn, welcome!" He gave me a sign to follow him upstairs. By the time we got to the second level, I had to do my best to not puff too loudly. These nerves were not doing me any favours. "How have you been?"

"Good, thank you."

"I'll present you to the dietician you will follow for the next few weeks. You will follow two dieticians, but you'll start with Linda." First, he gave me a little tour of the place. I did my best to listen closely, knowing fully well I wouldn't remember this in a few minutes.

Elijah stopped in front of a light wooden door, then knocked. A soft voice welcomed us inside. The office smelled like fresh coffee and soft perfume. A blonde woman who was probably in her early thirties gave us a wide smile.

"Linda, this is Evelyn, your new intern."

Linda took my hand, and unlike her boss, her touch was soft. Everything about this woman gave me a sweet and cosy vibe. There were many plants and framed pictures of her cats. Now this was exactly how I envisioned my future office.

"Linda especially takes care of diabetes patients."

Which almost seemed ironic as she gave me the most saccharine smile to ever exist.

"You can leave, Elijah. I'll take care of her."

My jaw almost dropped at the familiarity. She gave me a playful wink, and I smiled back, my nerves already getting under control. Elijah didn't take it the wrong way and went for the door.

"Very well."

Linda motioned me to sit in one of her plush sage green chairs. The perks of a private practice were that you could customize the place in the most awesome ways possible. I almost felt too dirty for her pretty interior.

"In half an hour, we will have our first patient," she

started, lacing her fingers on her wooden desk. "The first two days at least, I'll ask you to simply follow and take notes."

Easy enough.

"Once you've seen how it really goes, I'll let you handle the patients. I'll always be with you, in case you have questions or doubts, of course. Does that sound alright to you?"

She seemed to be one who would always try to help out others and give feedback in the most positive way. This was probably the best person I could've started with. I straightened in my chair. I would not let her down.

"That's perfect."

Her grin became toothy. "Great. Then let's get you a coat."

My eyelids were growing heavy. It was barely 8 PM, and I was so ready to sleep until the alarm would beep the next morning. My nerves had kept me going through the first day of the internship. Now that the adrenaline was gone, I felt like a ragdoll. The only reason I hadn't gotten to bed yet was because I had promised Danté and Jasmine I would tell them every single detail of my day around supper. Supper was over, so a part of me hoped that Danté would soon depart. He was helping Jasmine and I clean the kitchen when his phone chimed. The way his face became grave told me it was bad news. I silently asked Jasmine to leave us. She gave Danté a worried look before going to her room.

"Are you alright?"

Danté gave me his phone without answering. It was like he had barely heard me. My pulse quickened when I took the phone.

Dear Mr. Ortega,
Thank you for your interest in our association.
We regret to inform you that your application has not been accepted for our volunteer program in Sri Lanka. Although your profile is promising, your specialization is not what we are currently looking for.
Kind regards,
Laura Meskens from Global Volunteering HQ

Shit. I had never been good at comforting people; I didn't know what to do to lift his spirit. Though it wasn't the end of the world, I could see why he was so disappointed. Right now, his plans and dreams had been crushed. My heart hurt for him. I put the phone aside and laid a hand on his arm.

"I'm sorry you didn't get the spot."

Danté looked empty. Without thinking, I grabbed his hand and took him to the couch. He sat down, his eyes still unfocused. I pulled him closer, stroking his head.

"I'm really sorry. I know how important this is for you."

His arms found their place around my middle, and we stayed like that for a while. We never talked about his plans. The last time Danté had brought up his desire to travel and to volunteer, he had said he didn't want to do long-distance relationships. It had scared me to death. In the meantime, things had changed. Even if we never talked about it, we were a team. And team members didn't give up on each other. I wouldn't give up on him just because he would be far away for a while. There were many volunteering programs all over the world. Danté was a very skilled physiotherapist, so I was certain that he would be able to find something. It wouldn't be the first destination of his choice, but it could still be a wonderful experience.

"Just promise me you'll try again."

Danté let me go, his head slightly tilted to the side. "What?"

"This sucks, but don't give up on your dream. You'll try again, right?"

He stayed silent for a while. There was a war going on inside his head, one he had to wage himself. When he looked back at me, I didn't know which side had won. Danté tugged on my hand, and I ended up on his lap. A position that could've become saucy rather quickly, if he hadn't buried his face in my neck, hugging me closer.

"I'm sorry, love."

My heart did a flip at the nickname. This was the first time that he didn't call me by my name, or Squirrel. Luckily, he couldn't see my blush.

"What are you sorry for?" I asked.

"Not telling you I applied, and for ruining your night."

"You didn't ruin my night. But I wish you'd told me."

His breaths were irregular, so I left it at that. His embrace tightened around me. "Can we stay like this a bit longer?"

I flipped my legs over his knees and nestled closer until my head was resting against his heartbeat. Danté laced his fingers with mine, still waiting for my reply. When I gave him a smile, the lines that creased his face smoothed out a bit.

"We can stay here as long as you want."

Danté was scrolling on his phone while I went through my wardrobe. Jasmine had suggested we watch a Disney movie. I, of course, had agreed without even thinking. Danté on the other hand, had shot a look at Theo, who had just answered something along the lines of "Meh".

"The girls always watch Disney movies. Better get used to it," he had said, already bored at the mere idea of watching yet another "kids movie".

The only difference was that Danté wasn't comfortable enough yet to suggest something else. So after our workout, we both showered.

"Are you wearing the squirrel onesie tonight?" he asked without looking up. "I haven't seen it in a while."

Yeah right. That had been the whole point. I grabbed a pair of sweatpants and a hoodie from my wardrobe. Danté didn't know it yet, but I had other plans for us tonight. Plans that didn't involve a squirrel onesie or pyjamas. I hadn't scrubbed and waxed for nothing. It had been a bit more than a month. I was tired of waiting. I went for the door and looked over my shoulder.

"Actually, I was thinking about wearing nothing at all after the movie. But if you prefer the onesie…"

His head went up so fast I feared he'd injured himself. His

blue eyes locked with mine, a gorgeous pink now dusting his face.

"Nothing."

"Are you sure?" I asked innocently.

The blue of his irises had almost been consumed by his dilated pupils. If I asked him to take me now, he would.

"Don't wear anything. Please."

I had no doubt that waiting and not letting anything show must've been hard for him. So tonight, I would let him do whatever he pleased. We both deserved it.

"I love it when you beg." I could hear him swallow, and I gave him my prettiest smile. "Fine. You can undress me later."

Then I slipped out of the bedroom to put on the least sexy outfit I owned. Everyone was already sitting on the couch when I emerged from the bathroom. Jasmine and Theo were talking. For once, Danté wasn't participating in the conversation, his thoughts elsewhere. I bit my lip to keep from smiling. I knew exactly where his mind was. He didn't care one bit about the movie we were about to watch.

As soon as *Atlantis* started, I nestled against him. His body was taut under my fingertips. When I looked up, his pupils were still as large as they were before. But like the gentleman that he was, Danté wrapped an arm around me and let his hand rest against my ribs.

Theo was flipping through the menu of a Chinese takeout after the movie. I did my best to ignore Danté's growing impatience. It had been hard to focus on the screen when he was that close; I was just as restless. Tonight would be the night. It was something I had fantasized about way too many times. The only difference was that I was better at hiding my eagerness. Jasmine shot him worried glances every now and then, and Danté didn't even see it. I followed Jasmine to the kitchen.

"Is he alright?" she asked in a hushed voice.

I leafed through a pizza takeout menu. Sex and fast food were always a nice combination. Maybe we could order something later. It was better to have the garlic bread afterward rather than before.

"Yes, why?"

"He seems stressed. Like he actually has something more important to do than being here."

I closed the menu. Better to keep her aware of what was going to happen. I took a deep breath. "I told him he could undress me tonight."

Jasmine burst out laughing, and I made a sign for her to be a tad bit more discreet. She dabbed at her eyes with a tissue, a big smile blooming on her face.

"Alright. I'll sleep at Theo's tonight."

Thank the gods.

"Thanks."

"Enjoy."

"Trust me, I will. I probably won't be able to walk tomorrow."

And I was fine with that.

"I'll expect some spicy details."

"Anything you want."

Theo didn't get why Jasmine had suddenly decided to sleep at his place. From the shy smile Danté gave us, he did. My best friend gave me a kiss before practically running away from the apartment. Once they were gone, Danté waited for me to make the first move. I pressed a kiss to his lips, and his face lit up like a kid with a present. He pulled me down until I had no choice but to straddle his lap. Yet even now, he waited for me to set the pace. My heart almost burst with love and wanting. I kissed him again, pressing closer to him. His fingers trailed lines on the skin under my sweater.

Danté kissed my neck before lifting me up. I was ready to tear his clothes off when he laid me down on the bed. His touch was slow, agonizing. Goosebumps erupted on my skin everywhere he touched me. When he claimed my lips, the words almost stumbled out of my mouth.

"Make me see stars, Danté," I whispered. "I'm yours."

His gaze was so soft it made me tear up. Even if three words were left unsaid, in this moment, I knew he felt them too. His smile made my stomach tighten.

"Thank you."

CHAPTER 33

The mattress dipped beside me, and I jolted awake. The first thing I saw was Danté watching me with wide eyes. Why was he looking at me like that? It took me a few moments to chase the sleepy haze off my mind. Then everything that happened last night came back, and my toes curled at the memories. Danté sat back down on the bed, removing some wild hair strands from my face.

"Good morning," he whispered and leaned down to kiss my forehead. "Did you sleep well?"

The sweetness made me smile. If this was how waking up with him was, I wanted this every morning of my life. I hummed and appreciated the heat of his hand against my neck. He pressed another kiss to my mouth. Danté smelled like toothpaste. His hair was still wild, and I wanted to make it even wilder, to have another round before Jasmine came back.

"Why are you up so early?" I asked as I yawned.

"It's past 9 AM."

Great. He was one of those horrible people who could get up early and thrive in the morning. After a nice stretch, I let myself fall back against my pillow.

"That's what I said."

Danté watched me with amusement. "What are your plans today?"

The list of everything I needed to do unfolded in my head. Starting with scrubbing off all the sweat and other residues that probably still clung to my skin. Then, of course, breakfast, going to the gym, cooking, cleaning the apartment, doing the laundry. Now I could also add "having mind-blowing sex with my boyfriend" to it. Because wow. He had not disappointed. No wonder so many girls had come back so many times.

I cleared my throat. "Oh, you know, the usual."

The way his grin turned catlike indicated that Danté had caught on to where my thoughts were headed. I touched my cheek. Yep, definitely blushing. The gesture only made his amusement grow. I waited for him to comment on it, to make fun of me.

"Let's go to a cat café," he offered instead.

"A cat café," I repeated dumbly.

Post sex Evy wasn't the brightest light out there.

"You know, like a date."

I did my best to not grin like an idiot, not that it really worked. There went the extra round. I couldn't mind. As long as I spent my time with him, it was all good.

"Oh, okay. I'll need to shower first."

I got out of bed and rummaged through my wardrobe to

pick up a comfy outfit. If we were going to spend the next few hours with kitties, there was no need to be all dolled up. I looked back at Danté and his dishevelled look.

"If I remember correctly, you offered to carry me once."

His attention that had been on his phone, was now mine and mine only. The phone slipped from his fingers, already forgotten.

"I hope the offer still stands," I continued in a soft voice.

Danté practically jumped from the bed. A second later, I was pressed against the door.

"Oh babe, I'll do anything you want and more," he purred. "All you need to do is ask."

His teeth raked down my throat. Danté looked up as his fingers caressed my breasts, and my breath hitched. He let out a hiss when my hands roamed over the hardness in his pants. Danté grabbed my hands and placated them against the door. I couldn't help the whimper that escaped my lips when he pressed his erection against my core.

"Come on, love, what are you waiting for?" he asked in a whisper.

"Fine," I choked out at the next movement of his hips, unable to move or touch him myself. "Please take me now."

My cheeks grew hotter, but I didn't care. I would beg for him if that was what he wanted.

Danté's hot breath tickled my neck as he laughed. "There you go."

Without wasting any more time, he picked me up. My legs wrapped around his middle and I went for his mouth. I could barely register the water being turned on, too lost in this haze. It was with care and patience that Danté helped me undress, like no matter how much he wanted this, he would take all the time in the world. The moment we were both under the hot water, Danté peppered kisses to my cheeks, my neck, my shoulders. My skin burned everywhere his lips touched me. He kept going farther down until he was on his knees. It was with utmost gentleness that he placed my leg and hand on his shoulders. Oh, gods. Danté looked up once, his grin wolfish.

"Hold on tight, love. You're going to be here a while."

CHAPTER 34

As always, there were traveling flyers lying on the table in Danté's living room when I walked in. I smiled as I imagined him with his backpack and his luggage strolling through the airport, looking like a real tourist. A sight I would've loved to see and take a picture of before grabbing his hand and running to catch our plane. Then my gaze fell on a red booklet. His passport. The front door opened and closed, and Danté walked to the kitchen with a bag in his hands. His eyebrows got up in surprise. Probably because he thought I'd be waiting at my own place.

"Got your coconut ice cream."

He dropped a kiss on my cheek. The familiar prickle of his stubble on my skin was something I liked way too much.

"You're going abroad?" I asked, still looking at the papers scattered on the table.

I waited for an answer that didn't come. Hadn't he heard me?

"Yeah." His voice sounded so hoarse. "I am."

"Where are you going?"

"Australia."

I jumped in his arms, laughing. His dream was finally coming true. I hadn't really thought about going to Australia. If that was where he wanted to go, it seemed like that would be my next destination as well.

"I am so happy for you."

His arms wrapped around my middle, but there was no soul in his embrace. It felt forced. I let him go. Something didn't feel right.

"When are you leaving?"

"In less than two months."

Two months. The words echoed in my head. Over and over again. My heartbeat picked up an uncomfortable speed.

"How long?"

When I looked up to face him, his wide eyes were fixed on the wall behind me. He resembled a deer caught in the headlights. And I was the car about to crash into him. My throat constricted.

"Danté?" I pleaded.

"I don't know yet," he rasped. "Maybe a year, maybe longer. I haven't bought a return ticket yet."

His words hit me like a punch in the gut; my breath hitched in my throat. What was happening? The ground under my feet had disappeared. Now I was freefalling, and the hand that had become so familiar wasn't there to catch me. I stumbled back.

"Why didn't you tell me?"

He rubbed the back of his neck, still not looking at me. "I

forgot, I guess?"

I gaped at him in disbelief. This was the goal he had been working on for years.

"You truly believe I am that stupid? You've dreamed of this for years, and you "forgot to tell me"?"

Danté came closer, trying to touch me, but I dodged him. This couldn't be happening.

"Evy, listen, it's not what you think."

"How could it not be what I think it is? What reason could you possibly have to not tell me this? I thought you and I were a team."

"We are," he said slowly. "For now."

Realization hit me. Who would have thought that it would hurt so much? My shoulders sagged. How could I have been so blind?

"You don't want me in your life."

Anger flashed in his eyes. He took a step in my direction, and I took a step back.

"Don't put words in my mouth!"

I could taste the tears. Heartbreak had a flavour after all.

"Then tell me!" I yelled. "Why haven't you told me?"

Please, tell me you have a plan for us. Please.

"Because there is no place for me in your life!" he yelled back. "Can you say you want to leave behind everything you've worked so hard for to be with me?"

I opened my mouth, but no sound came out.

"I…" I tried.

It would have been a lie. I had never thought that my life would not be like I had planned it, like I had dreamed it would be. Delayed, maybe. Danté tore at his hair.

"That's why I didn't tell you. I didn't want to waste the little time we had."

How long had he known that our time was running out? Had he known this every time we had kissed? Every time he'd held me close to his heart? My stomach churned and my vision blurred.

"You should've told me."

"I know. I'm sorry."

"That's not enough."

He took another step towards me, and I darted for the door. Warm fingers gripped my arm.

"Evy, can we at least talk about it?"

A choked sob escaped my lips. I shook my head. "So now you want to talk about it? Well, I can't."

"Please," he said, his voice trembling.

A part of me wanted to hit him with all I got. The biggest part of me wanted him to hold me. I wanted to hear him say that we would get over this, that everything would be fine. But maybe love wasn't enough. Danté had clearly said once he didn't want to be in a long-distance relationship. I couldn't be the weight that would hold him back. My fingers found his. This would be the last time.

"You know what's the worst? You didn't even give us a chance. You didn't give *me* a chance to choose you."

Something like hope shined in his blue eyes. "Would you?"

I felt like a monster for crushing that hope. The room around me started spinning. I wiped my cheeks before squaring my shoulders.

"I don't know. It doesn't matter anymore. You already

had our breakup planned."

A tear rolled down his face. I bit my lip as more tears fell down my own.

"Don't walk away," he pleaded.

"I can't look at you right now."

And I let go of his hand before I slipped back inside my own apartment.

"Evy, please open that door."

I quickly locked the door before crumbling down to the floor. This felt familiar, and yet this was the worst day of my life.

"I am begging you. Open the door."

I heard him slide to the ground. I don't know how much time passed, but as the sky grew darker outside, Danté got up and headed back inside. Jasmine walked outside her room, her headphones blasting music. When she saw me on the floor, she threw her headphones on the couch before taking me in her arms.

"What happened?"

I swallowed back my tears. It was over.

"We broke up."

CHAPTER 35

I had never really thought about where the term broken heart came from. It had always seemed more figurative than literal. When I heard the term "broken heart" I always pictured an emoji or a stupid pink picture of a heart torn in two. Today those words finally got a meaning. Maybe it was called a broken heart because it felt like our hearts couldn't deal with the pain. The rate of my ticker was always off; most of the time, it was going too fast to the point it felt like I would collapse, but when it slowed down, it cramped painfully. Now I also understood why the heart was ripped in the middle. It felt like mine was torn in two, one of the halves I had lost still with Danté, except that it had stopped beating. And there was nothing I could do to fill the hole in my chest where that other part used to be. Just thinking of his name made me breathless.

The first days, I didn't leave the house. Sometimes someone knocked on our door – I never opened it. I couldn't let myself see him. If I let Danté in, I didn't know what I would do. Would I scream? Yell? Ask him to stay with me? Or worse, would I ask him to take me back, even if he had planned our breakup for weeks, or maybe months? How low would I let myself fall for love? I knew that if he had asked me to leave everything behind and to go with him, I would have. Probably not forever, but I would have found a way. The worst part was that I had been the only one ready to compromise. I couldn't force Danté to compromise when his mind had been made all along. My phone had also been ringing all day. Sometimes it was messages, but mostly calls. At one point, I turned off the device. It was easier to pretend that the reality I found myself in was a dream when the buzzing didn't bring me back to where I stood.

Danté: *Please stop ignoring me. We need to talk.*
Evy: *There is nothing to talk about. We're not together anymore.*

My vision blurred once I sent the message. I was done pretending. Typing those words had been a wake-up call. We *had* broken up. It would take me a while to get over it; maybe it would be a scar that would always hurt. One thing was sure, I couldn't keep hiding in my room any longer. Not when I had to go to the cafe for my shift. So I did what I did best: I made lists.

> *Showering*
> *Skincare and dressing up*
> *Shift at the café*

I looked back at my attire. I had worn Danté's old sweater for days, to the point his smell had worn off. There was no point in keeping this up. I tore the page out of the notebook and started anew.

> *Collect Danté's stuff*
> *Showering*
> *Skincare and dressing up*
> *Bringing his stuff back*
> *Shift at the café*

Without wasting any more time, I grabbed a cardboard box from our pantry and went to the kitchen. I took his black mug from the shelf, then went back to my room. The first thing I threw in the box was the sweater I had been wearing. Then I went to the wardrobe and took out the few shirts and sweatpants he had left there. His wireless phone charger went in the box too. It felt like I put a piece of me in that stupid box, but I had to move forward. So I took a burning hot shower to scrub away the sadness. And I would ask Chloe and Kristen if they would agree if I changed my Tuesday shift to another day. Any day would be fine. I could convince Elijah too to slightly change my shift and internship schedule.

When I went into the kitchen with the box, Jasmine frowned.

"What is that?" she asked.

"Danté's stuff. I'm going to give them back."

"Are you going to talk to him?"

She had disapproved of me ignoring his calls. Jasmine was more straightforward than I could ever be. Here I was about to disappoint her even more. I shook my head. She let out a long sigh.

"Eves, you need to talk to him. Just dropping his stuff on his porch is going to backfire, and you know it."

"That is a problem for future me."

Even though she wanted to protest, Jasmine let it go. If she was more straightforward than I was, I was the more stubborn one. I dropped a kiss on her cheek before taking my jacket. Fake it till you make it, is what they say. I could do this. All I had to do was keep going, and I would get better. Someday. I could do this. I quickly looked in the hallway to make sure it was empty. I dropped the box in front of his door. Then I made a run for the entrance of the building. *Keep going. We'll be fine.*

I could see Danté storming towards the café and fled to the kitchen before he could even catch a glimpse of me here. Chloe saw me run and followed. The bell chimed, which meant that my short-lived peace was officially over. My heart was beating painfully fast in my chest.

"Evelyn Somers, you better get out here right now," he bellowed from the front room.

Chloe's eyes went wide at the aggressive tone. I felt my limbs freeze. The only time Danté had ever raised his voice at me was that night at the bowling.

"What did you do?" she whispered.

"I put his stuff on his porch without telling him."

She ran a hand over her face. This was as bad as it looked. Probably worse.

"Oh God, Evy."

"Please tell him I'm not here."

Chloe wasn't one to pity me, or to help me if she knew I could do it myself. If anything, she always pushed me to become better. Today was the day she understood that I needed her to support me, not to push me.

"Fine."

She went back inside.

"Hi, can I help you?"

Chloe was a boss when it came to being professional. I could practically see her calm demeanour and reassuring smile.

"Where is she?"

"Evy? She's not working today."

There was a scoff. *Please make it work.*

"Okay, I am not that stupid. She never misses a day of work. Evelyn, come out of that kitchen before I get you out of there!"

My colleague shot me a sorry glance. As soon as Danté saw me, he pointed an accusing finger at my face.

"You..."

A few customers shot us wary glances. I gulped under the sudden attention. This was *so* going to be a disaster.

"Let's not do this inside, please."

Annoyance flashed in his eyes, but Danté nodded before storming out of the shop. I followed him outside, heart beating too fast. *Oh dear.* Jasmine had been right. As soon as the door closed, he exploded.

"You broke up with me through a text!" he hissed. "And you left my stuff on my porch."

I'll admit it wasn't my smartest choice. Though at that time, it felt better to make a stupid choice than to face him. Now, I still had no idea what I was supposed to say to him. My plans hadn't gone that far into detail. For once, I found myself completely unprepared for what was happening, and no amount of lists and thorough planning could've changed that.

I shrugged. "And? No one would've stolen a few worn shirts."

No one except for me, that is. A part of me had wanted to keep at least one sweater. At least then, I would always have something from him. I also knew that clinging to the memory of us wouldn't help.

Danté scowled. "I am not talking about the clothes, and you know it."

"Then what do you want, Danté?"

"We're fucking adults!" he yelled, opening his arms. "You should've told me that in person."

Although my eyes were prickling, I had cried too many tears already. I forced out a fake laugh. Anything was better than crying.

"Oh, because you hiding the fact that you were going to break up was so much more mature."

Danté's temper seeped out of him, only to melt away like snow under a scorching sun.

"Evy, I'm trying to talk with you. Can you at least try to put your sarcasm aside for a few minutes?"

"Fine. I didn't know we were still together when I sent that message."

"You would've known if you opened your door when I tried to see you."

Again, that hole in my chest opened. I swallowed away the tears. The only thing that had kept me from opening the door was the knowledge that things wouldn't go differently, no matter what I did. It was better to stop seeing each other again.

"Danté, this doesn't change anything. Your decision is made. We might as well accept it and rip the Band-Aid off instead of postponing it for a few weeks."

"Does it really have to end like this?"

"Can it be any different? Can you accept the distance?"

I put my heart on the line by asking the last question. I wanted him to say yes. There was room for him in my plans. There always would be, but only if he wanted to try long distance. Except that he had been more than clear. He didn't want that. And I couldn't hold him back here. None of us could be happy that way. Danté knew it too.

"I'm sorry" was all he said.

If there had been anything left of my heart, it was completely shattered now. Who knew that a muscle could be so breakable? A single tear fell down his cheek.

"Once again, that's not enough. Enjoy your travels."

Danté pressed a kiss against my forehead. It felt like a brand.

"Be happy, Evy."

Then he turned away, taking half of me with him, never to be returned again.

CHAPTER 36

It was 9:30 PM. Most students and young adults were still wide awake at this time, and probably getting ready for a night out. It shouldn't have been a surprise that there was a lot of noise outside of our apartment. There was music, many people talking, and overall, just a lot of movement. I knew where the noise was coming from.

Against my better judgement, I opened the door to see what this whole commotion was about. Danté's door was wide open. Alex walked out of it, his arms full with boxes and bags. My breath caught in my throat. Danté was moving out. Alex tried to wave but almost dropped everything he was holding.

"Hey, Evy!" His tone was too light-hearted, too forced. He was Danté's best friend. I had no doubt that Alex knew every single detail of what had happened. If not told to him by his friend, then at least because he had been able to piece everything together himself with that annoying sixth sense of his.

I did my best to show him a smile. The way his face fell and his expression became clouded with pity, I hadn't done a good job at it.

"How are you?" he asked in a softer voice, just loud enough for me to hear. Because it was Alex, I didn't pretend like I was fine.

"I'm hanging in there. Do you need some help with those?" I asked, pointing to the many bags hanging from his arms.

Alex shook his head. "I'll be fine. Please know that if you need to talk, I'm there for you."

Since he came back from Russia – engaged, no less! – Alex had regained his usual calm and carefree composure. Gone were the sad boy days, and I was happy for him. I really was. If I had ever disliked the guy, things had changed these last few months. Alex was a busybody who often tried to meddle in other people's business. He was also loyal – I had ended up appreciating him. I was happy that he had found his happy ending. A foolish little part of me hoped that if it had worked out for Alex, maybe it could also work out for us. But what were the chances?

"Thanks."

Alex gave me a nod before leaving towards the parking lot. I watched him disappear. Would I still see him, now that Danté would be gone? There was some shuffling, then Danté stood there. Our eyes met, and I found myself unable to look away. He seemed... worried. His blonde hair was shorter now. Only a few steps separated us; they felt like miles. It took all my strength to not run to him, to hide in his strong embrace. My eyes burned with unshed tears. How was it that it had been over a month, yet it still hurt as if we had broken up yesterday? Danté was with me every second of every day as long as I was awake. And now he was leaving for good. It was probably the last time that we saw each other. I couldn't watch him leave. Danté opened his mouth to speak. Nothing good could come out of this, so I squared my shoulders and went back inside.

Lana Del Rey was singing about mountains and rivers in my headphones, about a place where she belonged, while I dried some mugs. *A place where I belong.* Funny, how a person had made me feel like I belonged, only for that feeling of home to be taken away. These days, I wasn't able to listen to Taylor. Her songs had accompanied every step of my life for as long as I could remember. Now that I was going through one of the roughest patches of my life, I couldn't listen to her. Her songs made me think too much about him. Danté had been able to taint almost every part of my life. Lana's music at least still felt like my own, untainted by his memory.

A white cloth was being shaken in front of my face, getting me out of my head. Chloe's lips pressed together with concern. I took out my headphones.

"What is it?" I asked.

"You've been drying that same cup for over two minutes."

The shine of the clean mug was mocking me. I almost

threw the object across the kitchen. Chloe took it from my hand, afraid I would actually chuck it against the wall. Once the mug was out of reach, Chloe took my hands in hers. Her skin felt fresh against mine. I had slowly been cooking in the steam of the dishwasher.

"Evy, go home. This isn't working."

"To do what? Study for my exams? You know I could pass them now and still make it."

The exams were mere days away. My internship was over, for now. Once I got home, I would bury myself in my books. It was easier to focus on that than on what I lost. That didn't mean I wanted to go home to study now. Being here at Hot Stuff made me feel at least a bit valuable. A bit useful. Which I wasn't, apparently. My shoulders sagged.

Chloe gently squeezed my hands. "You won't accomplish anything by pretending to be okay. Go home, have a good cry."

Here was the thing: if I let myself go down that road, I wasn't sure I would be able to come back from it. I would only end up in the same place as I always did: wanting to call Danté and ask him to come back. It wasn't fair to either of us. Chloe could probably see on my face that I didn't want to leave.

"Please, do something. I don't care if you need to go out and get drunk, or need to go for a run. But you can't stay here staring at the walls on the verge of crying."

I found myself nodding. There was no way I could argue with her. Chloe was capable of calling Kristen to force me to go home.

She gave me an encouraging smile. "Let's go get a drink

tomorrow, okay?"

"Not the College, please."

I hadn't gone to that bar ever since I had ended up in Danté's bed, hungover. Though going out and not thinking about anything sounded nice, I couldn't go back there. Chloe nodded.

"We'll go somewhere else." She gave me a tight hug.

"You will get through this, I promise."

CHAPTER 37

The ceiling was having a staring contest with me. Or maybe I was merely losing my mind. My exams had gone by in a blur. A few days afterward, I had gone to parties with Chloe or spent my time working extra shifts. Everything was fine, as long as I didn't have to spend hours with myself as my sole companion. Not able to take the calm anymore, I went to the kitchen. Jasmine was still studying at the table, lost in her books.

I took mascarpone and lemon curd out of the fridge and started making a lemon tiramisu. Every now and then, Jasmine shot me a worried look. I got a lot of them lately. Between her and Theo, it often felt like they were anticipating a mental breakdown. I was glad that I couldn't see myself the way the others did. Not that it would've been bad to be outside of my own head for a few hours.

My phone chimed. Not wanting to annoy Jasmine more than necessary, I went back to the living room. A new email from the school.

Dear student,
Your exam results are now online. Click on the link below to view them.

I clicked on the link, swallowing hard. After all these years, these moments still made me nervous. Had I ever failed an exam ever since I got into college? No. Did that make it any less stressful? Also no. The screen loaded, and my results appeared. I stared, and stared, and stared, until my phone slipped from my hand, falling on the floor. Then I hiccupped. Jasmine walked over to me, but I couldn't move.

"Evy, what's wrong?"

She picked up my phone and looked for herself. My skin prickled, suddenly feeling too tight for my body. Jasmine's eyes went wide. A second later, she was hugging me.

"You're graduating! That's amazing."

Then why didn't it feel so? I hiccupped once again. And again, only to end up sliding to the floor, with my head between my hands, sobbing. Jasmine's soft orange blossom perfume came closer. Her warm hand rested against my neck.

"Eves, talk to me."

"It's over," I choked out. "Everything I worked for my whole life... all my efforts have paid off."

"Then why are you crying?"

"My first thought was that Danté isn't here to live this moment with me."

What was the point in having joys and sadness, and not

being able to share them with the person you loved more than anything? What was the point of it all if he wasn't with me?

"What was the point of all these years? This?" I yelled. "That's bullshit!"

This was supposed to be a wonderful moment. Graduating and starting the career I had been working towards was supposed to be rewarding. The sobs never stopped. This was the first time that Jasmine was tongue-tied. For as long as I had known her, Jasmine always had something to say. Not today. Her eyes grew sad.

"I can't do this alone," she whispered before getting up.

She dragged me to my feet to make me sit on the couch. Jasmine called someone. It sounded heated, but I could barely hear her over my loud breathing. I didn't want to cry anymore. What good did it do?

I must have fallen asleep at some point because I jolted awake when someone knocked on our door. Jasmine practically ran to open it. My sister wasted no time and hugged Jasmine as she walked in.

"Thank you for coming so quickly," my best friend told her.

"What's going on?"

"I can't get through to her. *You* are her big sister, so man up and do something."

They both talked as if I wasn't there. It would've been nice if I had been somewhere else. Eleanor's grey eyes landed on me. I flapped my hand at her, more lethargic than ever. After my breakdown from earlier, I was drained. All I wanted was to fall asleep, only to wake up once the pain was gone.

My sister plopped down next to me. She was as pretty as always. Not a single strand of her dark and shiny hair was out of place, and her cheeks had a healthy glow. The way she cocked her head to the side as she checked up on me, it was clear that I looked like I had been run over by a bus. Funny, that was exactly how I felt.

"This is a first. I don't really know what to do," she admitted in a soft voice. Indeed, Jasmine had never called my sister to come and help her before.

"I'm sorry you had to come." I picked at a cuticle so I didn't have to look at her. If only I could regain control over my life. But what was the point? I'd had everything under control until Danté. Now that he wasn't here anymore, it felt like there was nothing left of me. Eleanor grabbed my arm and pulled me closer to her.

"Don't apologize. You're my baby sister. I'll always come when you need me."

For once, the term baby sister made me smile. She untangled and stroked my hair.

"Jasmine told me what happened between you and Danté. I'm sorry it didn't work out."

"Me too."

"Why did you guys break up?"

I told her everything. Him hiding the truth, the planned breakup. Would things between us have been different if I hadn't been such a control freak? If I had been less fucked up? Would we still be together if he had loved me more? I hated when my mind spiralled like that. I wouldn't have been me if I had been any different. If Danté couldn't be with me like this, maybe we were never meant to be. If only knowing this could make missing him less painful.

Eleanor drew in a sharp breath. "I am sorry, Evelyn. I made you like this."

I turned back to my sister, only to see her lips wobble as she did her best to keep from crying. Eleanor laced her fingers with mine.

"I took away your youth without realizing it. I can't give back the years that you lost, but I can give you this piece of advice. You need to take life one day at a time, and accept that not everything is yours to control. That's what makes life hard, but also worth living for."

Her words opened an old wound in my chest, and stitched it back together. Burning tears rolled down my face. My sister kept rubbing circles on my hands as the tears kept coming. When was this going to end?

"I'm so tired."

"I know you are. You love him, so it will take a long time for you to get over this. But you and I, we're fighters. You stopped living because of us. Try to live for yourself now."

"I'm scared," I admitted.

"Trust me, I know." She let out a long sigh. "Healing is a scary, slow process."

"Is this the moment where you say that it is worth it?"

Eleanor flicked me on the forehead as a punishment. When the fun of the moment fell back down, she cupped my cheek and put her forehead against mine.

"Healing is worth it. Being happy is worth it, especially because you deserve it. Enjoy life the way it comes at you. Surprises change your life. For worse, yes, but also for the better."

CHAPTER 38

Today was the day. A day I had dreaded so much that even if I hadn't marked it on my calendar, I knew exactly what would happen. My body was heavy and lethargic; it didn't really feel like my own. But while my body didn't respond the way it should, my mind kept racing. So did my heartbeat. It was beating in my ears and in my throat, making me nauseous. If only I could go back to sleep for a few hours, or a few days, until it was over. Then it wouldn't feel like I was awaiting a death sentence anymore. So I did what I knew best: I moved on autopilot. There was no need for a list. I wouldn't be able to get outside anyway. Anything was fine as long as I could keep my thoughts of him at bay. I put on Lana Del Rey, again, and started dusting off the house. I even did the dishes. Time moved in a blur until the door opened and Jasmine came back from her exam.

"How was the exam?"

"You're listening to Lana again," she said instead of

answering my question.

"A fine lyricist."

Listening to Taylor made me think of him, and right now, I couldn't bear it. It was easier to pretend like it wasn't happening now. Getting over him leaving was a problem for future Evy. This Evy only wanted to get through the day.

Jasmine stomped her foot on the floor, catching my attention. She was fuming. "You fucking dumbass! What are you still doing here?"

I scowled at her. "Did you just insult me?"

"Oh right, you're a *stubborn* dumbass. That's even worse!"

"Now you're pushing it," I warned her, crossing my arms.

We sometimes had an aggressive way of loving each other. Tough love was how Jasmine and I functioned. Most of the time, we hated fighting. Today, she was ready to throw me out of the window. She grabbed a pillow on the couch and hit my face with it repeatedly. I caught the makeshift weapon and hit her back.

"Can you stop?!"

"How can you sit here and simply brood while Danté is leaving?"

I shrugged. "We're not together anymore."

Jasmine grabbed another pillow, and I readied myself for a blow that never came. Instead, her hands kneaded the poor object so hard I feared she would tear it open. She breathed in deeply to keep her temper under control.

"Evelyn, that boy is the love of your life. You wasted two years. Are you really going to waste more?"

I wanted to scream that no, I didn't want to waste another minute. A whole lifetime with him wouldn't be enough. I loved him, and I had imagined us spending our lives together. But Danté had made his choice, without me. How could I counter that? How much I loved him didn't matter. I blinked the upcoming tears away.

"But he…"

She bit her lip, pacing in our little living room, her eyes shining too.

"I am not saying that what he did was right. Hell, I'd punch him in the face if he did that to me. But he loves you more than anything, so don't let that go. Even if he made the worst decision of his life by letting you go, Danté waited two years for you. The least you could do is be honest with him and tell him how you really feel."

"And if I'm too late?"

"Then that's on you. But you can't give up so easily and pretend to be happy with your lists and routines. You know this!"

A sob escaped me. Then another one, until I was a crying mess on the floor. Jasmine's arms found their way around me, and she held me, her embrace never faltering.

"I know you believe that no one will put you first. He didn't exactly nail that part. But that just is how love goes. We make mistakes, and we make amends. I know how much he cares. So please don't give up just yet."

"I don't want to live without him."

"I know, babe. That's why you have to go."

I looked at my watch. I still had some time to get there. "I know it's a lot to ask, but can you take me to the airport?"

She shook her head, her long dark braid hitting me in the face like a whip. "Sorry, but I can't. Theo planned something for our fourth anniversary."

Had I been such a terrible friend that I hadn't noticed that they had their anniversary coming up? Jasmine put some of my unruly curls behind my ear.

"Don't feel bad. I didn't tell you because I knew how sad you were. Now you better start moving."

I took a minute to splash my face with cold water before running out of the apartment. Thanks to Alex, who had sent Jasmine Danté's flight details, I knew to which airport to go. It felt intrusive to know they both had been talking about our future and planning this. I also knew that I would've hated myself for all eternity if I didn't go to the airport. And yet, self-loathing had been an easier option than to call Danté and talk it out. It proved I was that pathetic person who needed people to scheme behind my back and to make me move when I couldn't do it on my own.

At first, I thought that things might be fine. Well, *fine* might be a stretch if I looked at the whole situation. The only thing that seemed to go well was the bus being on time. Until we got stuck in traffic for ten minutes. I cursed but waited patiently. It seemed like the universe had other plans; we were stuck in traffic for so long that I missed the train that would bring me directly inside the station of the airport. Tears of frustration burned my eyes, and my palms were sweaty, but I couldn't give up now. I jumped inside a cab and promised the driver a tip if he could bring me there in time. A whole day of working at the café went into that thirty-minute drive. Hopefully, every penny would be worth it.

The cab had barely stopped when I jumped out of it and ran inside the airport. At this point, Danté had probably already checked in and was now waiting for the gates to open. Yet I didn't stop running until I reached the information boards, out of breath. I grabbed my phone to call. Danté – last seen three hours ago. Shit shit shit. I called anyway, praying for him to answer. He didn't. My heartbeat was still too loud in my ears, and I felt my shoulders sag. This couldn't be it. This just *couldn't* be over.

I waited inside the coffee shop. One hour went by, then another. So much time passed by, that the baristas had come to ask me if everything was fine. What could I say? Because no, nothing was fine. My heart shattered when the announcement that the gates would open was made. In less than an hour, he would be in the sky, and then it would be over for good. I bit down on my lip to keep from crying. There had to be another way. Maybe it was a long shot, an expensive one at that too, if I went to Australia. But I had to do something. Anything. This had been the reason why I preferred staying in a slumber rather than to face reality. It was easier to pretend that there was no hope for us. It was that sliver of hope that made me feel like my heart was hanging by a fragile, breakable thread. *That boy is the love of your life. You wasted two years. Are you really going to waste more?* If Australia was the place I had to get to to see Danté again so we could talk it out, or to get closure, then that was going to be my next destination. I could do this. I would not give up as long as we hadn't had one last talk face to face.

I grabbed my phone and started looking for flight tickets. My phone buzzed, and Danté's name appeared on the screen.

"Evelyn?"

My heart clenched at the name. Him calling me by my full name had never really been our thing. My eyes flickered to the board. The gates would close any minute now. Was there still time? I swallowed.

"Where are you?"

I grabbed my bag and left the coffee shop. I didn't know if I would get there in time, but hell, now would be the time to see how fast I could run if my life depended on it.

"At home. Why?"

I stopped in my tracks.

"At home?" I repeated, lost.

There was rustling on the other side of the call. Then a door closed. "Why did you call me?"

The adrenaline that had kept me on my legs until now was wearing off. My brain had a hard time following what was going on.

"I came to the airport to see you."

"I am busy right now. I'll drop by your house later tonight if that's alright."

"Sure," I answered numbly.

Then the line ended. People moved around me, but I found myself unable to react for some very long seconds. Someone bumped into me, forcing me back into motion. Unlike the journey to the airport, going home went by in a blur. I didn't remember a thing from the journey home. When I walked inside my apartment, Jasmine jumped up from the couch.

"Weren't you supposed to be with Theo?"

She hummed. "I was. But unlike you, some of us still have exams. It was a rather short anniversary."

Jasmine watched me with wary eyes, probably expecting me to explode. She put a reassuring smile on her face, but I could see it wasn't genuine.

"How did it go? You were gone for hours."

The sky had grown dark outside. More than a whole afternoon had gone by without me even noticing it.

"Danté is coming here."

"Wasn't he supposed to leave today?"

Danté was still in the country, but why? I had been too stunned to register that piece of information earlier. When I looked back at Jasmine, she was playing with her hair nervously. She hadn't known he wasn't leaving today either. I turned back to the city outside my window. Danté was coming. Hope fluttered in my chest, soon to be swallowed by fear. There was no place left for me to hide anymore. So I waited.

CHAPTER 39

I felt like a lion locked in a cage. My thoughts were getting out of control. It didn't matter how many cups of chamomile I gulped down, or how many times I looked around the apartment to see if there was something to clean. My body was buzzing with anxious energy. What was I going to tell him? What would happen after tonight? All the questions made me dizzy. Was I mad at Danté for not telling me he was leaving? Fuck yes. Did I understand where he was coming from? Also yes. What he did was not enough for me to give up on him. I had been foolish to think that giving up on him had been the best thing to do.

My pulse resonated loudly in my ears – so loud I couldn't hear Jasmine when she talked to me. She was supposed to study for her upcoming exam in two days, but instead of going back to her textbooks, she stayed by my side.

A knock made me jump from the couch, and my best friend disappeared down the hall. I swallowed before opening the door. My heart stuttered inside my ribcage. There he stood. Danté's back was slightly hunched, and he looked like he hadn't shaved in a few days. The sadness in his eyes only made my own amplify.

"Hey," he said in a hesitant voice.

My body moved on its own, and I wrapped my arms around his middle. Tears escaped as I felt the familiar warmth. Danté hesitated, and I stepped back before he could give back the embrace. I cleared my throat. Maybe he wasn't here for the reason I hoped he was.

"Hey."

I stepped aside to let him in. Danté took in the apartment, then turned to me.

"We need to talk."

Would I still have the courage to tell him how I felt if I let him go first? If he was here just to finish the breakup that he had planned?

"Can I start?" I asked, rubbing my arm.

For a second it looked like he was about to throw up, but Danté nodded. He sat down on our couch and watched me, pale as a ghost. My heartbeat picked up an even faster rhythm than it was already playing.

"I am mad at you," I blurted out. "Worse. I am absolutely furious and disappointed and heartbroken."

He opened his mouth to talk back, but no sound came out. I laughed nervously.

"Actually, I've hated your guts for the last few weeks. You lied to me."

"I didn't lie," he rasped out.

I raised a brow. "You lied by omission."

He showed me his palms as if to say "Fair enough". I let my back rest against the wall, watching his every move: the way he was leaning forward, ready to jump from the couch any moment, or the way he was wringing his hands. Maybe today would be the last time I saw him.

Which was why I said "I understand why you did it. I am sorry."

Danté lifted his head, eyes wide. "What?"

"I am sorry if I made you feel like there was no room for you in the life I had planned. Because I would have chosen you."

Tears ran down his cheek, and he buried his face in his hands. His breathing d quickened. Hope bloomed in my chest. I didn't know how things would go after tonight, but Danté loved me, that much was clear now. I couldn't give up. I dropped to my knees in front of him and took away his hands. Little droplets clung to his lashes.

"Hey," I whispered.

A wet laugh left him as he let his cheek rest in the palm of my hand. "Hey."

"I love you. I have for years, actually. So if you still want me, I will choose you."

He took me in his arms and buried his face in my neck; his stubble tickled my skin. The nervous beats of his heart made my own calm down. I rubbed my cheek against his collarbone. Then I remembered something.

"Why aren't you on the plane?"

"I cancelled my trip."

Dante let me go and finally sat back on the couch like he planned to stay. I sat back as well, crossing my legs.

"I couldn't go. At least not as long as I hadn't seen you."

His fingers played with mine while he was thinking. His lashes cast shadows that deepened his dark circles even more. When his attention was back on me, I held my breath.

"These last weeks have been hard. I know I said I can't do long-distance relationships, but I realized that missing you and still having you in my life is so much better than missing you and knowing I let you go. I want you, Evelyn Somers, more than anything. I'm not leaving until we figure something out."

"I'll come with you," I said before I could think it through.

It didn't matter. I knew I would follow Danté across the globe. Maybe not forever, but if he still wanted me, I would do it without any hesitation.

"Why would you do that?"

"I just told you. I love you."

His brows creased into a frown. I wiggled on the floor. Had I misinterpreted him?

"Why aren't you happy? You don't want me to come?"

"Of course I want you to come. But do you want to go? Won't you regret it?"

I held his hand between mine. The soul-crushing sadness from these last weeks was melting away, and that sliver of hope I had tried to drown was growing. Having all those possibilities felt wonderful.

"I'll regret not going. Don't get me wrong. I still want everything that I had planned, but I'll travel with you for a few months. If I like it, maybe longer. If not, I'll come back and do what I want, and we'll make it work, even if we're continents apart. How does that sound to you?"

His eyes were still shining when he said "It sounds like a dream."

I nudged his knee with my toes. "You know, you can say it back."

"Say what?"

"That you love me. You cancelled a trip because you want me, so you might as well say it."

There was that dimpled smile that had put me under a spell right from the start. "Didn't I just confess how much I care about you?"

I sighed loudly, but still couldn't help but smile back. "Why is it so hard for you?"

"It's not."

He got up from the couch, and I pouted. Danté fished something out of his back pocket. A piece of crinkled paper he gave me. My heart squeezed as I saw the words written in bold marker. The exact same I love you as in Taylor's "You Belong With Me" music video. I sobbed as I held the paper closer to me. Danté dragged me to my feet and held me closer.

"I am sorry, love. Sorry I made the decision for you, and sorry I didn't tell you I love you sooner."

"I told you he was in love with you from the start," a voice shot from the kitchen.

Danté jumped in surprise. I, however, wasn't even fazed that Jasmine had been listening. His cheeks burned when he realized that she probably heard everything he had said.

"Have you been listening all this time?" I asked, wiping my cheeks dry with a tissue.

"Pretty much."

I flashed Danté a sorry smile. The poor boy looked like he was about to combust any minute now.

"I am sorry. There is no privacy between Jasmine and me."

She walked over to us and hugged me. "Glad you guys are alright."

She hugged Danté, who still looked very uncomfortable. Yet he hugged her back. Funny how we had all lived a few meters from each other, and yet, they had never bonded.

"And happy to see you again. But hurt my sister one more time and I'll skewer you. With a rusty knife."

Gods, I could kiss that woman.

"Understood," he said in a solemn tone.

"And you know she's good at hurting people with knives."

Danté had the decency to pretend to be careful. He straightened his back, as if standing in front of a commander. "Oh, right. I forgot I had to take that threat literally with Jasmine."

"Will you guys ever get over it? We all know I would never hurt Evy on purpose."

It was that accident that had changed my life for the better, probably. If not for that one very awkward and bloody night, I would've never had the courage to talk to Danté, let alone tell him I was in love with him.

"I still have the scar on my finger," I told her, showing my hand.

Her mouth formed a thin line, and she went back to the hall. She shot me a dirty look over her shoulder. "Mention that incident once more and you'll have another scar in your collection."

"See? I am being abused here."

Before Jasmine could run away, I hugged her. She gave me back my embrace and patted my neck.

"Thank you for having my back."

"Always."

When my best friend was gone, Danté looked like he could breathe again. Even though it felt like we had been able to save our relationship, Danté stayed hesitant. It might take us a while to go back to where we once were, or maybe it was time for us to start all over. When our eyes met, a soft smile bloomed on his face.

"Would you like to stay the night?" I asked.

Him staying hadn't been something I had planned for today. In all fairness, I hadn't thought further than the conversation we needed to have.

"Would you like to stay forever?" Jasmine yelled from her room.

I let out a loud giggle. Apparently, I was the only one getting the joke. Danté shook his head. How he was a nineties kid and missed most Disney references was a mystery to me.

"I'd love to stay the night. Or forever, I guess."

Forever sounded nice, and now that he had agreed, there were no takes-backsies.

I hugged his arm. "Perfect. How about we watch Mulan, then?"

"I missed the reference again, didn't I?"

"We can fix that."

Instead of letting me grab the DVD, Danté caught me by the waist and finally kissed me. It was sweet, and short, and it tasted like more. I kissed him back until we were both breathless.

"How could I ever live without that?" he murmured before kissing me again.

His tongue caressed mine as he pulled me closer.

"Oh, fuck me."

The mischievous twinkle in his eyes lit up like a flame. There would be no movie for us tonight.

"I can make that happen."

CHAPTER 40

My leg was jumping up and down. Waiting rooms never did anything good for my anxious self. Minutes ticked by, and the skin on my arms prickled. Elijah appeared in the doorway, smiling warmly.

"Evelyn, please come in."

He motioned me to sit, so I let myself plop down on the stuffed chair. It was the very same chair I had sat on during my interview months ago, and I had been given the opportunity to get a job here.

"How have you been?"

"Good. I passed all my exams."

"Excellent. I'm sure you excelled at all of them."

Not that I really remembered much. After my mental breakdown, I'd pushed that knowledge aside. Danté had looked at the email with the results and told me I had an almost perfect score. Instead of looking myself, I had trusted him on the matter. I was graduating anyway so it didn't matter anymore.

"I did."

"What can I do for you?"

I breathed in deeply. It did nothing for my racing pulse. I had no choice but to just be upfront about it all. Even though I hated to disappoint.

"I came to decline the job offer."

If I wasn't sure I had caught Elijah's full attention, I was now. His brows creased ever so slightly. Elijah took off his glasses.

"Did another practice offer you a better job? If so, we can negotiate the conditions."

I shook my head. It was flattering to know that he didn't want to let me go so easily.

"I didn't search elsewhere."

Which was a first for me.

"Then may I ask you why you're declining?"

"My boyfriend and I want to travel for a while. While he does it to volunteer, I want to go for the adventure. I still want to work here, but if I don't try it now, maybe I never will. So I can't accept."

For the first time in forever, I had not made intricate plans for my future. I had given Danté free reign on the destination. He had come up with two.

"Are you sure? You would be a great asset to our team, but I can't guarantee the job offer will still be open when you come back. If we find another promising candidate, they will be the person that takes your place."

I exhaled, smiling. It was time to move on. Life wouldn't wait for me. Knowing that I might not get in here after our travel didn't seem as scary as I had feared. Even if this was still the dream, with Danté by my side, I would be able to live the life I wanted. No matter where that was.

"I am sure."

"Well, if I can't convince you to stay, I can at least ask you to come back after your adventure, if that is still what you want. I don't know if we can still offer you the job then, but please let me know when you get back. Maybe we can figure something out."

"I will," I promised.

Elijah opened the door and followed me to the front of the practice. "Where are you going?"

"Kenya, then Vietnam."

Danté had even convinced me to do some volunteering too. There was a program for nutrition in Kenya. In Vietnam I wouldn't do anything except for traveling and taking cooking classes. I would enjoy the six-month break and just live life without planning ahead too much. Weird, I know.

"Enjoy your trip."

It probably wasn't politically correct to do so with the person who might become your employer. I didn't care and gave Elijah a hug. The man patted my back before I let go.

"Thank you."

Chloe hit me in the face with a wet kitchen towel. Why did I always pick the aggressive friends out of the ocean of people? I grabbed the towel and took it out of her hands before she could attack me again. She scowled at me.

"I can't believe you're leaving!"

So Kristen had already told her. Last night, I had called her to ask if I could work full-time at Hot Stuff for a few months; I needed some extra money for traveling. Danté and I had agreed that we would leave the country as soon as I had officially graduated. And since the ceremony would be in October, it still gave me a bit more than three months to prepare. Kristen being Kristen, she had squealed in delight when I told her my new plans and had immediately accepted. It was weird to know that this part of my life would come to an end. Hot Stuff had been a second home, and Chloe had been like a second big sister.

"It was rather clear that I would stop working here after I graduated."

She let herself fall on one of the bar stools, her chin resting in her palm. Was she sad? I knew I was. That was part of growing up, I guess.

"I know, but I didn't think that you graduating meant you leaving the country. Why didn't you tell me that sooner?"

"I didn't know it myself until last week."

My father believed this to be the biggest mistake of my life: going abroad with a guy who had broken my heart a few months prior. My mom, on the other hand, had cried tears of happiness after I introduced Danté to her as my boyfriend. And like everyone else, she had been shocked when I announced that we were going abroad. Understandably. Unlike Dad, Mom said that this adventure would make me grow so much more than any job could do, that I'd be a fool not to do it. Needless to say, we both ended up crying on the couch, Eleanor, Danté, and Dad giving us concerned glances every now and then.

No one knew how things would go. Would Danté and I hate being with each other every single day? Would we still be together at the end of a year filled with travel? We would see. That was part of the adventure too.

Chloe gave me a hug. There was moisture on my neck where her face touched my skin. I rubbed her back while laughing.

"Don't be sad. I'll call you and send pictures."

"You better not forget about me," she sniffled.

"I could never. Plus, we still have a few months."

I imagined her waving a tissue while Danté and I went through the check-in at the airport, crying with my parents, my sister and Grandma, and Jasmine and Theo. I had felt so lonely and lost at times. Now when I'd look back, there would be a whole army of people who loved me standing behind me.

Chloe patted her eyes dry, doing her best to smile at me. The bell chimed, and Danté walked over to us. My heart still did a little flip every time he was near. He gave me a quick kiss, then looked at Chloe, confused. She sniffled harder.

"How dare you steal my Evy."

"She's my Evy, now," he said in a calm voice. Chloe shot him a glacial stare, and Danté had the common sense to avert his eyes. I snickered at how meek he was against my friend. "I promise I'll bring her back, happy and healthy." Danté placed a hand on the small of my back. "Are you ready to go home?"

"Yes. See you tomorrow, Chloe."

My friend returned behind the counter. I looked around Hot Stuff, at the wooden walls and the coffee cup lamps on the ceiling, the place I would be in almost every day for the next few months. Life really worked in mysterious ways.

Danté laced his fingers with mine, and we went back to my apartment. Since Danté's plans got delayed once again, he had taken back his post at the practice he worked at before and now stayed with Jasmine and me.

Now that summer was around the corner, nights were getting longer. A nice warm breeze ruffled my hair.

"That went well," Danté tried.

We both ended up laughing. It had gone better than telling Jasmine, that's for sure. The only thing that had made her calm down a bit was that if I moved out, Theo could move in our shoe box of an apartment not suited for four people. It was time for us both to have a new start. Though the thought made my heart squeeze.

"I'll miss them," I said quietly.

Never had I not seen Jasmine or Chloe for more than a week ever since I met them. This wasn't permanent, luckily. It didn't change the fact that it would be hard sometimes and that I would have to adjust to a new life.

Danté pressed my hand. "You can still change your mind."

"Why would I do that?" I asked.

"I won't break up with you if you decide to stay."

He would do his best to make this work was what he didn't say.

"I know you won't. But I still want to go."

It wasn't that I couldn't live without him. I didn't *want* to.

I hadn't known this before, but I wanted to travel, explore the world, and discover parts of me that I didn't know yet. Danté stopped outside of our building. The setting sun gave his skin a soft golden glow, and I couldn't look away. Yes, we had had a rough patch. There certainly would be more of them in the future, but gods was it worth it.

Danté's eyes were soft and filled with love. "Be my forever, Evelyn."

"I already was."

I had been here all along, just like he had. That was why I knew everything would be alright. Danté kissed me, and he tasted like chai lattes and new beginnings. My favourite.

EPILOGUE

People were hurrying around us. Soon enough, that would be us too. Danté and I waited with our luggage to see the whole clique coming together in the entry hall of the airport. A black one for him, and a neon pink luggage with a squirrel tag for me. There was no way I would not immediately find my possessions once we landed, unlike him.

It almost looked like we were about to go on a dangerous mission, and not going abroad for just a year. Our parents and my grandma were talking animatedly. It was fun to see how well they all had gotten along, and how fast. Auntie Aswaa also joined the group, smiling warmly. Her husband, on the other hand, shot Danté a wary glance. He would be the one needing the most time to get used to the idea that I would be traveling with my boyfriend. Especially since we weren't married. Danté being the sweetheart of us both, took Nadim's hand in his. I let them alone. Leave the guys to bond, or try to bond.

Jasmine grabbed me closer to her. "If only I could go with

you."

That wasn't in the cards for the near future now that Jasmine had found a temporary job in a school.

"Let's travel when I'm back, just us girls," I said.

Eleanor and Chloe both agreed to that. Theo scowled at the idea.

"Well, am I not good enough for you anymore?" he asked.

"Fine, if you really want to come, you can carry our bags," I said, looking at my nails.

The girls snickered. Jasmine stood on her tippy toes and dropped a kiss on his cheek. No hard feelings. Now that he was going to live with her in our apartment, I wondered how long it would take before they announced an engagement or a baby on the way.

I glanced at my watch. It was time to move. Danté, who had been swallowed by the group of parents, gave me a nod. Jasmine gave me one last tight hug, sniffling.

"I expect you to call me every week, and to send me updates and pictures on the days we don't talk."

"And if you meet a very handsome foreigner, do not hesitate to talk about us," Chloe added.

"Yes, don't forget about us old hags," my sister added.

Goodbyes were hard. Especially because there were so many people here for us. Many tears were shed, and many tissues were passed along. My smile wobbled when I waved at them for the last time.

Danté laced his fingers with mine. His gaze was open, happy. "Are you ready, love?"

I breathed in deeply. Oh, this was going to be so exciting. Especially with Danté at my side every step of the way. I tugged on his shirt to get him closer. Danté indulged me, pressing a soft kiss to my nose.

"The last one to arrive at the check-in is a loser," I whispered before taking off.

As we raced with our luggage like idiots, it didn't matter who would win. We never let go of each other. It was laughing and breathless that we went on to our next adventure.

BONUS

"For someone who's about to live his dream, you look like shit," Alex said as he walked inside the house.

Danté looked down at his threadbare grey shirt and grey sweatpants, his lips pressed together. This was the same attire he always wore when there was no need to go outside. And he hadn't planned on seeing people these days. Alex's gaze stayed on his face, a knowing smile tugging at his mouth.

"When was the last time you shaved?"

Danté shrugged. "Probably a week ago."

He hadn't really cared about his looks before Alex waltzed inside his parents' home. They both sat down at the kitchen table, sipping from their instant coffee. Danté grimaced. After years of drinking coffee from Hot Stuff, this beverage was a sad replacement. His friend's phone chimed, and Alex gingerly looked at the notification. Ever since he came back from Russia a month ago being engaged, Alex was his old self again. Gone were the mood swings and the sadness that had eaten him alive. It had been Alex's sadness and fear that had fuelled Danté's resolve to not try the long-distance relationship with Evy. The loneliness, the constant doubt... Seeing one of his best friends go through that had been enough to spook him, especially since Alex and Elena both hadn't been sure they'd make it. Now, they were getting married, and Danté had let his fears cloud his judgement.

"How is she?" he asked, swirling this sorry excuse of a coffee in his mug.

"Who?" Alex asked back, still typing away on his phone.

Danté did his best to keep from rolling his eyes and retorting something sarcastic like a certain dorky girl would have done.

Alex looked up from his phone. "Oh, you meant Evelyn? She's fine."

His breath hitched. Had she been able to get over him that fast? Danté swallowed hard.

"That's good."

Alex watched his every move. No matter how hard he tried to keep his thoughts and emotions inside him, Danté was certain that Alex could see right through the calm exterior. He always knew what he was thinking or feeling.

"She's nailing her exams."

Of course she would. Evelyn's future was set in stone. There was nothing and no one that would keep her from graduating and living the life she had envisioned for herself. Danté felt pride bloom inside his chest, just like it was easily replaced by regret. Maybe he should have fought harder to also have a place in that future Evy had seen for them. *You didn't give me a chance to choose you.* He could still see the tears shining in her eyes when her words had found their mark. It was too late now. Evelyn had moved on. Unlike him, she would be fine.

Alex cleared his throat. "You deserve a punch in the face if you believed that so easily."

"I beg your pardon?" Danté seethed.

Alex raised a single brow, hands clasped together. He might punch him, if he deemed it necessary. Alex wasn't the type of person to hesitate before acting or speaking up. That had been why Danté and Alex had gotten along so quickly in college. They always spoke true to each other, no matter how harsh their words could be. Today though, it didn't feel so good. If Alex noticed, he ignored how his words felt like acid thrown over burns.

"Evy is miserable, if you must know," Alex continued. "She cries a lot and avoids everyone. Just like you've been doing these last few weeks. She misses you, obviously."

"How would you know?"

"Jasmine told me."

Danté scoffed. It seemed like the world hadn't stopped spinning while his life had felt frozen in time.

"It seems like you two became great friends."

His friend laughed. Alex rested his elbows on the table, an eyebrow raised. "Jasmine is a sweet girl. You would've known that if you hadn't been simping after her best friend for years."

Alright, that was fair. Danté had pined after Evy ever since she flirted with him, her bloody hand wrapped in a kitchen towel. Her quirks and humour had drawn him in. Then her wits and kindness had made him stay around longer than he would've, had she been anyone else.

At first, Danté had tried to convince himself that letting her go was the best thing to do. Evelyn could get over him. She'd bounce back. Then why did the possibility of her moving on hurt so much? Was she really as miserable as he was?

"It's not too late to talk to her," Alex tried.

A part of him wanted to snap at Alex, to tell him to fuck off. But here was the thing: Alex could judge character like no one else. And Danté trusted the man's gut feeling. He abandoned the idea of finishing his coffee and dropped the mug on the table, sighing.

"When will you stop meddling in my love life?"

Alex clicked his tongue. "I'll stop meddling the day you get your head out of your ass and actually have a love life instead of running away from it."

A muscle twitched in Danté's cheek as he clenched his teeth. This was not how he had planned his day to go.

Alex softened his tone. "Are you really planning on leaving the country without talking to her?"

He wanted to say that his mind was made up, that there was no point in trying and clinging to the past. But he couldn't.

"I haven't started packing yet," he admitted quietly.

"Then you know what to do, brother."

His hands turned cold. There was no way Evy would take him back. Not after he fled before she could even decide what she wanted to do. Maybe she would've wanted to try the long distance, maybe she would've accepted to go overseas with him. Or maybe she would've just said no. The idea alone of her rejection had been terrifying. That was why it had been easier to break things off before she could do it. There was also a selfish part of him that didn't want Evelyn to one day look back at her life, only to realize that she had wasted her dreams on him. Danté looked up.

"I'm scared out of my wits," he admitted.

"Good. I'd think your love a sham if you weren't."

"What if she cannot forgive me?"

"Then at least you'll get closure. You both need it."

The very reason why Alex had flown to another continent: to either save his relationship or to get closure. Real closure. Danté hoped there would be anything left to salvage.

"Be sure to shave before you go. She might not recognize you like this."

Danté smiled, and for the first time in weeks, it was genuine. "Prick," he muttered.

Alex clasped his forearm, squeezing gently, and winked.

"Just for you, dumbass."

What now?

Thank you so much for picking up this book! This project was pure self-indulgence, and boy, I had a marvellous time writing it.

If you loved it, please leave a review on Amazon and/or Goodreads. It helps me out a lot.

Love,

Josie

About the Author

Josie Winters has been imagining stories since kindergarten. Her favourite books to write are the ones about characters with emotional baggage and quirky personalities.

When Josie's not writing, you can find her nestled on the couch with her cats, reading swoony love stories.

If you want to know more about when Josie's next book will come out, or what she's up to (it's no good, that's for sure), take a look at her TikTok or Goodreads page.

Connect with Josie here:

TikTok: @josie.n.winters_08

Goodreads: Josie N. Winters

www.ingramcontent.com/pod-product-compliance
Lightning Source LLC
LaVergne TN
LVHW030334070526
838199LV00067B/6272